He was a specimen of strong heritage.

Henrietta refused to fault herself for noticing the thickness of St. Raven's hair or the confidence in his stride. His skin shone with good health and his white, cared-for teeth hinted at a fastidious nature.

Yes, even a doctor could note such things. The churning in her stomach was very natural, she assured herself. Simply a physical and chemical reaction.

And then he turned and saw her.

She, quiet and unobtrusive, edged as close to a wall as possible, yet he saw her. Their gazes connected. She looked quickly away, eager to discourage him from approaching her.

The tactic did not work. Trying not to frown, she nodded a greeting as he neared.

"I see you are walking without pain," she said promptly.

"Is that why you were studying me so closely?"

Jessica Nelson believes romance happens every day and thinks the greatest, most intense romance comes from a God who woos people to Himself with passionate tenderness. When Jessica is not chasing her three beautiful, wild little boys around the living room, she can be found staring into space as she plots her next story, daydreams about raspberry mochas or plans chocolate for dinner.

Books by Jessica Nelson

Love Inspired Historical

Love on the Range
Family on the Range
The Matchmaker's Match
A Hasty Betrothal
The Unconventional Governess

JESSICA NELSON

The Unconventional Governess

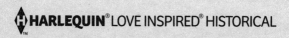

HARLEQUIN® LOVE INSPIRED® HISTORICAL

LOVE INSPIRED BOOKS

Recycling programs
for this product may
not exist in your area.

ISBN-13: 978-1-335-36965-9

The Unconventional Governess

Copyright © 2018 by Jessica Nelson

www.Harlequin.com

Printed in U.S.A.

And let us consider one another
to provoke unto love and to good works.
—*Hebrews* 10:24

I would like to dedicate this book
to Denise Petrovich, my very unconventional
mother. Life would be quite boring without you.
I love you and thank you for all of the creative ways
you support my writing.

Many thanks to all of my fabulous writing friends,
including the members of my Sunshine State
Romance Authors group (Loretta Rogers,
Darlene Corcoran, Barbara Cairns,
Michael Ditchfield and many others), who one
October Retreat night helped me brainstorm my
hero into the unique and fabulous guy that he is.

Thank you to Emily Rodmell, editor extraordinaire,
who is both kind and wise with her advice.

Final thanks to Jesus, my main squeeze.
He is a God who is constantly teaching me
in unconventional ways.

Chapter One

England
Spring 1814

No conventional daughter of an earl desired to become a physician.

Henrietta Gordon did not fool herself into thinking she was conventional. As a woman of limited funds and genteel birth, there were very few socially acceptable dreams to dream. And while dreams were all well and good, accomplishment came by setting goals and pursuing them.

Which was why, despite the increasing suspicion that in order to avoid matrimony she might have to take on a governess post, she was determined to prepare for the life she wanted, rather than the life being foisted upon her.

If there was one thing she had learned in her twenty-four years that served her well, it was to persist in what she wanted.

On this brooding English afternoon, Henrietta had taken refuge in Lady Brandewyne's expansive library. To her great delight, she found a copy of *A Practical Synopsis of the Materia Alimentaria and Materia Medica*. No sooner had she curled up in a plush wingback chair than Lady Brandewyne swept into the room.

The dowager countess, an old friend of Uncle William's, had kindly allowed Henrietta to stay with her while she recovered from a bout of rheumatic fever. Uncle William had gone to London to teach a medical seminar. He'd promised to return to collect Henrietta, but it had been a month since he left, and she began to doubt his intentions.

Especially with Lady Brandewyne's daily insinuations.

The fearsome lady now paused when she saw Henrietta reading rather than practicing the pianoforte, or performing some other expected feat of ladyhood. She sniffed, her regal, powdered chin tilted to display her disapproval more effectively.

"I have received a report that a man was found wounded nearby. His servants are bringing him here. Since the apothecary is on another call at the moment, it seems as though I may have need of your expertise." She delivered the words stiffly, and Henrietta hid a smile behind the professionalism her uncle had taught her to display.

"Do we know the nature of his wounds? Will he require sutures?" She placed the book on a side table and stood.

"No, and I do not want you overly involved with his care. As soon as the apothecary arrives, you will remove yourself."

Henrietta felt her eyebrows fly upward at Lady Brandewyne's dogmatic tone. She hadn't practiced medicine in England thus far. She'd been too focused on recovering from illness and Lady Brandewyne disapproved of her chosen vocation, at any rate. While here, she must observe propriety much more strictly than she had in the Americas.

Not for long, she comforted herself. Soon she'd be assisting Uncle William again, propriety be hanged. There were lives to be saved. Soldiers' hands to be held while they verbalized their final goodbyes. Mothers to comfort as they birthed their children.

Her throat tightened.

As though noticing her discomfort, Lady Brandewyne drew near. "Calm yourself, my dear. I'm sure the apothecary will care for him completely. Let us speak of a happier subject. I've arranged a house party in two weeks' time to relieve the tedium of your convalescence. You may want to consider encouraging a suitor."

"A suitor?"

"It is past time for you to marry."

Before Henrietta could remark on that most outrageous statement, the butler appeared in the doorway. "They have arrived, my lady."

"Bring them to the front door. The servants' hall is too narrow."

Henrietta rose quickly, following Lady Brandewyne out of the room and through a hall lined with antique oil paintings of ancestors, down the ornate, curving stairwell to the entrance of her Elizabethan-shaped home.

As soon as she saw the large man being carried in, mental images assaulted her. The battery was unexpected. She had no time to arm herself against memories of assisting Uncle William during the War of 1812. She willed the pictures of war and death away.

This is not Newark, she assured herself firmly. Memories from that deadly skirmish rushed her. Fire, screams, black smoke blanketing the sky…and then the deaths. So many deaths…

She squared her shoulders. She was a person of great practicality and self-control. Thus equipped with logic, she took a calming breath. Thankfully, no one noticed her angst. Everyone followed the orders Lady Brandewyne snipped out.

Henrietta pressed herself against the wall as the entourage shuffled past.

She noticed a girl in the group, her eyes wide and frightened. She was ushered away by a female servant. Perhaps her nurse?

Henrietta followed everyone up the stairs again, all the way to a room in the east wing facing the gardens. Two footmen laid the prone figure on the bed. Lady Brandewyne glanced over at Henrietta.

"It is Lord St. Raven," she said quietly. "A neighbor. What do you suggest our first steps to be?"

Henrietta stepped closer. His wavy black hair was in disarray. Twigs and debris were tangled in the strands that curled over what looked like a fashionable collar. In fact, the closer she came, the more she realized this man might qualify as a dandy. Had she ever seen such a perfect knot on a cravat?

Truthfully, she couldn't claim any knowledge of what was considered fashionable these days. Nor had she ever cared. But his longish hair and tanned skin were at odds with the lifestyle suggested by his clothing.

A lifestyle of vanity, certainly.

His lips, unfortunately, were the color of ash. Blood smeared his jaw. His whole body was so completely still that she felt certain he must have passed on. She touched his neck. His pulse limped quietly beneath his skin.

He lived, but for how long?

"We will need to remove the soiled clothing and clean his wounds. That should allow us more information."

The dowager sent for hot water while Henrietta continued her cursory examination.

Rumpled clothing. Dark smears that constituted a combination of dirt and blood. She saw no fresh oozing. A blessing. Perhaps the dirt had acted as a bandage, stemming the flow.

His eyes fluttered. A moan crumpled between his lips.

"Shh." She placed her palm upon his brow. "You are safe now, sir."

At her touch, his eyes opened, revealing jade irises. She inhaled quickly, struck by the intensity of the coloration.

"Beautiful…" The word came haltingly, his voice unsteady, but the way he looked at her sent her nerves on a tumbling spiral.

She and Lady Brandewyne exchanged a glance.

"Nonsense," she said briskly. "I've been plain since childhood, and plain I shall be long into spinsterhood." A term she loathed, but nevertheless, she lingered on the cusp of being labeled a spinster by society. "Now save your breath, for you are wounded and I know not the gravity of your injuries."

"Bandits."

"They say you led them a merry chase, my lord." Lady Brandewyne came to his side. Recognition, and perhaps relief, flared in his eyes.

"Is my…attire irreparably beyond repair?"

"If that is your main concern, then your problems are far greater than I feared." Henrietta pressed her lips together, refusing to let his cavalier comment perturb her. "I shall need to fetch supplies. Perhaps comfrey as an astringent for his wounds."

"A fresh cravat," Lord St. Raven groaned, and then the poor man fainted.

Dominic Stanford, reluctant earl of St. Raven, woke from pleasant dreams to even more pleasant humming. He stretched before a spasm of pain in his ribs reminded

him of his unfortunate altercation with a group of vaga-
bonds. He'd almost had them beat, too, he remembered
with a half-edged smile.

With that comforting thought in mind, he opened his
eyes a crack, just enough to find the source of the humming. The woman's voice was melodic. Husky and flavored with a depth rarely heard in young ladies. She came
into view, her unassuming clothes attesting to her station.

An ordinary housemaid.

A seemingly productive one, though. She wore a ser-
viceable cap in which strands of hair escaped in tendrils
about an ordinary face. In fact, there was nothing about
her to draw his attention, and yet he could not look away.

Perhaps it was the sound of her low humming that welcomed him. Or the purposeful way in which she moved.
It was not that she bustled, as he'd often observed the servantry doing, but she glided with a purpose. A singularly
minded woman.

"You're awake," she said, without even turning to look
at him. She stood at a small table at the side of the room,
clinking metal against cup, as though mixing something.
He could not see what. Her voice was as soothing as her
unworded song. "How do you feel?"

A good question. How did he feel? He tested various
parts of his body, flexing his fingers, drawing a deep
breath that ended shortly with a stab of pain in his side.
"I believe I've a broken rib or two."

Full consciousness returned. He jerked upward, then
fell back as daggers sliced across his torso. "My niece,"
he rasped. Had he protected her? Had he saved her from
those men?

"She is fine, my lord. Safely here at Lady Brandewyne's."

He struggled to breathe past the pain still lacing his

chest. "She is safe. And we are at the dowager count-ess's home?"

"Correct."

"Where is the doctor?"

"The village apothecary is on his way." If his question surprised her, she showed no sign of it. "I am your nurse, for the present moment. You have been unconscious since yesterday, when you were brought here. You've a few con-tusions and most likely some bruising to your internal or-gans, though no hemorrhaging that I can tell."

"So, for now, I shall live," he said drily, his body relax-ing as he was convinced that Louise had not been harmed. He suspected the convulsions that had plagued him these last months would be the death of him, anyhow.

"Indeed, you shall certainly live." She chuckled, and once again, he was struck by the cadence of her voice. Her pronunciation was rounded with a foreign flare. Amer-ican? She did not speak like a servant, but neither did she sound wholly English. For the first time in what had been months of a terrible lethargy of the spirits, the tini-est flicker of intrigue stirred within.

Swallowing against a throat that had gone dry, he said, "Fetch me water."

Her gaze flew up to meet his, her fingers pausing. Such direct eyes, a deep brown at odds with her lighter hair and fair skin. They chastised him. "No manners?"

He lifted an eyebrow. "You dare criticize me?"

At that, the corner of what he realized was a very pretty set of lips tilted upward. A housemaid he had not no-ticed in the room brought her a different glass filled with water. The woman turned to him, a sparkle in her eye. "Your lack of observation is forgiven, as you're no doubt groggy, but I am not a maidservant. I shall speak to you however I wish."

"Point taken, madam."

"As well as it should be." She reached behind his head, gently lifting him to allow his mouth to connect with the cup. "A gentleman always admits to being wrong."

He almost choked on his water, but managed to swallow without his laughter killing him. The chuckle that had bubbled up at her words was quickly sobered by reality. In truth, he was no gentleman, but he did not intend to disclose such a thing.

He drank deeply, ignoring the ache in his midsection and concentrating on filling the thirst that beset him. All the while he was aware that she studied him. Not in the way he was used to being studied, though.

He was well aware of how ladies used to ogle him. They wanted his family lineage, his wealth. They liked his darkly handsome features and green eyes, telling him so on numerous occasions in which propriety was lightly skirted. With their fluttering lashes, their colorful fans, their shallow giggles, they admired his elegant cravats, his French tailoring, his expensive rings.

And he had enjoyed it until ten months ago.

They knew nothing of his damage now. And he enlightened no one, for should society know, it was almost certain that he'd be sent to an insane asylum. Or at best, confined to his estate, talked about with condescending pity while someone else enjoyed his title, his lands and his inheritance. Little was known about his disease, but most assumed it stemmed from mental illness.

He knew he wasn't crazy, but he couldn't return to his old way of life until he found a cure.

Therefore, due to the uncertain nature of his illness, he had hidden away at a little cottage he owned in northern England for these past few months. He had ignored his duties, both to Louise and to the St. Raven estate where she lived.

Until he'd received the letter from his sister threatening to take Louise from the St. Raven estate and send her to a girls' school on the Continent. That threat, combined with yet another governess quitting, urged him to leave his self-induced solitude to collect his wayward niece from St. Raven and take her back to his cottage in the north.

Then they'd been attacked by bandits. He'd successfully coerced the criminals to follow him away from his party, but alas, had not been able to keep them from attacking him. Thankfully his party had followed at a distance and found him.

He shuddered to think of what might have become of them all, but this woman insisted Louise was well. She was his main concern.

He grew aware of the woman staring at him. Her gaze was intense. Scientific, even. Completely devoid of personal feeling. As if he was a specimen beneath the light. He shifted, handing the cup back to her.

She took it, a puzzled expression on her face. "Forgive me if I speak out of turn, but whatever are you doing so far from London in such finery? Especially with the Season in full swing."

She did not sound contrite over her impertinence. He met her curious look with a crooked smile. "Ah, that is a question I do not care to answer… Mrs.?"

"How is our patient, Miss Gordon?" A man who looked to be the epitome of physicianhood walked into the room. He must be the village apothecary. He came to stand above Dominic. The man rubbed at his finely tuned mustache, studying him with all the objectivity of a cat studying a mouse.

These people were all the same.

"Your patient is fine." Dominic wrestled himself into an upright position, despite the razor-edged pain beneath his ribs. "I must be on my way to London. Duty calls." He couldn't stay here. Should he have an episode, there was no telling how this doctor might respond.

"Hmm." The apothecary turned to Miss Gordon, who looked a tad perturbed that Dominic had answered for her. Or perhaps he imagined the peevish set to her mouth. The woman amused him for some very odd reason. He had been gone from society too long, he supposed.

Nothing had ever induced him to take residence in the cage of responsibility foisted on his older brother, the earl of St. Raven, until his brother and sister-in-law had died in a tragic carriage accident, leaving him heir to the estate and guardian to one little girl, who refused to do what she was told.

And yet he adored her. His brother had entrusted him to care for Louise, and he was not going to allow anyone to take that responsibility from him. Not even his little sister.

"Duty?" asked Miss Gordon.

"Yes, a twelve-year-old girl in need of a new governess." He paused, eyeing the woman before him. "You don't perchance know of someone looking for a position?"

Chapter Two

"I do not." Henrietta set her jaw, eyeing Lord St. Raven sharply. Did she have a sign on her head proclaiming her situation? Either way, she'd already ascertained that he was not someone she wished to work for. No doubt the girl was as difficult as he was, and she had no experience with children anyway.

What did she know of teaching? Nothing, which was why it was best to find a position with a sweet, biddable child.

"In that case, bring me Jacks and ready my carriage for departure," he said in a voice that resonated with an irritating earl-like authority. He was a man obviously used to being obeyed.

"You are not going anywhere." Annoyed by the determination on her patient's face, she gave him a stern look. "There is no telling what internal damage you may have suffered. To get up, to be active, could worsen your condition."

The man scowled at her. And it was a dark scowl indeed, on such a handsome face. She crossed her arms and sent the apothecary a pointed look. "Do you not agree?"

"I do agree." He stroked his chin. "Are you sure we

should not bleed him? His humors are visibly imbalanced. His coloring, for example."

"We will not be using leeches. My uncle, Mr. William Gordon, says they are ineffective, and that conclusion is based on years of observation and experience."

"A fine physician. I've seen his works in various medical journals." The apothecary dipped his head. "No leeches, then."

Grunting, their patient pushed himself to a sitting position on the edge of the bed. She examined his physique for any other weaknesses, any inordinarities. Pain whitened his lips, but did not soften the stubborn jut of his well-defined jaw. He was a larger and broader man than Henrietta had realized. When he'd been lying down, it had been easy to forget his size. Her own stature had often been called average, as had most everything about her besides her intelligence.

"I've business to attend while you are wasting time discussing bloodsuckers and the humored color of my skin. Send for my valet. Instruct him as to my needs."

A rustling of skirts and a perfumed puff of scent announced Lady Brandewyne's arrival. She entered the room, forcing Henrietta to move toward the foot of the bed. Though comfortable, the room was hardly spacious, and with their medical tools set up, the space further shrunk.

"He's awake! How unfortunate, how terrible that you were attacked by bandits on my property. Those roving groups of perfidious miscreants...but never mind. After all you've been through, and now this. We are all deeply sorry about your family's loss." She clucked her tongue. "How can I see to your comfort, my lord?"

He lifted a pointed look to Henrietta. "My valet, if you please."

"But certainly." The lady called for a servant. "What else?"

"Louise must be ready to go within the hour. It's paramount I return to my northern estate."

"Why, yes, yes, of course." Lady Brandewyne cast a searching look to Henrietta, who felt tempted to shrug her shoulders and leave this beast to his wildness. This might be her last opportunity for nursing, however. If she had to find a post… The depressing thought weighed upon her.

"It is my opinion—" she gave St. Raven a steady look "—that the jostle of a carriage will be quite painful and his wounds might reopen. Keeping them clean will also be problematic. I cannot recommend he be moved."

He looked about to retort when a commotion outside their room ensued.

"Oh, my." Lady Brandewyne pressed a hand to her bosom and exited, followed by the doctor. Henrietta remained in the room, along with her lady's maid—an extravagance she had insisted she did not need, but Lady Brandewyne would not hear otherwise.

St. Raven leaned back upon his pillow, weakness overcoming his pride. Foolish man. Of course a man who asked for a new cravat while half-conscious with pain would refer to going to his estate as *paramount*.

Henrietta pursed her lips, peering out the doorway. Downstairs a girl with thick raven hair and an obstinate expression wrestled with a servant. Behind them, Lady Brandewyne's butler, housemaid and three other servants watched the tussle. Henrietta leaned forward, attempting to listen without leaving her patient. For all she knew, he was just waiting for an opportunity to sneak away.

Like Uncle William. How could he have done such a thing to her? All because she contracted rheumatic fever… such nonsense to fear for her life. Risks were always present, no matter where one lived. She'd much rather face death on a field with her uncle than waste away as a companion to a crotchety rich person or, worse, governess to a spoiled child.

"Eavesdropping?"

Henrietta's attention flickered, but she did not turn toward that voice. And what a voice. Husky and laced with humor. His scowl earlier had seemed out of character. This man acted like a coddled prince, dressed like a dandy and spoke like a…well, she wasn't sure, but she knew one thing: no patient of hers was going to be harmed due to willful ignorance.

"Yes," she finally said, keeping her eyes trained on the situation below. "I cannot leave you here alone."

"You have no regard for my station."

He obviously wanted to converse. Sighing, she turned. He sat resolutely on the bed, his hands spread upon the mattress for balance. A curious smile played about his lips.

"Should I? You are an injured man. Your title and your wealth have little importance in a sick room."

"Come now, Miss Gordon, do not be serious with me. Your brows are knit so tightly that I fear they shall remain forever stuck that way."

"You are impudent."

"I am bored and, most unfortunately, beset upon by many responsibilities not of my own making. It appears your word is more revered than the town doctor's." His eyes, that striking rich green, regarded her laughingly. "Release me. Give permission."

The town apothecary was a nice man, but he had not updated his medical knowledge in years. It had not escaped her notice that he had *seen* rather than *read* her uncle's articles. He was slightly better than a self-taught surgeon. Heat flushed through her, turning her palms sweaty. Lord St. Raven befuddled her.

Had she ever met such a charming personality? She could not recall, though, when one was dying on a battlefield, she doubted charm was of any importance.

But how very annoying to be almost swayed by this man's smile, by his persistent eyes.

"No." A high-pitched girl's voice came from below stairs. "I insist on seeing him at once." The shrill proclamation was followed by the patter of footsteps on the long, winding staircase that served as the centerpiece to Lady Brandewyne's home.

Determined footsteps, Henrietta concluded. She put her back to the wall, bracing herself for the child about to burst into the room. Lord St. Raven regarded the entrance with interest, his arms propped on his knees.

The girl flew into the room. She was a wisp of a child and shot directly to the earl's sickbed.

"Oh, Dom, how could you?" She threw herself against him, eliciting a pained grunt from the subject of her emotions. "First you leave me for months on end, and then you act the hero, taunting criminals until they chase you and leave you practically dead on the roadside, beaten to a bloody pulp by pernicious ruffians."

Henrietta felt her eyebrows raising at this exclamation.

"I'd hardly call myself close to dead. Roughed up a bit, that's all."

"That is not what Jacks said."

"Dear one, you've been listening in on adult conversations," Lord St. Raven murmured, his hand patting the girl's back, belying the censure in his tone.

"And I've had to deal with insipid servants all week. I declare, Dom, you are perfectly horrid to have left me by myself at St. Raven in the first place. You shall never leave me again."

After that impassioned declaration, the child swiveled around and leveled a sharp look at Henrietta. She quickly smothered any existence of laughter.

"Who are you?" Eyes the same shade of emerald as the earl's regarded her with distrust, but where his twinkled in immature mischief, hers were intensely serious.

A grudging admiration for her pluck rose within Henrietta. She inclined her head ever so slightly. "I am Miss Gordon."

"You don't look like a lady."

"And you do not speak like one."

The girl's eyes narrowed. "Who are you to answer thus?" The imperious quality to her tone suggested an unfamiliarity with conflict from those she deemed less than her equals.

Henrietta squared her shoulders. This little girl did not bother her. After all, how many people had doubted her abilities as an adequate nurse? Men considered her silly and women accused her of misplaced priorities, going so far as to suggest she lacked femininity.

"My lord." Lady Brandewyne came into the room, nursing a frown. "The girl refused to stay in the nurseries."

"The girl has a name." The child's eyes blazed green fire.

Oh, the impertinence! These two were most certainly related.

For Lady Brandewyne's part, she puffed up her chest, cheeks billowing with suppressed irritation. "What manner of child is this to speak so? Someone must take her in hand, at once."

"Louise." The earl placed his hand upon the bristling girl's shoulder in a reproachful manner, but Henrietta did not miss the betraying quiver of his chin. She pressed her lips together to keep from uttering an ill-timed criticism. Or chuckle. "Go with Lady Brandewyne to the nursery, please."

"The nursery? Why, I am practically upon my thirteenth year. The time for this nonsense has passed. You almost died. I cannot be apart from you any longer."

At that, Louise's eyes moistened and Henrietta felt a deep compassion overwhelm her. "Your father is quite healthy and should recover nicely as long as he rests these few days."

She gave him another hug and then sailed past Henrietta with a toss of her head, in which the hair looked almost as unmanageable as the personality.

"Dom is not my father."

Dominic sat back against the pillows, palming the sore place in his ribs and containing a wince. No need to let the dragon nurse in the man's profession see his discomfort. How he loved Louise, but she'd exacerbated his pain in more than one way.

He could not let Barbara have her, but somehow he must find a way to be well again. To be a fit guardian.

"Are you in pain, my lord?" Miss Gordon edged near his bed while the doctor did something at the makeshift table they'd set up at the side of the room. "Can I offer you relief?"

"Now you're solicitous," he muttered. What an inconvenience this entire fiasco was. He'd been invited to several parties this week, but had sent his regrets. His past friends would never understand his illness. "When my valet has freshened up, send him to me."

"I shall do so." Her brisk tone left no doubt she would. That serious look on her face…did she ever laugh or make merry? He squinted up at her, scrunching his nose in such a way as to draw the lightest bit of humor to her dark eyes.

She did not smile, but an attractive blush stained her delicate skin. Almost too delicate, as though she'd been ill. He studied her more thoroughly as she turned to the doctor, murmuring in a low tone. Yes, her clothes hung a tad too loosely about her frame. They were not of the best quality, though certainly better than what a maid would wear.

He would know, as in the past he had made it his business to ensure his household was dressed to represent him. An illusion of perfection that, until the accident, he'd taken great joy in creating.

A groan caught up to him, gurgling inside. *Louise.* Whatever was he going to do with her? She absolutely hated his sister, Barbara. But could he really raise her when he had no idea of his future? If Barbara discovered his epilepsy, then he'd have a battle on his hands.

As though hearing the subject of his thoughts, Miss Gordon came back carrying a drink. "Who is the child?"

"What is this?" He took the cup, peering at the foul-smelling brew.

"Tea with a tincture of herbs to soothe the pain you're in. The girl?"

The reiterated question was rude, yet Dominic found himself amused by her plain speaking. He sipped the tea, ignoring the wretched taste for the sake of his aching muscles.

"She is my niece," he finally said, meeting Miss Gordon's frank gaze. "Bequeathed to me last year when her parents died."

"Bequeathed? What a terrible thing to say."

"One more mark against me shall not make a difference. It is all adding up, is it not?"

"What is?"

"Your blatant disapproval. You do not know me, and yet you find fault."

"Nonsense. I simply asked about the girl." She had the grace to look away from him, as though acknowledging a slight deviance from the truth. "Your niece is—"

"A terror, I know."

"Not at all." She looked up then, a warmth to her eyes. "Her manners are lacking, but her absence of guile is appealing and she obviously holds a deep love for you. I can commiserate with her, as my own parents died when I was about her age."

Dominic did not know what to say. Perhaps this explained the odd accent, the plainness of her clothes despite her regal bearing. "What happened?"

Her eyes flickered. "A fire. My father pulled me from the house. He went in for my mother. Uncle William took me in afterward. I assisted him in the medical field. I have traveled around the world with him and intend to continue to do so." There was a shadow to her features, and her gaze lowered.

Neither of her parents had come out of that house.

The implication soured the air between them. A clench of empathy stirred within, and Dominic then experienced the most curious urge to know what she was thinking. He could not recall ever wondering such a thing about a woman. What made her different? Perhaps her obvious lack of artifice. The simplicity of her presentation combined with the gentility of her manners? Or perhaps it was such a simple thing as her refusal to fawn over him.

His ego could not recall such a neglect.

She cleared her throat. "Where is your niece's governess?"

"She unexpectedly quit."

"The governess gave you no warning? No time to hire someone new?"

"It all became too much for her, I suppose. I myself would never wish to teach children."

"You never know what you must resort to in difficult situations, my lord." Henrietta's smile looked suddenly sad.

"That reminds me… I shall need to write her a letter of recommendation. Could you have writing utensils sent up to me?"

"You would reward a governess who has quite effectively left you in the lurch?"

"Why, no, dear Miss Gordon, but neither will I punish her. No doubt she is already fretting over her future. She will perhaps wonder what is to become of herself? A genteel woman of good family and no money, fallen on hard times. Who will take her on now that she has left her current situation? Without a letter of recommendation… suffice it to say, England is a harsh place for those caught between the servant class and the peerage."

"You are very astute for one who wears such expensive clothing."

"Another jab." His lips quirked. "Miss Gordon, I think you should count yourself very fortunate that you are not in need of employment, for that sharp-edged tongue of yours could very well be your downfall."

"Fiddle faddle," she rejoined, but an odd expression had crossed her face.

"And what is the meaning of your distaste of the finer things?" he continued, enjoying her discomfiture. He thought she might deserve a bit of perturbation. "I enjoy silk cravats and well-made clothing, and there is nothing wrong with such enjoyment. You would begrudge me my clothes, but have me refuse to recommend my governess?

Even knowing that Louise can be trying? You're a hard woman, Miss Gordon."

She searched his face, and so he kept his features blasé. Her inability to correctly discern his intentions showed upon her features. "Perhaps one must be strong to survive in this world."

"Hardness will certainly deflect any arrows to that armor you're wearing," he said easily.

Behind them, the apothecary coughed. Or perhaps it was an ill-disguised laugh. Scowling, Henrietta set her shoulders. "I shall return this evening to check your dressings."

"Please do," he called out, chuckling at the stiff way she left the room.

At the very least, she would amuse him while he contemplated how to find Louise a governess while searching for a cure for his illness.

Chapter Three

What a positively bothersome man.

His outlandish comments followed Henrietta the rest of the day.

Tea with Lady Brandewyne that afternoon furthered her agitation. Only moments into the expected social tradition, and Lady Brandewyne reached into the pocket of her dress.

"A letter came for you today. From your uncle." She held out a thick square, her eyes keen despite her advanced age. "I have news."

"News," Henrietta repeated, sounding just like her uncle's pet parrot. There was a sinking feeling in the pit of her stomach, rather like the jostling of organs when a ship took a sudden dip into boisterous waves.

"Would you prefer to read your letter first?" The lady sipped her tea, eyeing Henrietta expectantly over the rim of the cup.

Swallowing a smart retort, Henrietta opened the paper. Her shock increased with every line. Her fingers trembled as she read. Her heartbeat strummed to a near stop. Feeling very grim indeed, she set the letter to the side. "I suppose you know all about this?"

"It had been discussed."

According to the letter, Uncle had left England without her. He had gone to Wales in order to instruct more students, but felt that Henrietta was in no shape to be traveling. He asked Lady Brandewyne to watch over Henrietta until he returned. He worried for her safety. He no longer believed a woman's place should be assisting him at wartime, serving the poor souls of wounded soldiers. Henrietta's battle with rheumatic fever had shown him that he wanted her safe in England, away from illness and the ravages of war. He did not believe her heart could sustain the exhaustion of working in the field again.

"Well?"

"He wants me to stay in England," she said flatly. As she had expected, but to have it confirmed was more of a shock than she realized it would be.

"A wise decision. You are of marriageable age. The orphan daughter of an earl. Your plainness is not detracting, and your form is comely. We shall get you to London, spiff you up and find you a baron in no time. Perhaps even a viscount?"

"I have no dowry, nothing to bring to marriage but my bloodline. An engagement is out of the question."

"A baronet, then."

Henrietta squared her shoulders. Her life was with Uncle William, practicing medicine. He might not want her there, out of misplaced fear, but she would prove those fears to be unfounded. Time for her alternate plan.

"I shall search for a post until I have the money to join my uncle. Will you write a letter of recommendation?"

"Certainly, but I cannot approve such nonsense. This makes me quite unhappy, Henrietta."

"Happiness is ephemeral. I have no doubt it shall return to you shortly. In the meantime, I will begin searching for a position somewhere." She paused. "I would ask discretion from you on this matter. Please do not say anything to my uncle at this time."

Lady Brandewyne's hand went to her mouth. "You are not telling him?"

"I think it's best to find the position first, and I do not wish to worry him."

She nodded, but there was a worried glint in her eyes. "Secrets are unwise."

"It is not a secret," Henrietta assured her. "I would like to tell him myself, though."

"Very well."

Satisfied, Henrietta nodded. After tea, she immediately wrote two letters of inquiry to nearby neighbors whom Lady Brandewyne intimated were looking for governesses. She left them with the butler to be delivered later.

Knowing that Lord St. Raven was now without a governess offered a slight temptation. She disliked his effect on her nerves, yet she found herself reflecting on his unexpected kindness toward the governess who had left.

No doubt Louise would prove an apt pupil. Very bright and most likely challenging. And then they were both orphans. Oh, how she sympathized with the child. She did not want to teach her, though. It would require a great deal of stamina, patience and forethought. And time.

Then there was St. Raven... She did not want to be a governess in his household. Only the most severe of circumstances would change her mind. She prayed he healed quickly so that he could leave.

An uncharacteristic restlessness plagued her. Dinner was not to be ready for several hours, so she wandered into the gardens. Lady Brandewyne kept a well-stocked pond at the edge of the path. Succulent flowers hugged the stone walkway, growing in wild, colorful profusion.

The path itself was neatly groomed, creating a relaxing walk for Henrietta. She had not been outdoors yet today, and the gentle breeze riding on muted sunlight that filtered through the leaves of ancient oaks soothed her thoughts.

They had been hard to ignore.

She supposed she could be a companion of sorts to Lady Brandewyne, but their dispositions were so very different that no doubt it would not be long before they came to a disagreement. Henrietta felt no inclination to hold her tongue, and though she'd had lessons in deportment and the requirements of polite society, when her parents died, everything changed.

She no longer had the patience required to be an English lady.

She had discovered that good manners were unnecessary when struggling to save a soldier from death's embrace. One did not need to wear the proper style to nurse back to health a child ravaged by fever. While helping Uncle William in the Americas, she had grown used to making her own decisions and speaking her mind without the petty rules of etiquette she'd been raised to hold dear.

And now he'd left her to the clutches of a traditional Englishwoman bent on finding her a husband. How could he?

She sank down onto a pretty stone bench nestled beneath a poplar some distance from the pond. Butterflies danced in fluttering abandonment around her, blissfully unaware of the bitter disappointment that tainted their visitor's respite. She sighed deeply, closing her eyes to pray in the personal way she'd discovered overseas.

Treating God as a kind and heavenly Father was not something she'd learned from her family. Rather, a soldier recovering from an amputated leg had introduced her to a new perspective of God. She'd found the discovered relationship with her creator healed a void even Uncle William could not fill.

There was still pain, though. The loss of her parents remained a bruise within, sometimes unnoticed, but always tender to the touch.

She prayed now for wisdom, for forgiveness, because she resented that Uncle William had left her. She prayed that God would open a way for her to join him. Provide the funding.

The earl had called her a hard woman. The comment resonated uncomfortably, and she pushed thoughts of him from her mind.

When she finished praying, she simply sat and breathed. It was a lovely day, to be sure. Too lovely to squander. Nearby, a twig cracked. Then another. Louise emerged on the far side of the path, from a small copse of flowering bushes. Leaves stuck out from her hair and dirt stains smeared the front of her dress.

"Good afternoon," Henrietta said.

"What were you doing with your eyes closed?"

"I was praying."

"I don't pray anymore." Louise plopped beside Henrietta without any consideration of space. Her dress brushed against Henrietta's hand. "Did you know that when my parents' carriage crashed, Father was decapitated?" She paused for dramatic effect. "I plan to visit the place where they died. I overheard the servants saying it was a gruesome sight." The girl stared wide-eyed at Henrietta, perhaps waiting for her to faint from a fit of the oh-so-feminine vapors.

Henrietta had never been afflicted by such a malady.

She felt a deep empathy for the child, who was obviously struggling with coming to terms with her parents' death. Instead of allowing herself to heal, she tried to remove herself from the pain by speaking about the situation in an objective way, by covering the terrible tragedy with a blanket of detachment and, to some, shocking commentary.

She thought it best to match the child's coping with equally objective answers.

"Death is never pretty." She met Louise's aggressive expression with a sober look. "Charlotte Corday is rumored to have looked at her executioner after her beheading at the guillotine."

Louise gaped.

"However," Henrietta continued calmly, "you are quite right in your comment that a beheading is a messy affair. Unless you're a chicken. Then perhaps it would be less untidy."

"A chicken?"

"Due to their anatomy, it has been rumored that chickens can live for some time after the severing of their heads. It has to do with the spinal column, you see, and the location of the brain stem."

Louise's nose squished and her eyes narrowed. "You are not like other ladies."

"I am not a lady. I am a doctor." Or as close to one as society would allow.

"You are very blunt."

"'No legacy is so rich as honesty.'" At the girl's befuddled look, Henrietta sighed. "Are you not acquainted with Shakespeare?"

"That boring old dead man?"

"I can see your education is greatly lacking. Perhaps because you are running around the gardens rather than working on your lessons?"

"My governess quit." Louise jumped up from the

bench, making a scoffing sound in her throat. "Deportment and manners, bah. They are for stuffy old ladies."

Henrietta worked very hard to keep her eyebrows from raising. How closely the child echoed her own sentiments. To hear them so unabashedly touted was startling. Louise was looking to shock the adults around her, to horrify them and alienate them, because of her own sorrows. Henrietta would not succumb to the child's manipulations. The girl was hurt and grieving, and such behavior might be expected.

When Henrietta did not respond to that outburst, as Louise so clearly expected her to, the girl sent her one last brooding look before she ran off to chase butterflies.

She would need more than what Henrietta could offer. Although they had shared a connection…

Henrietta walked back to the house, deep in thought. A servant informed her the dowager countess was waiting for her in the parlor. She found the lady of the house at her desk, penning a letter.

"Ah, Miss Gordon, I have just heard of a perfect opportunity." Lady Brandewyne looked over the rim of her spectacles.

Sweet liver ague, she was surely referring to the earl's need for a governess. "Indeed?"

"Lord St. Raven has no governess."

Henrietta fought the grimace that tempted her lips.

"As I thought." Lady Brandewyne sniffed. "Your uncle is a very dear friend, and your parents were pillars of society. They would be horrified to see what's become of you. A governess is not the best position, but in time, perhaps, you will meet a kindly vicar or man of business. You are not completely plain."

"Thank you," she said drily.

"No decision must be made now. It is not impractical

to believe you could garner an offer from a baronet, perhaps at the house party in two weeks' time."

"I have not the slightest interest in rejoining society," she said in a firm voice, the one she used as often as needed. It was quite effective, even on Lady Brandewyne, whose posture stiffened. "A companion or governess position will suit me."

"Why not the governess position with Lord St. Raven? He is a good man. A fair man. He would compensate you adequately. He's not a stickler for propriety, which would allow you more of the freedoms you're used to. Before the accident, he spent most of his time in London, at any rate."

Shopping, no doubt, but Henrietta kept the uncharitable thought to herself. "He does seem as though he has a kind heart, but we would not be a good fit. Louise is in need of more than what I can offer. I am not good with children"

"My dear, I hardly think that. Your education is extensive and while your manners may have rusted, you were raised in a genteel fashion. Had your parents lived, you would have had your come-out and the pick of the Season."

"Even though I am not completely plain?"

Lady Brandewyne looked positively affronted. Her intelligence was such that she understood the sarcasm, but her ego was such that she could not believe it had been directed at her. Unable to decide how to answer, she settled for a nose-in-the-air glare.

Henrietta sought to relieve the tension with softer words. "It is very kind of you to have taken me in, but as you know, I have written several letters to nearby landowners and will no doubt find employment in record time."

"As you wish, my dear. I recommend that you do not make any decisions until after the house party, though."

Lady Brandewyne's lips pursed and for a moment, Henrietta had the strangest feeling that the lady was laughing at her, and that she'd been duped somehow.

Blackmail.

Dominic stared at the apothecary, who stood in the dark corner of the cottage, where he'd requested they meet.

The return to the St. Raven estate had been painful, just as Miss Gordon had said it would be, but after three days he'd decided to leave. At the mention of going to his estate in the north, Louise had begun weeping. She claimed to miss her home, and so, despite his reluctance to live at his dead brother's estate, he'd taken her back to St. Raven.

It was now her home, after all.

Old John, who'd been in the village near St. Raven since Dominic was a young boy, smirked a yellowed, rotting smile.

Dominic crossed his arms. "Let me understand this correctly—you are wanting a monthly stipend from me, and in exchange, you will not tell anyone of my condition. You realize the penalty for blackmail?"

The apothecary shrugged. "As I see it, if word gets out that you're afflicted, you'll lose the estate and the niece."

Dominic laughed coldly. "What makes you think I care?"

"Seems to me that niece of yours is going to get shipped off if you don't keep her here. I've heard talk. She can't keep a governess and her aunt wants to send her away." Old John sidled closer, his eyes gleaming wickedly in the morning light that streamed through the windows of his ramshackle cottage. Apparently being in the medical field didn't pay enough.

"I don't deal with blackmailers."

"Ah, but for the sake of the child? Will you let her be

sent off, her spirit crushed by well-meaning adults? She will be, you realize. On both counts." Old John cocked a brow. "And you will be ostracized. Epileptics scare society."

"Is that what you think I am?" he asked slowly.

The apothecary cackled. "You've been moping in northern England. I happen to know someone who witnessed one of your fits and he promptly wrote to me. I can see you're thinking about what I've said. My partner will give you three days to decide what means more—the girl's happiness or a bit of coin each month."

Dominic's jaw was stiff. His first instinct was to tell Old John to rot. He didn't care what society thought of him and he didn't care about the estate. He just wanted to find a cure.

But he loved Louise. He just hadn't realized what taking care of a child entailed. He'd always been the fun one, who brought her trinkets and cakes, who whisked into her life and whisked out with nary a cross word from her.

He glared at Old John and stalked out of the cottage. The ride back to the estate gave him time to realize that some of what the man had said was true. If word got out about his illness, Barbara would swoop in and take Louise. She might even have legal grounds, especially if he was taken against his will to an asylum. And then what?

He knew already, because Barbara had been sending him weekly letters urging him to send Louise out of the country to a finishing school for "difficult" girls. When this last governess quit, he had finally realized that if he didn't go and get Louise, his sister would. The situation could turn ugly, indeed.

He dropped off his horse at the livery, but there was no one in the stables to greet him. Frowning, he surveyed his surroundings, noting the disarray and general filth. Edmund's stables had never looked this way before his death.

He stabled the horse himself, pondering. Could he care for Louise, even with his illness? Could he oversee the estate while searching for a cure?

And the biggest question of all: Could he keep his illness a secret from the *ton*?

For some reason, Miss Gordon entered his thoughts. Strong and plucky, making her way in a man's world. If anyone knew how to accomplish something, she would. Perhaps he ought to meet with her.

When he returned to the main house, Jacks greeted him with a letter and a squirming Louise.

"I simply wanted to have tea with you," she said crossly, speaking before the valet. "I've missed you. Are you home for the rest of the afternoon?"

"Yes." He eyed her.

She twisted away from Jacks. "I shall meet you in the solarium, Dom, and we can discuss our new life together over tea." Flashing a smile that looked just like her father's, which stabbed pain through Dom, she pivoted and ran down the hall.

He opened the letter, which was an invitation to a ball hosted by Lady Brandewyne. Miss Gordon would be there, he realized. And suddenly, it felt imperative that he speak to her, face-to-face.

He handed the invitation back to Jacks. "Send an acceptance."

Chapter Four

Henrietta had definitely been duped. As the time for the house party drew closer, Lady Brandewyne's intentions became completely clear.

She was trying to marry off Henrietta, no doubt with Uncle William's blessing. His reasons for leaving were obviously a strategic tactic to aid Lady Brandwyne in her matchmaking.

Had he stayed, Henrietta would have been able to talk him out of this madness. But he had left to avoid the conversation, a realization that put her in a decidedly black mood.

To make things worse, Lady Brandewyne seemed to think Henrietta had forgotten the most basic tenets of *How to Behave Like a Lady*. When Henrietta emerged from the library or returned from a walk, invariably the woman gave her not-so-subtle etiquette lessons. Henrietta gritted her teeth and bore the verbal onslaught. After all, she was a guest in the dowager's home.

It was not as though she had not considered leaving for London. Uncle William let a house in Mayfair, but the Season was in full swing and Henrietta had no desire to stay in an area where carriages would be bumping across the roads into all hours of the morning. If not for that, she'd leave at once for a more peaceful setting with less marital hints.

"The house party shall be a small affair, really." Lady Brandewyne had called Henrietta in for tea in the parlor. She eyed Henrietta as though examining an infectious wound.

"I am expected to attend?" She knew she was, but she asked anyway, some puckish urge overtaking her mouth.

"But of course! It is, in a way, in your honor." She ignored the horrified expression Henrietta could not stop from displaying. "I've taken the liberty of procuring gowns based on the measurement of your other dresses." She gestured to the maid, Sally, who came over. "Bring me those boxes that were delivered earlier today."

Sally left while Henrietta struggled to control her temper. She rubbed her temples, trying to ease the ferocious pounding. "You have bought gowns?"

"Only a few. I wanted to surprise you."

Henrietta barely swallowed her snort. Surprise, indeed. More like browbeating. She feared this house party would best her social skills in unanticipated ways. She drew a deep breath, willing herself to smile, though her cheeks bunched unnaturally and her lips felt tight.

She foresaw nothing good about the coming event.

And she was right. After over a week of thinly disguised lessons in deportment and conversation suitable to ladies, the house party began. Guests arrived in various types of carriages, some more fancy than others. Lord St. Raven was among them, to Henrietta's shock. Louise was nowhere in sight, as expected. No other guests had brought children, either.

A rich evening meal started off the party. The countess placed Henrietta next to a baronet. "My neighbor to the south," Lady Brandewyne explained with an encouraging smile.

Henrietta did not don a return smile. She had no need to pretend to be anything other than herself. The man looked her over as though sizing up a horse at market. After the necessary introductions, he asked, "What part of England are you from?"

"North. My father was Lord Iversley but after he and my mother died, the second brother inherited the title and estate. My uncle, the youngest brother, took guardianship of me. He's a physician and we spent most of our time in the Americas. On the battlefield," she added, noting the crease between the baronet's eyebrows. "Tending soldiers, keeping my uncle's records. That sort of work."

The man blanched and, satisfied she'd made her point, she turned back to her food. No member of the peerage, even a baronet who technically was not considered a peer, wanted a wife who had worked. Henrietta set about eating her meal, a delicious concoction of boiled fowl with oyster sauce. She ignored the pinched disapproval on Lady Brandewyne's face and savored her food.

It was possibly the only good thing about returning to England.

After dinner, music had been arranged in the drawing room. Somehow Henrietta made it through the rest of the night without displaying a bad case of manners. She did not speak to Lord St. Raven, though she felt his eyes on her several times throughout the evening. When it seemed he might walk over and start a conversation, she avoided him. She couldn't say what drove her to do so, only a curious sense of self-preservation. On Friday and Saturday, she escaped some of the more strenuous activities planned by citing physical weakness.

But Saturday night arrived, despite Henrietta's prayers

otherwise. She entered the ballroom with trepidation. It was not grandiose compared to London ballrooms, but for a country estate, it was fashionably large and comfortable. Sparkling chandeliers cleaned to luminescent perfection hung from the ceiling. A quartet played quietly in a corner, warming up their instruments.

The butler announced guests as they arrived. Off to the side, Henrietta sipped her punch and listened as each entrant's name was called out. "Lord Dominic St. Raven."

Her head snapped up. The earl strode into the ballroom, tall and confident. A grin filled with charisma and mystery shaped his lips. A smile carved a dimple into his cheek. His clothes emphasized the broad swath of his shoulders and the strong length of his legs. His hair gleamed. A strange sensation curled in Henrietta's stomach as she stared at him from her safe little spot, where, thus far, no one had spotted her.

He was as cavalier as she'd expected, she thought as she watched him bowing over the pale, uncallused hands of the ladies present. He was laughing yet searched the room, as though his attention could not possibly be wasted on one person.

She sipped again, the punch doing little to calm her sudden case of nerves. Would he talk to her? Why was he attending Lady Brandewyne's house party anyhow? Henrietta had assumed he'd leave the country as soon as he was well enough.

Unbidden, a memory of Louise chasing butterflies flashed through her mind. Perhaps she should ask after Louise. Their shared grief created an invisible thread and it had been difficult for Henrietta to forget the girl. Or the uncle.

She studied him as he wound his way through the room. It was a scientific improbability that she would not notice him. All of the other ladies fawned over him, and men regarded him with a certain mix of respect and envy. He was a specimen of strong heritage.

She refused to fault herself for noticing the thickness of his hair and the confidence in his stride. His skin shone with improved health and his white, cared-for teeth hinted at a fastidious nature.

Yes, even a doctor could note such things. The churning in her stomach was very natural, she assured herself. Simply a physical and chemical reaction.

And then he turned and saw her.

Quiet and unobtrusive, she edged as close to a wall as possible, yet he saw her. Their gazes connected. She looked quickly away, eager to discourage him from approaching her.

The tactic did not work. Trying not to frown, she nodded a greeting as he neared.

"I see you are walking without pain," she said promptly.

"Is that why you were studying me so closely?"

Heat rose to her cheeks. Oh, where was that infernal fan Lady Brandewyne had shoved into her hands earlier? "You are a former patient," she said, hearing a primness in her voice that quite pleased her. *Let him do with that what he will.*

"Which is why I've meandered over. To allow you all the inspection you may need." His eyes crinkled, laughing at her.

It was probably better she didn't have a fan or else she'd be tempted to swat him with it, and then Lady Brandewyne might need use of her smelling salts.

His proximity was sending her pulse speeding along her veins. He wore a light cologne that teased her senses, and his fashionable attire did not scream *dandy* as loudly as she thought it might. He looked rather dashing, and that was enough reason for her to lift her chin and straighten her backbone.

"I am quite finished. You are in the pink of health. You may go now and continue your flirtations about the room."

Those dratted crinkles deepened. "A good doctor would take more time with her patient."

"Former patient, and I am not a doctor," she huffed.

He inclined his head, accepting the response. Then he gestured about the room, his long, tanned fingers contrasting with the white crispness of his cuff. "So which man is to be the winner tonight?"

She followed the direction of his hand sweep, her gaze narrowing. "What do you mean?"

"Your conquest…your intended. Who is it to be?"

Henrietta tilted her head, trying to figure out how he'd discovered Lady Brandewyne's shenanigans.

His expression changed. "Don't tell me you are not aware?"

"Aware of what?"

"Ah, that cross, suspicious tone. It tells me all I need to know."

"You're beastly, Lord St. Raven. Quit speaking in riddles and be out with it."

"The guests here are a curious mingle of friends and men looking for a wife."

"There are plenty of unattached females." But her stomach was sinking. "Are you saying you know that this affair was created solely to marry me off?"

"There were several tells." He tipped his cup toward her. "Your clothes, for instance. You are very pretty in that frothy confection of blues and satins. And slightly overdressed."

"Says the man whose boots are reflecting faces."

"They are Hessians, Miss Gordon. Do not fret, they

can't compare to your pearl-encrusted slippers that positively scream 'marry me.'"

"I did not pick out the shoes, and the ruffles are a bit overdone."

"Men like ruffles."

She glowered at him, but then cast a surreptitious peek about the room, and realized he was correct. Several gentleman were staring at her. Waiting, perhaps? For her to finish her conversation with an earl who, by everything she'd overheard this weekend, had no intention of ever settling down.

To make matters worse, she had not heard from her governess-post inquiries. That left her at the mercy of Lady Brandewyne. Refusing to attend the dowager's events would be the height of rudeness, in light of all that her ladyship had done for her.

"You're looking very fierce, Miss Gordon," St. Raven said lightly. "Is marriage such a loathsome prospect?"

"I have other goals."

"When do you rejoin your uncle?"

Henrietta slid him a look. He had the appearance of sincerity, the clear green of his eyes inquisitive. "Why are you spending your time talking to me? Lady Anne is near the orchestra. She's a beauty. Go cast your charm about her."

St. Raven's hand flew up, as though warding off attack. "Sharp words, and they would deeply wound me if there had not been the admittance of charm to soften the blow."

Henrietta rolled her eyes, but a laugh escaped. "Of course, that is all you heard."

"I retain important statements," he said solemnly.

"Obviously not—" Her laugh cut off as she spied the baronet heading toward her. "This is a disaster."

"Future husband?" St. Raven puckered his lips in a way

that was both funny and attractive. "A bit mule-faced if you ask me."

"One cannot help the bone structure one is born with." She raised an eyebrow at him. "We cannot all have symmetrical features, my lord, nor look as though we have been made to model for a Richard Crosse portrait."

"You know your painters. I'm impressed. And I believe you've given me another compliment. Two in one evening are noteworthy."

"Facts are not compliments."

"Miss Gordon." The baronet had reached them, a hopeful look upon his face. "Would you care to waltz with me?"

Henrietta felt the worst sort of panic at that point. Not only because she had not expected to waltz, considering it a fanciful and slightly inappropriate dance, but also because she hardly knew how. Before she could formulate a response, St. Raven moved forward.

"I'm afraid Miss Gordon has already promised this dance to me."

Dominic slid his arm around Henrietta, guiding her to the floor as the musicians began the first strains of the waltz. They had hardly started when she stepped on his toe.

"You see," he said, leaning close so that his lips were near her ear. She smelled of roses, of something soft and tender and sweet. "It is a good thing I wore sturdy boots to protect my delicate toes from your adventurous feet."

"You are ridiculous, my lord." A dusky hue invaded her cheeks.

Satisfied for some absurd reason, Dominic shrugged. "Better to be ridiculous than a snooze."

"You should not have claimed a dance with me."

"I was bored and you were near, and the waltz happens to be my favorite dance."

They swept across the room, Henrietta doing her best to follow his lead. He slowed somewhat for her halting steps, intrigued. "It's not often I meet a woman who cannot dance."

"I have had no cause to practice," she said in a small, stiff voice.

A hard part of him, one he did not realize existed, softened like butter on a warm day. He had no desire to cause her to feel badly about herself. "You have been saving lives, not spending your time learning silly dances."

"Sometimes lives were saved." A sad look overtook her face, and Dominic felt instant regret. His fingers tightened around hers and he was acutely aware of the slenderness of her body beneath his palm. "You never answered about when you plan to join your uncle?"

He swirled her past the bandstand, containing his wince when her knee knocked into his shin.

"I'm looking for a position somewhere. My uncle has decided to leave me in England, and I fear he hopes I'll marry."

"But you won't."

"No." Her gaze flashed up to his for the first time since they began dancing. There were bits of gold hidden in the darkness of her eyes. They were forthright, honest eyes. As though no one had taught her the art of guile or flirtation.

"Whatever will you do?" The music was slowing, the song almost finished. He guided them to an alcove, fully visible to retain her impeccable reputation, but private enough to enable conversation.

"Governess, or a paid companion, I suppose. Just long enough to garner fare to join Uncle William."

"He will not pay for your travel?"

She looked away, and Dominic realized that perhaps this lady was not without guile after all. For some reason, the notion amused him. "Does he know you're coming?"

"To be frank, no, he has told me to stay here." Those lovely eyes, earnest now, and somehow compelling, grabbed him. "But I cannot. I absolutely cannot stay. The only way for me to explain to him what I want is to speak to him face-to-face. Then he will see logic. I am quite sure of it."

"So you will defy the will of your guardian?"

"Bah." She waved her hand. "You speak of defiance as though he is the master of me."

"Is he not?"

"No," she said firmly. "And he knows that, which makes this situation altogether perplexing."

The music had changed, and other guests crowded the floor, but Dominic found himself captivated by the determined purpose in Miss Gordon's words. For many, many years his life had lacked direction. He had feared pursuing anything because of his affliction. Knowing he might die or be transported to an asylum at any time had put a damper on long-term goals.

"Why are you here?" he asked abruptly.

Startled, her lips pursed. "What do you mean?"

"Staying with Lady Brandewyne?"

"I suffered a bout with rheumatic fever."

"Your uncle feared for your life and brought you home to England."

"It was a small matter. He overreacted."

But Dominic heard the doubt in her voice, and he had noticed the clothing that didn't quite fit. Was it fair that she must surrender her freedom due to an illness? Or to the fears of an uncle? A plan was forming in his mind. He had simply wanted to get around to asking her what she knew about epilepsy, to get her opinion, but now he saw another, better option.

He flashed a grin. "You are looking lovely tonight. One would never guess you'd suffered from anything but an abundance of beauty and grace."

She gave him a look, one that said clearly she saw past his flirtations and perhaps even found them tedious. The thought made him laugh.

"I presume you are cackling at your paltry attempt to charm me." She crossed her arms, skewering him with an expression he might start calling her *doctor* look.

"Never. You are familiar with Louise and all her various quirks?"

"I would not call them quirks, but yes, I am aware that she is a strong-willed child."

"Perhaps then, we can help each other?"

Chapter Five

Dominic paused, debating his next words. Most governesses were ladies of quality who had fallen on hard times. With no immediate family to take them in and no marital prospects, they were often forced to find employment.

He knew little of Miss Gordon's family history, but he could not imagine the woman, with her quick tongue and keen eyes, succeeding in subservient positions. Though certainly she was intelligent enough to teach. It would be a matter of her nature conflicting with the expectations of her employer.

She had a genteel upbringing and extensive educational experiences. She had kept that doctor from sticking leeches all over him…but could she keep Louise in line? Could she make it so that Barbara did not take Louise?

If Miss Gordon discovered his epilepsy, would she be the type to send him to Bedlam? There were many who would agree with the decision.

He frowned. Louise had been nothing but trouble in the few weeks they'd been home. She needed more than what he could give, but if he let Barbara send her away, she'd never forgive him. Did Henrietta have the education necessary to teach Louise the attributes of a lady?

If only his niece had not been expelled. A school in England was better than one across the ocean.

After her parents' funeral, Dominic had sent her back to the highly esteemed boarding school she'd been attending since she was ten. That had been his first in a long series of mistakes.

For whatever reasons—he could not pretend to understand the workings of a twelve-year-old female's mind—Louise had decided to cease all good behavior. Within three months, she'd been expelled. Any misguided notion of an easy guardianship disappeared.

Then Barbara began nagging him and threatening his newfound hermit existence.

Even though he had retreated to the country, he did love Louise. He'd been selfish, holing away by himself. He had heartily enjoyed the conversations, music and dance in the past. Epilepsy had taken that from him.

Tonight, he'd been overly conscious of himself, worried that he might have an attack until he'd been diverted by Miss Gordon's quiet figure lurking against walls. Avoiding dances. She piqued his interest. Why would a woman given the chance to partake in the upper echelons of English society shun it?

Now he had his answer.

And he might be able to offer a reciprocal type of help.

Which brought him back to this very moment, where Miss Gordon stood waiting patiently for his next words. He noticed a few inquisitive sets of eyes upon them. He'd have to leave her soon or run the risk of gossip.

"Louise has spoken highly of you. She is at a determining point in life, and is in need of a firm hand. Someone who understands her pain."

They began waltzing on the outer sides of the ballroom. "She is in need of guidance. She respects you and

perhaps what she needs is a more unconventional governess. One who does not bow to a child's whims nor fears
losing her position by speaking her mind. One with a
breadth of knowledge that will intrigue a girl with Louise's curiosity."

"Optimistic words."

He gave her a small bow. "Consider my offer. I will
pay you a wage that will allow you to join your uncle."

"Why are you offering this? I—"

"I admire your vision," he interrupted. "It is a rare
and precious thing in life to know what you want. Even
more, to pursue it. Perhaps I have not lived my own life
as fully as I ought to, and in a way I can't explain, I want
to help you."

She nodded, accepting his words even as he struggled
to understand them himself. "I will consider it, my lord,
and send you word."

Henrietta awoke in a foul mood.

She did not know how to answer Lord St. Raven. His
offer last night had taken her by surprise, though perhaps
it should not have. He had been needing a governess for
some time. She supposed it made a modicum of sense
that he'd asked her. She had been tempted to give him a
resounding no, but a few reasons stopped her.

One, the house party ended today, but Lady
Brandewyne had informed her that she planned for them
to take a trip to London soon. Shopping and whatnot, but
then she'd added that several gentleman had asked to call
on them when they were in town.

Henrietta wasn't sure why they would. She was no great
beauty and had no money, but her lineage was quite good,
she supposed. Stomach twisting, she rolled onto her back
and looked at the vaulted ceiling.

She had not lived anywhere so grand since childhood. Those memories remained locked away, and she never visited them. It would be easy to accept a lower position, and sleep in a tiny room, if she could hold onto her dream of studying medicine. She'd even considered going to Italy, where they were much more accepting of female students.

A tiny worry crept in. What if she found her uncle, and he sent her away?

She pushed the unruly thought to the back of her mind.

Her second reason for not outright denying Lord St. Raven is that he had made a good point. Louise needed someone who cared. And for some reason, perhaps because of their shared orphan state, she did.

Groaning, she rolled out of the bed to face the day.

And the handsome earl for whom she was going to accept a governess position.

The guests dispersed after an involved luncheon. Henrietta hardly noticed. Her mind was preoccupied. She saw Lord St. Raven at one point, and offered him a nod, but he looked peaked and wan. Perhaps he'd woken with a stomachache as well, she thought ruefully.

Her mind conjured multiple scenarios. She paced her room. She ate four scones and drank three cups of hot chocolate.

Finally, around the three-o'clock hour, she sent Lord St. Raven a note via a housemaid that she would accept his offer and be ready to leave whenever he required.

Then she found Lady Brandewyne resting in the solarium. The bright room captured sunlight with oversized windows and then painted glowing swaths of yellow across the terra-cotta floors. Fauna of varying colors lined the walls and a cheery bench sat in the middle of the room for those wishing to admire the views.

"What did you think of the house party?" The dowager countess looked up from her sewing.

"The guests appeared to enjoy themselves greatly."

"And did you?"

"That is what I've come to speak to you about." Henrietta slid onto the bench across from Lady Brandewyne. "I have decided to accept a governess position for Lord St. Raven."

If Henrietta had been watching the countess more closely, she might not have missed the strange little quirk at the corner of her lips. As it was, she was staring at her hands in silence and so did not realize that Lady Brandewyne was not altogether unhappy.

"My dear, I shall miss you, but this is for the best. He shall treat you well."

"Is there anything I must do before leaving?"

"Do? Of course not." Lady Brandewyne waved her diamond-encircled fingers. "The servants shall see to your trunks. Are you leaving today?"

"Whenever Lord St. Raven is ready. I shall leave a letter for my uncle for you to post, if that will do? And we will keep this between us?"

Lady Brandewyne nodded, and the matter was settled. The rest of the day passed with a flurry of activity. She had been staying there for several months and had much to pack. Her lady's maid would not be going with her. Governesses did not get such a luxury.

A note arrived from the earl stating that they'd leave at first light in the morning, as it was half a day's travel to reach the St. Raven estate from Lady Brandewyne's. For the first time, Henrietta felt a flurry of nerves. She'd been traveling for half her life, from one place to another, but always with her uncle.

When morning came, and she found herself safely

ensconced in the earl's unsurprisingly plush carriage, the feeling still had not abated. She waved to Lady Brandewyne out of the gold-rimmed windows before closing the curtain and settling back against the squabs. She'd brought a book to read, but the passing countryside, with its verdant slopes and kaleidoscope of flowers, snared her attention.

Perhaps an hour or so had passed when the carriage slowed, then pulled to the edge of the road. Henrietta opened the door before the footman did, peering out. The earl's valet walked toward her, a grim expression on his face.

"Miss Gordon, his lordship has requested we stop for a moment. He is in need of rest. Might you like a small repast by the creek?" He pointed to a sparkling creek in the distance. A few trees stood sentry on its banks.

Henrietta blinked and then reached for her book. He had looked tired last night, she recalled.

"I hope he is well?" she murmured.

With the valet's assistance, she climbed out of the carriage. The balmy summer day stood in stark contrast to the concern on the valet's face. The sound of hooves grew louder as St. Raven pulled his horse up and dismounted. The sunlight drew attention to the pallid taint of his skin, the grooves at the corners of his eyes. The whites of his eyes were not yellow, though, and his pupils appeared normal.

"What are your symptoms, my lord?"

His lips pressed together. He shook his head. "Jacks, make sure Miss Gordon has all she needs."

"Are you sweating?" She reached to touch his skin, but he jerked back. There was a strange sheen to his coloring. "Let me check your heart and lungs. Jacks, if you would be so good as to retrieve my leather satchel. Be gentle, for I've valuable items inside."

"Go with him, now." St. Raven's words came out funny. Slightly garbled.

The carriage door remained open and Lord St. Raven stumbled toward it, in a lurching stagger that caught Henrietta by surprise. She slid to the side, allowing him room, but already she could see his eyes rolling back in his head. He fell into the carriage, drawing his knees up and lying on the floor.

His left arm jerked, the hand curled into clawlike rigidity.

Henrietta glanced down the road, noting the valet still digging in the other carriage for her medical supplies. The footman helped, and the coachman was nowhere to be seen. She grabbed the carriage door and half closed it, blocking the opening with her body. Lord St. Raven convulsed on the floor, his head knocking against the seat in a macabre, uneven rhythm.

Henrietta forced herself to keep looking, to watch even though her palms dripped and her heart wrenched in her chest. She had seen this before. The strange contortions, the stretched grimacing of the face.

In an asylum in France. When she was sixteen.

Epilepsy.

Finally the fit ended. St. Raven's body relaxed, though guttural noises were coming from him. She wanted to go in and check to make sure his head had not been injured, but the valet was bringing her medical bag. She closed the door more, shoving the earl's boots inside the carriage to do so.

"Your supplies, miss."

"Thank you. The earl does not feel well and is lying on the floor. I shall need something soft, a blanket perhaps.

Fetch Alice, please, as I will need to go in and examine his lordship." It seemed forever, but finally the female servant Lady Brandewyne had sent to protect Henrietta's reputation arrived. She'd ridden with the trunks in the other carriage. She wore a put-out expression that Henrietta ignored.

"If you will just stand right there." She pointed to the side of the carriage, where it could be reasonably said that Henrietta had been chaperoned, and yet Alice would not be able to see the earl. She opened the door and climbed in, shoving her skirts to the side and hefting her bag onto the seats.

A bluish cast to his face told her he'd stopped breathing at some point, though now the forceful exhalations of sound indicated steady respiration. She put her ear to his chest. No distress. Perspiration stained his underarms.

Henrietta examined him quickly, gently putting the blanket the valet brought beneath his head. She kept the door slightly closed, leaving a mere crack, and waved away the worried eyes of his staff. When she emerged, she shut the door firmly behind her.

They stood at the side of the road, the bright sunlight drawing attention to their somber faces. After all, it had only been a few weeks ago that he'd been attacked. Their worry attested to their regard for their employer.

"Does he have these episodes often?" She set her bag on the ground and studied them, particularly the valet.

"Episodes? What do you mean, ma'am?"

Every face reflected confusion. Sighing, Henrietta tapped her hips as she thought of what to say. She didn't care for the ratlike curiosity in Alice's beady eyes. A gossiper, no doubt. She suspected his lordship's condition was a secret that even his valet was not privy to.

Or else he was doing a splendid job of acting ignorant.

Either way, Henrietta had no desire to reveal St. Raven's infirmity to this group. She cleared her throat. "Tiredness and fatigue. Perhaps it is a side effect of his cracked ribs. Let us take a short break and then be on our way. I shall ride with Alice and we will leave the earl to rest."

"Will he be all right?" That from Jacks.

Henrietta nodded with force. Yes, he would be fine as long as no one in English society ever found out about his epilepsy.

She did not know much of the condition, but one thing she did know: those with it were often ostracized from polite society and confined to an asylum for the remainder of their lives.

How he had managed to escape detection, she could not fathom, but she would not be the one to expose his secret.

Chapter Six

An *epileptic.*

Henrietta could hardly believe the truth. A rare condition that she longed to research, but instead she sat quietly in the carriage with Alice. The loaner from Lady Brandewyne, while nicely made, could not compare to the comfort of St. Raven's carriage. Alice's company was not particularly enjoyable, either. She spent the rest of the ride clicking her knitting needles while Henrietta churned the facts over and over in her mind.

She knew very little about epilepsy. Only enough to recognize the symptoms. Surely St. Raven was resting now. He hadn't emerged. The carriages had kept up a steady clop and now it had grown dusky and cool, a hint of rain in the air. They turned into a long drive lined by trees and statues. Henrietta's window encompassed a view of the St. Raven estate. It was a smaller version of Lady Brandewyne's. They rounded up the drive and then slowed to a stop.

Perhaps she'd be brought around back to the servant's entrance? She gathered her bags, prepared to get out when told. Alice watched, her mouth a crimped line, reminding Henrietta that she was no more a servant than she was a peer.

In the middle. That was her new position. Neither privy to the confidences of the servantry, nor entitled to the privileges of the *ton*.

The carriage door opened and St. Raven peered inside. "We're here," he said, his grin lopsided. He looked no worse for wear. His cravat had been straightened and his skin had regained its color, as far as she could tell in the twilight.

With his help, she exited the carriage. Alice was behind her and then St. Raven guided her to the front door. "This is it. My humble abode."

"Humble, indeed." Square-shaped beds of grass decorated the front yard, carefully trimmed and verdant. The house itself was composed of rectangles and squares that sharply jutted into pointed roofs. The typical country home, resplendent and tight-angled.

A butler came out to greet St. Raven. She observed the earl, hanging back to watch his loose-limbed gait. He did move slowly, as though tired. There was no other evidence that only a few hours ago his body had contorted outside of his control.

Yes, she'd have to research more.

Behind her, the carriages rolled away and she realized that she was to follow St. Raven into the house. She joined him at the doorway, looking past him to the gilded entryway lit by several lamps along the walls.

He ushered her in, his eyes shadowed, belying the curved dimple in his cheek. "My childhood home."

"It is lovely," she said. "If you'll show me my rooms, I'll get situated."

"Would you care for tea first?" His question was not

a question. He guided her to a small parlor before she could say no.

St. Raven's eyes were tenebrous in here, without the sun to make them sparkle. One could almost mistake them for a dark green.

He did not shut the door. He meandered to a corner of the room, next to a lit golden girandole whose worth appeared to be more than the annual earnings of a governess. The furniture was ornate, heavy. Strange lionlike creatures rose from the edges of the couch. All in all, an uncomfortable, auspicious room.

She faced St. Raven, and was reminded of his overall largeness in comparison to her size. She'd been called slight. Never had she felt so, until she stood next to St. Raven. A shiver crept through her at the intensity on his face. She rubbed her arms, conscious that her medical bag remained with her belongings.

"About earlier…" He trailed off, stroking his chin with long, well-manicured fingers.

Henrietta pulled herself taller. "Yes, your epileptic attack."

"You saw." His eyebrows narrowed, ebony lines against tan skin.

"It was a shock, to be sure. You have lived with this condition unbeknownst to your staff?"

He shrugged, a curiously unaffected movement. "To most, yes. It is not something I want bandied about." He paused. "Are you familiar with epileptic disorders?"

"The only fits I have seen were in an asylum." An honest answer, though it emerged slowly.

"And is that where you think I belong?"

A strong, undeniable current pulsed between them. A moment of energized tension that illuminated the cost of this secret and the fortitude it took to maintain a cover of health and normality. She swallowed, her heart drumming, her fingers picking at her skirt.

He had given no indications of madness. His staff cared for him, as evidenced by their worry. She wet her lips, meeting his eyes, which bored into her, questioning, seeking. She drew from the wells of her authoritarianism on all things medical. Perhaps she had no experience with society, but she knew patients.

And despite the rocky planes of his face, the stiff cut of his shoulders, fear hid beneath it all.

"You are not a madman, my lord, and I do not believe you should be institutionalized."

His gaze flickered. The jaw that had been granite-hewn relaxed ever so slightly. "I quite agree, Miss Gordon. You will keep this information between us?"

Another question that was not a question.

"I shall do my best." After all, he was her employer now. And quite possibly, her patient.

He locked his arms behind his back, regarding her so seriously as to make her wonder how she'd ever thought him careless and lacking in soberness. "That will be all, Miss Gordon. I will ring for Mrs. Braxton, the head maid. She will show you to your room, the schoolroom and the general layout of the servants' quarters. I trust you will tell me should you feel unwelcome in any way."

"How I feel is of no consequence. My job is to teach Louise, and that is what I shall focus on." Speaking of the girl, she hadn't seen or heard her. Which struck her as immensely odd. "Where is she?"

St. Raven paused. "It is odd that she has not come to greet me."

He called for the head housekeeper. She appeared promptly.

"Where is Louise?" asked the earl.

Her fingers fluffed the folds of her dress. "She heard she was to have another governess, and to prove her lack of need for one, she ran off again."

"How often does this occur?"

"As often as she wishes."

"And you allow it?"

His housekeeper looked surprised. "She did it with her parents and they were not alarmed."

"Well, they should have been," he snapped. "Assemble the servants in the hall at once."

Henrietta nodded with approval. Until she could do more research, there was nothing more to be said about his epilepsy. Standing there looking into his handsome face accomplished nothing. He wasn't even trying to be charming, and yet she found herself studying the lines and curves of his features, storing the scent of his cologne in the back of her mind.

It was positively the most disturbing response she'd ever had to a man, and becoming a governess was probably the worst idea she'd ever had, but Lady Brandewyne had backed her into a tight and inescapable corner.

Besides, she now felt a deep concern for Louise's whereabouts. "What do you mean to do?" she asked St. Raven.

"I mean to find the girl." He pivoted, leading Henrietta into the hall. Mrs. Braxton stood as stiff as a marble statue, her features settled into a frown. "Don't you ever look for her? Doesn't anyone chase her down and tell her to stop running away?"

"My apologies, my lord," she replied. "But why on earth would we do such a thing when her parents allowed it? Where can she go?"

"Those questions are irrelevant. She should not have left at all. When she returns, she shall have warm tea and biscuits waiting for her. Mrs. Braxton shall put hot irons at the foot of her bed to heat her toes, and it will not be allowed again."

"Hot irons? Tea and biscuits?" Henrietta crossed her arms. "You are rewarding negative behavior. This simply will not do."

His head tilted, then his gaze shifted past her. "Mrs. Braxton, call the servants. We must find Louise."

At that moment, a crack of thunder shook the house. Rain tapped the roof, picking up speed and then turning into wild dance of sound.

"This weather is not good for her lungs."

"We will find her," he said, his features strained.

Servants filed into the hallway, lining up by rank.

St. Raven crossed his arms behind his back, posture ramrod-straight and mouth firm. "Please welcome Miss Gordon. She is Louise's new governess."

She did not miss the exhalations of relief many of the servants tried to hide. Was Louise so terrible? Perhaps these people just did not know how to contain an excitable child. Not that Henrietta had much experience with child-rearing, but common sense told her that consistency and a gentle attitude went far toward taming mischief and being spoiled.

"We will be looking for my niece, and she is not to run off like this anymore. Does anyone have an idea of where she might've gone?"

"She likes the horses," a young footman volunteered.

"Or the pond," said Mrs. Braxton. A portly woman with a severe set to her chin, she nevertheless carried a twinkle in her eye. "Always catching the minnows, though I tell the young miss it isn't sightly."

"Excuse me?" A maid at the back stepped forward.

"I've seen her at the folly…a few times, my lord." She bowed, looking apprehensive as she did so.

"The folly?" St. Raven stroked his chin. "That does sound like a good place to hide and it would appeal to a twelve-year-old's imagination. Very good, thank you. Stay here and set out tea and sandwiches for when the others return. Check the stables and the pond. Look through the house. I will search the folly."

"I will ready the horses." A whiskered man bowed and left quickly.

Henrietta lifted her skirts, prepared to follow the man.

St. Raven put out a hand to stop her. "Not so fast, Miss Gordon. You've just overcome a lung disease. You'll stay here."

"It was an infection." She narrowed her eyes, dodging out of reach of his imperious touch. "I certainly will not stay. I am going with you. I'll wear an extra layer. You might need me. Louise could be hurt."

"Don't you think I know that?" His voice was harsh, his eyes glints of green. Another shock of thunder resonated.

She took the thick shawl a footman handed her. The butler opened the door and rain sluiced into the house, pelting the floor in huge, splattering drops.

St. Raven gestured her out and, summoning fortitude, and aware of a simmering panic for Louise's safety gaining ground within, she stepped into the storm.

Dominic didn't think he'd ever felt such intense fear in his life. His jaw ached from clenching, and his neck kinked. The ride to the folly had been arduous and bumpy, the carriage traversing the rain-slicked path and mud holes with ferocious dexterity.

The folly loomed behind the flickering lightning and

sheets of rain. It was as though someone had shattered the sky. And Louise was out in this.

The carriage came to a stop and he exited, then turned to help Henrietta out. Her bones were as light as a bird's, and he felt her shiver when he put his arm around her waist. Mouth tight, he set her gently on the ground. A maid stayed in the carriage with warm blankets and hot tea, for when they returned.

He turned, trying to see past the torrential waterfall drenching the landscape. The folly's artfully constructed columns rose like pale sentries against the smeared horizon. His brother had constructed the thing at his wife's request. Many in the *ton* created ornamental buildings in their gardens. This was located a bit farther from the main house and had been designed to look like a Greek pavilion. With this wind-driven rain, however, the odds of the pavilion's interior remaining dry were low.

He swiped his hand across his face, seeking relief from the stinging nettles of precipitation. "We shall look within," he shouted.

Henrietta replied, her words lost in the noise. The downpour slammed against the ground, making hearing anything impossible. They trudged toward the folly, picking through debris strewn across the path.

Jacks held a lamp, but the flickering light did little to ease the way. Henrietta moved ahead of him, her steps nimble and quick. She dodged up the steps of the folly, disappearing into the cavernous blackness that was its entrance.

Dominic muttered under his breath and picked up his pace. Infuriating woman. He'd have two to worry about if she wasn't careful. He eased into the darkness, taking the lamp from Jacks and holding it up to see inside the oval-shaped orifice. Henrietta stood in the middle, eyes wide.

She shook her head when the light fell upon her face. She was speaking but the words were silently whipped away into the night.

Leaning close, he put his ear to her mouth to hear her better.

"She's not here." Worry crowded her syllables, and his chest tightened.

"We'll find her."

He straightened, pushing back the urge to hug Henrietta and tell her everything would be fine.

Before he knew what she was doing, she grabbed his hand and Jacks's. He glanced down, and realized she was praying. Holding up the lamp, he saw that her eyes were closed and her lips were moving softly and though he could not hear her words, he felt them.

The pattering of rain and the growling of thunder all coalesced into one strange moment of peace in which he wondered if God would hear this unconventional woman. Would He answer in the way they wanted him to? He closed his eyes, her small hand enfolded in his, her fingers tiny yet strong.

And then she let go.

Jacks met his eyes, shrugging as though the foibles of woman fazed him not. For his part, Dominic just wanted to find Louise. The more time that passed, the more likely she'd caught sick.

She could be at home, of course. Just because she was missing didn't mean she'd been outside. But the twisting pain in his gut told him otherwise. She was out here, somewhere, alone.

Henrietta had left the center circle. She explored the circumference of the folly, going from pillar to pillar, her skirts wet and dragging.

Dominic gave the lamp to Jacks. "Stay here in the mid-

dle. If Louise is out there, she'll see your light." He strode
to the stairs and, shielding his eyes, looked out over the
landscape for anything that could be construed as human.
Nothing but rocks and trees and sloping land in the gray-
ish dirge.

A shout filtered through the noise of the storm. Pivoting, Dominic saw the light swinging crazily back and
forth.

He strode back into the folly and there was Louise,
lying in Henrietta's lap. They were shivering and when
Henrietta looked up, he couldn't tell whether her eyes were
wet with rain or tears. Louise's hair was plastered to her
head, and violent spasms wracked her body.

He kneeled, taking her from Henrietta. His niece snug-
gled into him, not talking, which was worrisome in and
of itself.

"Her ankle is twisted."

Dominic followed Henrietta's pointing finger to Louise's right foot, which was without a shoe and garish in
the flickering, black-blue light. As round as an orange,
and puffy. He pulled Louise closer to his chest, beckoning with his chin for the others to follow.

Henrietta took the lamp to lead the way, and Jacks attempted to hold his coat over Louise as they stumbled
back to the carriage. Jacks went in first, then Dominic
handed Louise up to him. In the carriage light, her lips
were tinged blue and her eyes closed. He had never seen
such pale eyelids, devoid of coloration.

He helped Henrietta in, then followed. Jacks laid Louise on his lap, and every so often, her body shook with
tremors. Tension rode back to the house with them, and
Louise said nothing. Dominic could not recall ever feeling so helpless in his life, except in the aftermath of his

own seizures. The full scope of humanity's fragile hold on life glared at him accusingly.

Louise might have died. Could still die.

He would do anything to keep her safe. Including paying the blackmail demands so that Barbara did not find out about his epilepsy. Now that he had a governess, he simply needed to find a cure.

Jacks and the maid were silent spectators in the carriage, their eyes huge with worry. But Henrietta reached over and smoothed hair from Louise's forehead. She took the girl's hand and rubbed it between hers.

"Keep her warm, St. Raven."

"I'm trying." His voice cracked. "Will she die?"

Henrietta looked up at him then, her pupils giant black orbs. "Not if I have anything to say about it."

Chapter Seven

"I am not going to let you die."

"It is a possibility?" Louise's voice rusted out the question, dry and cracked.

Henrietta dampened a cloth, wrung it, then wiped it gently over her clammy forehead. "Perhaps it would be, if you did not have such a skilled nurse at your side."

The little girl's lids closed, blue-veined and papery thin, but a tremulous smile shook her lips. After a scary night, her fever had finally broken this morning.

"She's awake." St. Raven appeared in the doorway.

"Yes, you leave for ten minutes, and she opens her eyes." Henrietta placed the cloth back in the washbowl, then wiped her hands on a towel. "I think she may have gone back to sleep. Did you finish your work?"

St. Raven lifted one shoulder casually, as if he couldn't be bothered to notice if he'd finished or not. "An earl does not work, Miss Gordon."

She nodded, though in truth she didn't understand. Work carried various connotations. Everyone worked in one way or another.

"Have you come to sit with her again?"

"Yes, and to inquire if you have need of anything."

The fever that had invaded Louise had been alarming, but she already showed signs of improvement. A good thing, as Henrietta had been up with her for much of the night. So had St. Raven. Purple crescents shadowed the skin beneath his eyes.

"She may wake and ask for water. I have been bathing her forehead, but she is no longer feverish." Henrietta glanced down. Louise looked so very frail beneath the covers. Helpless and tiny, a wisp of a human on the cusp of adulthood. Heart twisting, Henrietta stood. "She will be well within days. Then she will need to be taken to task for her antics."

His eyebrows rose. "Are you on that again?"

"Do you enjoy seeing this?" She swept her hand in an arc. "Do you wish to repeat this situation every few months? If not, then take her in hand, my lord. Teach her how to handle disappointments."

"As you were taught?" he asked quietly.

Who was this serious man? She almost hoped he'd return to the bantering, superficial creature of days ago. "No," she returned. "As you were."

"Touché." He made way as she slid past him. "You will put this entire house in order?"

She stopped at the doorway, hearing the amusement in his voice and strangely glad for it. "Will you be paying me? Because the breakfast was cold. The oatmeal gelatinous. And there is dust along the windowsills. Someone needs to take charge here."

"I have a housekeeper."

"Mrs. Braxton, yes. A busy woman."

He nodded, but she could tell that she had sobered his levity. That had not been her intention. "Louise shall awaken again and I've no doubt she will be happy to see you. In the meantime, I will rest before preparing the schoolroom, though she's a bit old for it. I would recommend that she be put in a private school once I've left. Not a finishing school. Those are becoming obsolete. There are places you can send her where she'll learn more than the art of being a man's decor."

St. Raven appeared startled, and indeed, Henrietta had surprised herself with the bold words. Heat suffused her face, but she refused to take back the opinion.

"Your advice is noted." He studied her further, his handsome features pensive. "Rest assured, she attended a prestigious school before the headmistress dismissed her."

"Dismissed…that does not surprise me. This was after her parents died?"

His eyes flickered in acknowledgment.

She gave him a gentle smile. "She's a strong-minded young lady who will need to be carefully handled. Your brother and his wife would've been proud, my lord."

He looked down. "Her aunt feels that Louise would be better off in a school on the Continent. She has asked me several times for guardianship of her."

What to say to such a confession? It was not that she disapproved of a girls' school, but she could not help but think that such a place would stifle Louise's natural enthusiasms.

"And what do you think?"

"I have spent the last few months in northern England at my cottage, but I had no intention of allowing Barbara to raise the girl." He glanced down at the sleeping girl, contemplation a heavy curtain across his features. "Now I wonder if I am up to the task."

"Raising a child is a monumental feat," she murmured, thinking of her own family and how she'd maneuvered them into letting her live with Uncle William.

"Indeed. We are in a strange situation. One in which you are a governess who is not really a governess."

"Not really a governess? Really, St. Raven, that is slightly offensive."

"I insist you call me Dominic." Sunlight glinted off his hair, the shiny strands as dark as a raven's wing. Not a hint of brown in there, she realized obtusely. He wore an inscrutable expression, his lips serious, his eyes fastened upon her. "It is not my intention to offend, but surely you understand my meaning."

"I simply do not see the point in using our Christian names. Yes, the Americans are not so formal and it is true that I prefer informality, but I am trying to teach Louise the value of her cultural mores. The correct use of titles is important in English society."

"But it is not important to a family, nor to a child who needs to feel involved."

She pursed her lips, studying him, and the earnestness that had blotted out the teasing. Why did she feel uncertain, as though he was asking her to cross an invisible line?

And yet didn't she find him intriguing? The idea of using his name was both thrilling and terrifying. A comfortable segue to their relationship.

"Very well. *Dominic.* And you may call me Henrietta. But in society, we must adhere strictly to expected standards. This is for Louise's benefit."

"But of course," he murmured, dipping his head.

She gave him a terse nod and left the room.

For the next week she busied herself setting the schoolroom to rights, finding outdated books that might still retain some kind of pertinence for Louise. Her bedroom was small but comfortable. Set near the nursery, she had few opportunities to encounter servants and she had discovered that the sitting room was rarely used. Although she'd been out of England for many years, she was familiar with the duties of a governess. Including the desired goal of teaching her pupil to be ready for marriage to a peer.

What she had not expected was the distance with which the servants treated her. In fact, they hardly spoke to her.

And consequently, Henrietta felt the first stirrings of loneliness. The library became her sanctuary. One evening after dining alone in her room, she perused the available books while ruminating on her day. It had been a good one. Louise had eaten all of her meals and taken a careful walk around the gardens. Perhaps tomorrow they might begin lessons.

Which was another reason why Henrietta found herself in the library. She wasn't certain where to start. Literature or arts or sciences. Sewing could wait for a rainy day. Dancing… Dominic would have to hire a dance instructor.

How easily his first name flowed into her thoughts. Sighing, she pulled a novel from the third shelf. A cloud of dust billowed outward and she sneezed. Waving her hand in front of her face, she turned and encountered the earl.

His silent presence took her by surprise. "My lord, what are you doing in here?"

"I thought you might wish to have company."

She looked past him. No servants nearby, but the door to the library remained open. "I am looking for tomorrow's studies. Something interesting. Botany, perhaps. Or the study of insects. Louise enjoys butterflies."

"Pinning them to her collection, you mean?"

"I shall encourage her to study them whilst they are alive."

"You were in the gardens today."

Henrietta's gaze shot up. "You saw us."

"Yes. Louise is recovering well. Her ankle has healed?"

"It was a minor sprain, enough to keep her stuck in that…folly. Is that what you call it?"

Dominic laughed, a husky sound that tickled Henrietta's senses. What scientific reason could she attribute to such a reaction? Wetting her lips, she smiled back.

"Yes, a folly and it is the most ridiculous thing I've ever seen. I try to forget it's there."

"Louise quite likes it. I believe the fanciful nature of such a place stimulates her imagination and will provide a good backdrop for multiple history lessons. Perhaps even philosophy, if I can get her to believe it to be a place where Plato might hold his lessons."

"Who?"

She gaped, and Dominic laughed again. "I jest. Do not look so affronted. I am sure whatever you have planned will be beneficial." His lips quirked. "Am I to understand you believe in flights of fancy? That hardly sounds practical or scientific."

An acute sense of embarrassment stole over her in hot waves. Surely this was not the usual banter between an employer and his governess.

Squaring her shoulders, she looked up her nose at him. She could not very well look down as he stood a good head taller than her. Nevertheless, she attempted a stoic and tutorial look. "You would be surprised by the wide range of studies in the academic field. There is room for many objects of study."

"Chemistry, for instance?"

"For those with an interest, I suppose."

Dominic ran a finger along the shelf, picking up dust and staring at it with a lazy grin. "Some of us, Henrietta, are more interested in chemistry than others." His gaze met hers, and the mellow lights of the candles caught the sparkle in his eyes.

Swallowing, she clutched the book to herself.

"It is quite a bit of dust," he murmured.

"More than what is acceptable." She had noticed other problems as well, but it was not her place to mention them. With great purpose, she pressed her lips together to avoid speaking out of turn. "If that will be all, I shall go up to my room now."

He turned to her, brow furrowed. "All is to your liking?"

Words jammed against the roof of her mouth. She squeezed the book, pressing her fingers into it as though she could halt the flood of opinion fighting to be freed. "My room is comfortable. Good night, my lord."

He nodded, his eyes watchful, and she felt his gaze boring into her back as she skirted out of the room.

Dominic shoved the papers on his desk to the side. The piles seemed to grow every day and so did his frustration. He jammed his fingers through his hair, groaning. Sunlight streamed across the desk that used to be his brother's.

Edmund had most likely kept it much neater.

He plucked the note that had been delivered this morning, rubbing it between thumb and forefinger. In a burst of temper, he swept his arm across the surface of the desk, scattering everything to the floor. Inventories and bills and documents to be signed.

Now the desk gleamed at him, dust gathered in the spots where the papers had not sat. He didn't want an earldom or epilepsy. He wanted to be in London. Lounging at White's with his friends or sitting at Ascot to marvel at the horses primed for racing. Right now, he could use a few pugilistic bouts to release the tension building within.

But no. He was stuck in the country. Getting blackmailed.

How it rankled to be threatened with losing Louise. At least she was thriving beneath Henrietta's tutelage. He would continue to resist both Barbara and his blackmailers until he could find a cure.

Getting up, he stalked out of his office. He prowled the house until he spotted his niece and Henrietta from the huge window in the breakfast nook. They were on the lawn. Playing some sort of game.

Last night had been dangerous. He needed more to divert his attention. When he'd wandered into the library and found Henrietta's delicate features absorbed in the books, then her dark and forward eyes fastening on him, he'd felt a strong current of attraction that had been difficult to ignore. They were growing closer. Perhaps he should not have told her to call him by his given name.

Frowning, he stood at the window and watched them running across the grass, apparently laughing if one could judge by the thrown-back heads and happy movements. The arms across the stomachs as they bent at the waist, trying to contain something that could never be contained.

Henrietta was good for Louise. She understood the girl, somehow. What he'd felt for her was nothing more than appreciation of her good looks mingled with respect. That was all. He'd been gone from London too long.

This attraction to Henrietta, his governess, could be nothing more than boredom. In fact, he'd go outside and prove it to himself.

It took only minutes for him to reach the two females. By the time he'd walked up on them, they had collapsed on a sizable blanket, where their hats were strewn and a lunch basket was filled to the brim, their giggles feminine and irresistible.

He loomed above them, the noon sun casting very little

shadow to announce his presence. "Shouldn't you two be in the schoolroom?"

Their laughing ceased.

Louise jumped up. "Dom!"

She propelled herself into his arms and he hugged her, thankful for the energy pulsing through her, the life, the healthy shudders of exertion rather than fever.

"This is our schoolroom." She twirled, her skirts fluttering. "Henrietta says we'll learn more out here than we ever will in a stuffy old room."

He let himself look at Miss Gordon then. A jolt jerked through him. Her hair was a messy mass of blond-streaked strands floating about pink-stained cheeks. Her flushed lips looked like roses after a spring rain and her eyes shone like melted chocolate.

"I hope you don't mind, my lord, but I gave her permission to call me by my given name. It seemed appropriate considering the circumstances." Her smile was plucky, and a twinge wrenched its way through his chest.

"It's unorthodox." He managed to squeeze out a coherent answer, though he wasn't sure how as his heart galloped faster than the racers in the Royal Ascot. Yes, he needed to escape back to his home in northern England, away from the emotions assaulting him.

"But not uncommon in America." She pushed to her feet, swiping at her skirts as if she could undo the wrinkles growing there.

"In my presence, Louise, you are to call her Miss Gordon."

"That's very crotchety of you, Uncle." Louise put her hands on her hips. "She says in America no one uses titles. People are practical and on the same social level."

"She's teaching you already, I see."

Henrietta's grin widened. That spontaneous curve to

her lips quickened his pulse, sent his thoughts flying into a mass of confusion. Louise grinned, too, her top teeth a tad too big for her face, giving her a puckish, piquant air.

"Everything in life is teachable."

"Then shall we resort to nicknames? We can't let those Americans have the upper hand." He waggled his eyebrows at them both. "I hereby dub you Retta."

"Retta?" Louise squealed and grabbed him in a hug. Her face turned up to him, nose wrinkled. "That's atrocious."

"If I pronounce it like the French, will you like it better?" He said in a deep and guttural voice, his *r* a throaty purr, *"Retta, Retta."*

Louise collapsed into a fit of giggles, dropping on the ground and throwing her head back in the most unladylike, unrestrained fashion he'd ever seen. He chuckled, noticing how the smile on Henrietta's face was like sunlight first breaking through a cloud, one timid crack at a time, until she laughed, too.

"If you speak to me with a French accent, then I shall certainly not dissuade usage of the name."

A crackle of emotion traveled through him when he met her eyes. How bright and cheery they were, as if she had never known sadness. But she knew his dark secret. His future was, in a sense, in her hands.

Did she know how much power she had over him? The thought sobered him as he realized suddenly that the word of this woman, this doctor governess, could alter his life forever.

Chapter Eight

Henrietta was going to dredge up a talk with the earl.

She surveyed the unrepaired cottage, its roof sagging in the middle beneath a crookedly hung front door. Her horse, Starlight, shifted beneath her, stomping its hooves as if feeling her exasperation. It was the third cottage she'd found like this.

A chilly breeze nipped at her cheeks as she dismounted, tying Starlight to the post.

Louise slid off her own horse. "Can I pick flowers?"

"Find four different species to take home. We will catalogue them. I have a very good lens with which to study them." Henrietta tied Louise's horse up as well, watching with approval as the girl scampered across the grass to a patch of flowers near a copse of trees.

Their afternoon ride had proven fruitful in countless ways, but was also eye-opening. They'd need to head home soon as clouds gathered in slate-gray bunches and the wind slowly grew chillier.

"Missus, can we help you?" A woman appeared in the doorway of the cottage, her skirts as threadbare as the poorest farmers Henrietta had met in the Americas. Brown hair pulled back, the woman sported an infant on her hip and a toddler with smudged cheeks at her side.

Henrietta strode forward, holding out her hand. "I am Miss Gordon, Louise's governess."

The woman stared, as though having no idea what to say. Her gaze skittered to the girl, then rested on Henrietta once again. As if taking in the quality of Henrietta's riding habit, the cultured cadence of her voice, the woman dropped her head and knees in a quick, dutiful curtsy.

"Pleased be to meet you. I'm Mary Smith."

Henrietta had to listen closely to understand her due to the strength of her accent. "And I'm pleased to meet you."

Mary stared in a wistful manner at Louise. "I have not seen 'er since the accident. Her parents used to bring her out to visit. Those were good days, 'ey were. Nice people. Took care of their tenants." She pointed to the roof. "Do ye happen to know if his lordship be fixin' this soon? My 'usband has had a request in for months."

"That is not why I am here, but I shall certainly mention it to the earl." Though she hadn't ridden an estate in years, the state of the cottage caused concern. She noticed a mark on Mary's arm and moved closer for a better look. "How long have you had that on your arm?"

"Oh, this?" Mary held up her arm, examining the purplish rash as though unsure. "Months, and it itches something fierce. The apothecary gave me a cream, but it hasn't done nothing for the better, nothing for the worse."

"May I see this cream? Did he say what's in it?"

"Aye, come in, if you'd like. I'll make you a spot of tea."

Henrietta waved at Louise to let her know where she was going, and then stepped into the cottage. Small and square, the homey atmosphere stood at stark odds with the exterior untidiness. A clean sideboard held a bowl of fruit and nuts. A neatly made bed sat against the far wall, its bright quilt suggesting the owner's skill with a needle.

She waited near the door while Mary rummaged through a wooden chest on the other side of the room. She brought back the cream, handing the glass container to Henrietta with a frown. "The smell is something awful."

Henrietta sniffed it. Camphor and sage. Hardly beneficial for a rash. Perhaps the apothecary had mixed other things within, but one sniff told Henrietta all she needed to know. She gave it back.

"May I examine your arm?"

Though clearly surprised, Mary held out her arm, shifting her babe to the other hip. He gurgled, his toothless grin bringing a smile to Henrietta's heart. "You've a lovely family here."

"Thank ye, miss."

After one more thorough look at the skin, which was dry and scaly in some places, yellowish with a putrid smell in others, Henrietta straightened. "I will bring you a special soap. You must wash with it, using clean water, three times a day, keep the rash dry. I also have a liniment that may prove useful, and it smells much better than what you're using now."

Mary nodded, but doubt was evident on her face.

The English did not trust a woman for anything but help in childbirth, evidently. "My uncle is Mr. William Gordon. I have studied with him for many years. Would you be willing to try my methods? If they don't work, you can continue using what the apothecary gave you." Even though that obviously had not worked, either. But Mary's wide eyes and clutching of the baby said some verbal compromise was in order. "I don't like the look of the scaling of your rash. Do you see that yellow crusting? It could be infection."

"Infection?" Now Mary sounded panicked. "Could ye please just ask his lordship to fix our roof. We've paid our rent every month, and the leaking is damaging the floors." She gestured to a spot nearby.

"The message shall be passed on," Henrietta said courteously. Obviously dismissed, and feeling curiously let down, she walked back outside. Mary waved and shut the door.

She'd bring her the supplies tomorrow and hopefully Mary would use them. She didn't want to arbitrarily call the village apothecary a quack, but his cream didn't appear to be helping Mary at all and smelled odiferous.

Sultry clouds crawled across the sky, blocking out the sunlight. The air had grown heavy with humidity while she'd been inside. Frowning, Henrietta called for Louise. They had better get home, and fast, before this moving, moody sky opened up on them.

The ride went quickly and just after they'd dropped the horses at the stables, the first drop of water plopped against the ground. Louise squealed, and her look of genuine happiness inspired Henrietta's own smile.

They ran to the house, laughing and out of breath by the time they reached the side entrance. The lunch basket containing their pickings weathered the dash, but hopefully the flowers had not been crushed. She would need to take them up to her room to put the herbs in her medicine chest, and then the flowers could be arranged wherever Louise preferred.

As usual, the servants had little to say when she and Louise trekked through their space, though Cook did take a second glance and one of the housemaids hid a smile behind her hand.

Henrietta glanced down. Mud soaked her skirts. Louise burst ahead of her into the main hall, her splattered skirt flapping against the backs of her calves in reproachful whacks. Jacks approached them and bowed, effectively stopping Louise.

"His lordship wishes to see you in his study." His gaze roved over them, undisguisedly disapproving.

Feeling the weight of that look, she plucked at her skirts. "Should we change first?"

Before he could answer, Louise giggled. "Let's go now. If we are messy, he will not lecture for so long." She skipped around Jacks, giving him a friendly pat on his shoulder.

Trying to get the image of a lecturing Lord St. Raven into her mind, Henrietta followed. The earl had his moments of seriousness, but mostly when she thought of him, she thought of crinkling eyes and crooked smiles. Did the man even know how to lecture?

They entered his study. Or rather, Henrietta entered. Louise was already there, her voice a steady chirping as she regaled Dominic with their afternoon adventures. They had explored the wooded areas, gathering mandrake for her herb chest, and other flowers for decoration.

Henrietta set the basket on the floor, observing his lordship's personal space. A large, oval-shaped room, it boasted plenty of intricate candelabras for light and a sitting area near the fireplace. His desk, a mahogany giant, faced the door.

Dominic was not behind it. Rather, he and Louise stood near the window as she gesticulated with her hands. An indulgent smile played around his mouth. The tips of his fingers rested in the pockets of his trousers and the strong slopes of his shoulders were relaxed.

Not for the first time, she saw how deeply he loved Louise. The observation made her like him. Uncle William had often smiled at her in such a way. They had spent many evenings discussing medicines and the newest surgical techniques. She hadn't heard from him since she left Lady Brandewyne's. Had he even received her letter? She should pen another. A nondescript one with no mention of her plans to join him.

The last thing she needed was her guardian telling her no. If she could but see him face-to-face. Explain her position. Then surely he would understand that her place was next to him.

"You are deep in thought."

She focused on Dominic, noticing the mischievous glint in his eyes and the dimple carving a crescent in his stubbled cheek. The man had not even shaved this morning. He should not look so dapper, so utterly charming.

Biting back a scowl, which intellectually she realized he did not deserve because it stemmed from her own frustrations, she fixed a placid look upon him. "There are many considerations to be taken in my life, my lord."

"You don't have to call him *my lord* here," said Louise.

Dominic turned to his niece, but not before Henrietta caught the unprofessional wink he slid her way.

"Although we are using our given names, it is not entirely appropriate for me to do so with your uncle." Discomfited and yet feeling a strange urge to smile, she crossed her arms. "I must refine my mannerisms to reflect my current society. Such as the proper use of titles. Even you should refer to your uncle as Uncle Dominic or as *my lord*. That is what is proper."

Louise snorted, an unlikely noise coming from her twelve-year-old self. "Stuff propriety. The Americans do."

Henrietta's eyes widened. Thus far, perhaps due to her accident, Louise had been amenable. Now a stubborn, persnickety note crept into her voice. Dominic's expression grew stern. Louise ducked her head, an abashed look entering her eyes.

"Tell me more about these Americans?" he asked.

Louise shrugged, digging her terribly soiled slippers into the carpet. "They don't have dumb rules."

"Use your words," Henrietta advised. She rather enjoyed being the teacher. "*Dumb* is not expressive."

"On the contrary." His lordship turned to her, obviously preparing to argue. She took a deep breath, fortifying herself for the smug retort which no doubt would roll off his precipitate tongue. "The word *dumb* expresses quite a bit. It is a small yet strong word. Why use fancy when simple will do?"

He made a legitimate point. Aware of Louise's eyes upon her, she inclined her head in acquiescence. "For the most part, I do agree with you. But I would wish Louise to expand her vocabulary, for a command of language is a boon to any young lady. As well as deportment and good manners."

"What about hygiene?" Dominic cocked an eyebrow and Louise covered her mouth, failing to hide her sniggering.

"We just came in from outside. Louise shall change shortly."

"And you?"

Another snigger from Louise.

Of course this egotistical earl would care about his governess having a soiled hem. Feeling somewhat stiff and put upon, Henrietta jutted her chin. "Certainly."

"While you are tending to your hygiene, you may want to consider washing your face."

Henrietta schooled her features while calculating the sensations upon her face.

He was clearly laughing at her, his fine eyebrows practically wiggling like shaved caterpillars. "Your nose, Retta."

"My name is Henrietta." Oh, how she wanted to rub her nose. Now that he'd pointed it out, she did feel a dry crustiness upon its tip. She twitched, curling her fingers against her dress, resisting the quick itch that would dispose of the offensive mark. How long had it been there?

Dominic's shoulders shook. His former nurse—now governess—had turned a surprisingly becoming shade of pink, her normally porcelain cheeks suffused with color and her dark eyes glinting. Not with anger, but annoyance. Perhaps even feminine embarrassment, which he was certain was a foreign feeling to her.

Such a smart and interesting lady.

The smudge of mud on her nose was not the only imperfection. Small splatters dotted her cheeks, and a long smear ran across her forehead. Henrietta fidgeted while his niece giggled. Forcing his grin into some semblance of sobriety, he moved toward her.

"There is no need to feel ashamed for playing in the mud with Louise. She quite likes getting dirty, and I'm sure no other governess has ever traipsed in the dirt with her. What do you call this lesson?" He raised a brow. "Geography? Soil-ology?"

The way she wrinkled her nose, one side of her pretty lip curling up with the movement, intrigued him unaccountably. Did she have any idea how pretty she was? How her intelligence glowed out of her small and fine-boned features, coupled with a soft compassion that stirred the hardest of hearts.

Namely, his.

He could not recall the last time anyone but Louise had made him laugh. Bending down, so that he and Henrietta's eyes were level, he grinned. "I do not object to your lessons. They are quite…relevant."

Her eyebrows narrowed and even with that disapproving expression, he realized she was quite pretty in an understated way. One had to look closely and pay attention to see the beauty. From the Cupid's-bow lips to the slightly exotic shape of her eyes, all lost behind the serious expressions she often wore. Or perhaps her busy movements and constant opinions hid the quiet details of her loveliness.

And, he realized, still a little closer than necessary, she smelled good. Like summer. Like flowers and woman and sunshine.

"No more, *Lord* St. Raven." She put emphasis on his title, as if that would deter him from his antics. "We will be observing English manners, and that is enough of the matter."

"Ah, but you started this with your talk of the Americas." He straightened, putting a little space between them. With a wide gesture, he said, "In this house, you shall be Retta. I shall be Dom. And Louise shall be…" He put his finger on his chin.

Jumping up and down, Louise circled them. "Lou, Lou. Call me Lou?"

"This is nonsense. Utter nonsense." Poor Miss Gordon, with her smudged face and aromatic smell, looked flustered.

"Come now, surely you must know that pet names are signs of affection."

She shook her head, mouth pursing as though she'd just sucked a lemon. "May I be excused, my lord?"

He held up a finger. "I called you in here for a reason, then you may go. I must know—how are the state of affairs between the two of you? Is Louise behaving as she ought?"

Louise's face scrunched. "I shall behave just as long as Henrietta does."

Dominic sent his niece a hard look. "That's unacceptable, Louise."

"I'm sorry, Dom. I shall do my best." Her shoulders sagged.

"It is all I ask." He touched her head, guilt churning his gut. He should have been here with her, but the St. Raven estate reminded him of Edmund. Even Louise, with her dark hair and stubborn chin. The looks she gave him sometimes...

If he left, then perhaps Old John would cease demanding money. After all, he'd be gone and if Louise had Henrietta, then perhaps Barbara would leave him alone.

"Go change, and we shall work on arithmetic next," said Miss Gordon.

"Again?" Louise's pitch soared.

"Would you rather sewing or singing or pianoforte?"

Glum, Louise kicked the floor with her toe. "No."

"We shall be quick about the sums, and then you may choose the next lesson."

"Really?" Her head shot up, a bright hope in her eyes that touched Dominic. It had been months since she'd shown any interest in learning.

"Really. But first I must speak to your uncle."

His niece gave him one more hug, then skipped from the room while attempting, not very successfully, to whistle.

The earl crossed his arms. "You're doing remarkably well so far."

"There is still time to fail. I have not been here very long," she replied. She paused, as though examining her next words before uttering them. "I think your presence curbs her anxieties. She is better behaved when she knows you are here. It is a security issue, I believe."

"Did she say that?" A very real panic was filling his chest, ballooning inside, making breathing more difficult.

"No, no, I have not spoken to her about this. It is merely an observation. There is another issue."

Another? He just wanted to leave. Leave for north England and consign himself to hermitude until he could find a cure for his epilepsy.

Being here oppressed him. And Henrietta, with her practical, no-nonsense air, looking at him, demanding things of him. Making him feel emotions he was unwise to feel.

"Go on," he said in a short tone.

"There is the matter of your estate."

"My estate?"

She walked past him, gesturing to his desk, where papers spilled haphazardly across its surface. A small bust that he'd given his brother took residence in one corner. Dominic had a sudden and irrational urge to throw the thing. To shatter it.

Just as his family had been shattered when his brother died.

Henrietta trailed her fingers along his desk, her gaze fastened on him. Reproachfully, he thought. "While riding with Louise, we met a Mrs. Smith."

"Who?"

Yes, most definitely reproachful now. "One of your tenants."

"Ah, yes. The Smiths. No idea who they are."

Her eyes flashed. "How can you be so flippant? These people rely on you. She came out and introduced herself. Her roof is in disrepair. Leaking. She has two young children."

"Isn't there a steward who takes care of these things?"

Her mouth moved, and then as though thinking better of saying whatever she had planned to say, she snapped it closed and glared at him.

"You're furious," he remarked. Perhaps he should be, as well. He had assumed these issues were being overseen by someone. He had put off meeting with his solicitors due to his illness. Unwise, he was beginning to realize. He moved closer to the desk, scanning the various papers. "Have they requested repairs? I would think Mr. Smith could handle a simple thatching."

"They're your tenants. Do you even have a steward?"

He waved a hand, studying the papers, seeing nothing about a roof.

"My lord, to be so unconcerned for your tenants is appalling. I realize it's not my place to speak thus, but I have also noticed that the house is unkempt and the servants disorderly. Even lackadaisical and slow. Something must be done. Immediately."

Chapter Nine

"By all means, do not mince words." A knot was slowly growing inside Dominic, dark and hungry, eating a hole in his insides. His temples pounded as any trace of good humor fled. "Since this household does not meet your satisfaction, why don't you devise a list of your perceived wrongs and leave it on my desk. I'll get to it when I'm ready."

Henrietta crossed her arms. "It does no good to be oversensitive about these matters, my lord. I am not attacking your abilities, nor do I intend this as a personal critique. I am merely drawing your attention to issues which require noticing. Pouting is unattractive," she added, as though that tidbit would uncarve the lines he felt gouging his forehead.

He gathered up the papers, jamming them into a semblance of squared order. "You may leave your list here, Miss Gordon. Your concerns are noted."

Though he was not looking at her, he felt her move from the desk. A small swish of air that told of retreat. He had spoken in a hard voice. One he did not care to use, but her prodding annoyed him. Everything about her annoyed him. He turned, and saw that she had not left after all. Indeed, she had moved closer and when he faced her, he caught again that flowery scent.

The aroma wrapped around him, twining like ivy, drawing him closer when he should be walking away. Her eyes widened, but she did not back away. An invitation. His senses sharpened, narrowing into a single focus, that of getting closer to her.

Only the sight of mud on her nose brought him back to reality. The reality in which she was his temporary governess. She was not of the society he kept and she would not take his flirtations lightly, if she took them at all.

Pulling in a deep, shuddering breath, he stopped inches short of her. Annoyance still traipsed through him, but that other feeling, the one he would do best to ignore, was fading beneath the bitter wipe of reality.

"Was there something more, Miss Gordon?" His voice remained unyielding. Good. She would not argue with him now.

Irises almost indiscernible within the black of her pupils, she nodded. "Yes, I would like your permission to treat Mrs. Smith for a rash."

"Given."

Unsurprisingly, Henrietta continued talking. Dominic was torn between several equally terrible urges: stomping out of the room like the pouting child she had accused him of being, great concern that his tenants had suffered due to his own, selfish negligence and hauling Henrietta up against him and stopping the talking in the most elemental way possible.

Her lips, pale rose, did not seem to realize the havoc they wreaked on Dominic's thoughts as they moved, forming words. He struggled to bring his mind to the present.

"The apothecary has given her an ointment which is making her rash worse, in my opinion. I'd like to meet with him and discuss his medical training. He obviously has no idea what he's doing." Her foot tapped.

"Uh." Dominic pushed his fingers through his hair. "The apothecary?"

"Your village doctor? Surely you know his name, though on the other hand, you probably do not."

It made no sense that her peevish tone could make Dominic want to hold her, but it did. His arms ached with the sensation. His legs begged permission to move forward, to gather her in his arms and inhale the sweetness of her hair. He blinked, bringing her face into clarity. That foot of hers still tapped steadily against the floor.

"My lord, are you okay?" Before he could stop her, she closed the gap between them and pressed her palm against his forehead. As quickly as her cool skin met his, she removed it. A blush stained her cheeks, as though even she, impervious to societal dictates as she was, recognized the impropriety of touching him outside of a sickroom.

"Overwhelmed," he said.

They stood quietly for a long moment that stretched thin and taut.

She broke the silence and said, "This dirt is making my face itch. I suppose I should refresh myself and carry on with Louise's lessons."

"Yes." He rubbed his forehead. "I know I'm going to regret this, but this evening we shall take a ride about the property. Take me to the Smiths and I will see what needs to be done."

"Why don't you have a steward?"

His jaw tightened. He weighed her words. "I wrongly supposed that I did. Because I did not want this responsibility, I did not pay particular attention."

"Did you ignore your responsibilities in hopes they

would disappear?" The tease of a smile tugged the corners of her lips.

"Ignoring problems has been my chosen method of living."

"That does not surprise me in the least."

Now they were both sharing smiles, and in some odd way, he felt lightened. "Be ready at four."

She dipped her head, then turned and left the room, her skirts swishing in that no-nonsense way she had about her. He turned back to his desk, went over to it and sat. The chair groaned beneath him. Had it done the same for his brother? He tried to imagine Edmund sitting here. Working. Keeping up an estate, raising a daughter, loving a wife.

And not for the hundredth time, he wondered why Edmund had left him in charge of Louise.

He sifted through the papers, going more slowly, until he found one with the name of Smith. Submitted a fortnight ago. His head dropped into his hands as he realized how greatly he was failing.

Perhaps he deserved to lose it all, but that didn't mean he would go down without a fight.

Henrietta waited in the carriage promptly at four o'clock. On her lap she held a jar of ointment. She'd mixed it up earlier, moving slowly under Louise's scrutiny, explaining each ingredient and its medicinal qualities. Now Louise sat across from her, swinging a foot.

"Where is Dom?"

Drawing her watch from her reticule, she said calmly, "He is only three minutes late. Be patient."

"I can't." She threw back her head. "He is always late. It is his greatest downfall."

"That is surely not true."

"Whose downfall?" Dominic opened the door of the carriage and popped in. "Henrietta's watch is probably set early to keep her from ever being late."

She sniffed. How had he known that?

Grinning, he wagged a finger. "I know your type."

"Fustian nonsense." She slid the watch back into her reticule. "Let us be off."

They bumped through the countryside, Louise's chatter causing the earl to laugh in deep tones that rolled through Henrietta in bursts of awareness. He was a strange man in some ways. Difficult to dissect. Which made him all the more intriguing. Like an unknown illness. Familiar symptoms, but put them all together and she still could not make a diagnosis.

Turning to the side, she watched as the land flattened into emerald swaths of grass. Cottages peppered the land, little squares of ivy-laced homes, sometimes well-tended, mostly not. Gardens and rectangles of farmland speckled in neat order.

As they neared the Smiths', Henrietta pointed out their cottage. Dominic gained the driver's attention. The carriage rolled to a halt. When she placed her hand in the earl's to step out of the carriage, it seemed as though he held her a millisecond too long.

Long enough for her to glance up at him, questioning, thinking he had something to say. But no, his face was shuttered.

Mrs. Smith met them at the door. She looked less haggard today, her hair neatly parted into a bun and her dress clean and pressed. Her home had been straightened, but the hole in the roof trickled afternoon sunlight.

"My lord," she said, sweeping a deep bow.

"Mrs. Smith. It has come to my attention that you're in need of thatching."

"Ay, yes."

"Is Mr. Smith about?"

"No, my lord. Mr. Smith has taken a job in Suffolk at the factory, for a wee bit."

"He doesn't farm here?"

Mrs. Smith startled, her fingers plucking at the apron. "There wasn't any work to be had. No one to…" She trailed off, looking miserable and helpless at the same time.

Louise skipped out of the house, bored. Henrietta took pity on the poor woman. She touched her shoulder. "May I see your arm? How is it?"

Now the woman grew more red, visibly uncomfortable.

"My lord," Henrietta murmured, understanding the situation at once. "Would you be so kind as to check on Louise?"

His brows lifted, but understanding filled his eyes. He left, and she gestured Mrs. Smith to the table. The woman lifted her sleeve and Henrietta had to stifle her gasp. A hot, viscous anger poured through her as the smell of the apothecary's mistreatment rose from the rash. What had been crusty yesterday now oozed pus and odor.

She had seen worse. But she shouldn't see it here, not on a prosperous estate. This was completely unnecessary. Swallowing the distaste and anger that kept rising in her throat, she wet her lips. "You will need to clean this with hot-water compresses three times a day. Stop using the cream he gave you. It's completely ineffective."

She fumbled in her reticule until she found the jar of ointment. "I have made you a liniment, and I will be back to check your arm tomorrow morning. Keep your rash covered with clean cloths, changing them after every hot compress. You must let me know immediately if the rash spreads."

"How did this happen? Did the apothecary cause it?"

Mouth tight, Henrietta shook her head. "No, most likely there was broken skin from the rash, which could have been caused by a minor irritation. But infection got into the skin and the ointment he gave you did absolutely nothing. I'm not certain what's in it."

Mrs. Smith tilted her head. "Ye're the governess. How is it ye know of these things?"

"I was trained in nursing and doctoring. The governess position is temporary." Henrietta frowned. "Let's clean this first."

Sometime later, Henrietta left the cottage. Mrs. Smith's wound was cleaned and covered. She'd shown her how to apply the ointment.

She felt alive. Useful.

"You're glowing." Dominic came up to her from where he'd been lounging against the carriage. His gaze skipped across her face.

"That apothecary of yours is inept."

"And yet happiness is fairly leaping from your face."

She lifted a shoulder, unable to keep from smirking. "My true calling is doctoring. Mrs. Smith will recover if she does as I say. Shall we be off to tour your estate? I'm sure your tenants would appreciate hearing from you."

The crinkles at the corner of his eyes disappeared. He shuffled his feet in a surprisingly unsure movement, as though he wanted to run but could not. Perhaps that urge to run was inherited, she mused. Like uncle, like niece?

She pulled her bonnet more securely across her brow as the sun had not yet sunk below the horizon. Its orange-hued rays bounced brightness across the earth's surface. "You do not wish to see your tenants?"

Dominic effected a sigh surely too deep and overdone for such a simple question.

He was saved from answering when Louise bounded over. "Retta, look what I have found? What is it?"

She bent forward, examining the shiny brown hide of a lepidoptera pupa. "It appears to be a caterpillar undergoing metamorphosis. We shall find a book to discover which species, as I am not well-versed in the study of insects. Keep it safe. We do not want to harm the pupa."

"Pupa," the girl said reverently. The oval-shaped case was cradled in her palm. "I shall be very careful." She walked away slowly, cautiously, treating the developing moth as though it was a precious jewel.

"She is tenderhearted." Henrietta blinked at the sting in her eyes. An ache had started pumping within, for well she remembered that age. The wonder, the sweet agony of newly discovered joys. The pain of loss. When her world had ended, her heart had kept pumping. The sun had continued its unsung rhythm.

"I doubt the servants share your sentiment." St. Raven's eyes glinted in the setting sun, looking somehow more dangerous, an emerald mirror to the grassy floor around them.

"She adores you," Henrietta said quietly. She watched as Louise climbed gingerly into the carriage, her fingers cradling the pupa. "If you leave, she may revert to her old antics."

"I hired you because you relate to Louise. You understand her. I'm no longer needed."

"That is what you would like to think, because it is easier to dismiss her than to love her."

His face turned to stone, his eyes reflecting jewel-toned hardness. "You speak too familiarly, Miss Gordon."

"Do you expect less from me?" She met his jagged gaze with a firm and steady look. "You have avoided your tenants and their needs. These people are depending on you for their livelihood. The cottages are in need of repair. The fields lay barren. Is this what your brother would have wanted? Is this why he left you in charge?"

"Challenging words for a mere governess." A tic tugged at his jaw. She only saw it because somewhere in her lecture she had lost contact with his eyes, knowing she crossed a line yet unable to stop herself. It was one thing to be stern with a patient. Quite another to criticize your employer. But her principles would allow nothing less.

She forced herself to look at him again, ignoring the clench of her stomach, the tightness of her throat. "These people deserve a landowner who cares for them. At least hire a steward to handle the paperwork puddled across your desk. Someone to care for the people since you cannot bring yourself to do so."

He shoved a hand ruthlessly through his hair, mussing it and grimacing at the pain. Or perhaps her words. She refused to play with the edges of her reticule, though her nerves screamed and her fingers itched to move, to wiggle, to crawl away. Someone must tell him these things. Someone must make him see how the estate was falling apart without his leadership.

She inhaled a shaky, uncertain breath. "I can't leave here without being honest, my lord. I hope you understand."

He groaned then, a surprising sound that struck her as both mournful and wounded. Aggrieved. A sober reaction for someone determined to play his way through life. "Though you are impertinent, your opinion has merit. I will meet with my solicitors and determine what is to be done."

"It would be good for the tenants to meet you. To feel that their futures are secure. Mrs. Smith's husband is working at a factory. I'm not well versed on English economics—"

"Crops are failing throughout England. Add in the bad harvests and farmers are struggling," he said crisply. "I will do what I can, but the world is changing and we must change with it. Perhaps you're correct about the tenants, though. After my brother died, I didn't visit the estate for several months. And when I did, it was short. Mostly to see Louise."

"Then you are past due."

"I'm sick, as you know. It seems…" His fingers jogged again through his hair as though searching for words. "Perhaps a waste of time to invest myself when there is no guarantee I will be here tomorrow."

"Are you referring to your illness? I do not believe it to be a terminal disease, though I've yet to perform the research." He looked so stricken, and she felt helpless to wipe that despair from his face.

"Yes, this cursed disease that has plagued me. Who would have guessed a bump on the head had the power to forever alter the course of my life."

"When did you first exhibit symptoms?"

"The day after my brother and his wife died. I was riding with them."

"Oh, I did not realize." She swallowed, understanding the pain of losing those you held dear in one fell swoop.

"I am hoping to find a cure."

"Why?"

"Why not?"

She dipped her head. "Fair words. However, you cannot neglect your duties simply because you don't know what the future brings. I will watch you closely, my lord, and guard your secret. Never forget, He holds us in the palms of His hands."

"Who?"

"God. Be anxious for nothing, but in everything let your cares fall upon Him, for He careth for you."

Dominic's brow rose in a mocking manner that Henrietta found rather annoying. She put a hand on her hip. "I'm simply giving you good advice. The future is unknown. If we visit the tenants today, then tomorrow, if you have not suddenly died, you can go about hiring a steward."

"Sarcasm. Very ungoverness-like." He regarded her with narrowed eyes. "You were quoting the Bible."

"Yes," she answered defensively. "I enjoy reading it."

"As I have never turned a page of it in my life, I will trust you when you say reading it is enjoyable. Louise is waiting and the day is waning. After consideration, I have determined that it is far better to face the tenants than your wrath."

Her wrath.

Shooting him a glare and refusing to respond to the challenging spark she saw in his eyes, she marched to the carriage. She had accomplished many things today. When she left this place, it would be knowing that she'd done her part and been useful.

If she could not doctor bodies, the next best thing to fix was a broken family.

Chapter Ten

Henrietta certainly had a way with words.

Her chastisements had plagued him, nudging him into action.

Dominic peered out the window of his office, staring at the governess and Louise sitting in the tiny squared-off garden below him. A servant brought them a tray, and it appeared that Henrietta was instructing his niece on the art of pouring tea. Louise seemed interested, her head bent in concentration, her body very still as though she absorbed each detail with her entire self.

Should he go down there and tell her he'd found a steward? Quite easily, in fact. The butler knew of one at a nearby town, and the housekeeper had seemed thrilled. How long had they been hoping for this? What kind of earl was he to have shirked duties for so long, and would the estate prosper now that he'd taken a step forward? Now that he'd committed himself...

Frowning, he turned from the window and left the room. Only time, and perhaps this new steward, would be able to give him an idea of which changes, if any, would bring prosperity again.

He crossed the hall and took a turn in the solarium.

Greenery and flowers overflowed the small space. Someone had been caring for the plants in this room. He made a mental note to find out who and thank him or her.

At the edge of the solarium, he opened the door and took the cobbled path, which led directly to where Henrietta sat with her pupil. No time like the present to help himself to some of their dainty snacks and to let the fearsome governess know that she could save her lectures for his niece.

A lick of anticipation lapped up his spine. He was looking forward to tangling wills with her. Very few women in society, especially the debutantes, engaged in verbal sparring. He had a notion they were told to act vapid and smile insipidly until they'd caught a husband.

Not bothering to hide the grin he knew edged his face, he sauntered into the area where the ladies sat. Louise had just replaced the teapot on a silver gilded tray that reflected sunlight rather uncomfortably into his eyes, almost ruining his saunter. He recovered, angling toward Henrietta, who watched him knowingly.

He bowed to Louise. "Miss Stanford."

She responded with a deep and surprisingly smooth curtsy. "Lord St. Raven. Won't you join us for tea?"

"It would be my pleasure." He took the seat next to Henrietta, noting the slight wiggle she made to move away from him. Ah. The thrill of the chase. Even if she was only here temporarily, she provided an escape from boredom. "Anna, another cup if you will?"

The maid curtsied and hurried away.

"Are you taking a break from the schoolroom?" he asked.

"It is ever so tedious, Dom." Louise sent Henrietta a petulant look, but the recipient merely took a sip from her teacup. "She has been making me memorize sums and multiples. I told her that I shall not be using them. Why would I have need of that? She says if I don't learn them, my brain will be reduced to mush."

"Mush?" He turned, catching the governess's lips twitching behind her cup. "Is that the medical term for the malady?"

With a methodical care, Henrietta set the cup on the tray. "The brain is a remarkable organ, and each section must be exercised daily to prevent atrophy."

"Well, that certainly explains what has happened to mine."

Henrietta coughed, her fingers covering her lips as though holding in an unfortunate and inappropriate laugh.

A fierce desire to make her laugh again rushed through him, but he couldn't think of anything to say. Louise looked between the both of them, her face as confused and blank as his supposedly mushy brain. The maid set the cup on the table and retreated.

"My lord, a spot of tea?" Louise quirked her brow at him, lifting the teapot. She poured flawlessly, a lady in every way.

"Well done," he said, taking his cup, no sugar. "Henrietta taught you how to do this?"

"My parents died when I was fifteen. I had a governess for several years before that, so yes, I am versed in the art of pouring tea," she said.

"Did she make you do math, too?" Louise's nose crinkled like an accordion.

Henrietta smiled quite charmingly. "Yes, any woman who may one day run a household should have solid accounting skills. There are many duties a lady must know to be effective in her home."

"Sounds boring," Dominic drawled, just to see Henrietta's eyes flash at him. "Much like my meeting with the steward today."

The flash subsided the tiniest bit. "So you've decided to hire one?"

"Yes, and another maid or two. The food is cold because apparently there are not enough servants. When my brother—" He caught himself, glanced at Louise, who was picking at a hole in her dress, and continued. "When everything changed, apparently several servants left for a neighboring estate and towns."

"Very good." Henrietta sounded too prim and self-satisfied. It made him want to get the smirk off her face by any means necessary. "Does this mean you'll be leaving now?"

Louise's head popped up, and Dominic held in his groan. He hadn't said anything to Louise, but Henrietta did not know that. As if realizing her mistake, her face flushed in apology.

"But you just got here? Why must you always go to that dreadful place?"

He pulled at his cravat. "I have a home there."

"This is your house, too." Her voice went high, desperate. She stomped her slipper-clad foot, a scuffing noise that did little to ease the strain in Dominic. "I'm your home. Tell him, Henrietta."

Henrietta stood and brushed the wrinkles from her skirt. Dominic immediately followed suit. "Why don't we talk about it later, when you've calmed down."

"Calmed down?" Louise crossed her arms, twisting her lips into a mulish scowl. He reached for her, but she pivoted out of reach. "You can't go, Dom. Please." And then her lip quivered, and it felt as though that quiver was an arrow to his heart. Pain lanced his chest.

"I have to. I have to go."

Louise shook her head, hard, shaking his words from her ears. Then she ran, disappearing down the path. He groaned.

Henrietta expelled an exasperated sigh. "We really must teach her better coping skills."

Louise returned after dinner had been taken away. Henrietta had been waiting, her heart beating a nervous pitter-patter for every hour the girl didn't show up. St. Raven had gone to his study to go over the books with his new steward, who had shown up shortly after Louise threw her fit.

He had been visibly upset but after an hour of searching and not finding the girl, they'd decided to see if she returned home for dinner. A few servants had been posted at various spots on the estate, in hopes of spotting her.

Henrietta paced the parlor, awaiting word of her charge's arrival. She'd brought a book, an anatomical study of the human body, but her eyes kept stuttering on the hippocampus drawing.

Was Louise hurt somewhere? Broken? She hadn't been able to speak with Lord St. Raven about consequences for his niece's behavior, but as she turned about the room, she formulated a plan. She had already informed the staff to send Louise directly to the parlor. No food, no stops.

A dusky sunset splayed through the curtains, bathing the room in an overripe peach glow. The faint sound of servants moving through the house reached her ears. Even St. Raven's voice, low and muted, could be heard as a threadbare echo through the walls. Still, she strained to hear Louise's excited footfalls, her chirping voice.

She hadn't fooled herself into thinking Louise had changed, but she had hoped the girl was happier. She should have guessed Dominic hadn't shared his plans with anyone. Why had she opened her mouth?

Sighing, she went and sat on the fancy settee in the corner. Brocaded and stiff, the cushion made sitting more uncomfortable than standing. She stood up again. Better to address the behavior now. To teach that running away only caused more problems and that when Louise was upset, she must stand and face her fears.

Face the opposition.

Setting her jaw, she waited. Then there were footsteps down the hall. Strong and firm, but light. Henrietta rushed to the door and found Cook, her fingers hooked around the collar of Louise's clothes.

"Tried to sneak some tarts from the kitchen," said Cook.

Henrietta had not actually spoken to the cook in her time here, and now she understood why. The woman exuded disdain. With a contemptuous sniff, the servant released Louise and pounded away.

Though her head felt light with relief, she kept her face placid. "Go sit down, please."

Louise stalked past. Her hair hung in disarray and though the lighting in the room was dim, Henrietta was quite sure there might be a sunburn on her nose. Which would result in freckles. Unseemly for a girl whose debut was in only five years. Lemon juice might lighten the marks, perhaps, though Henrietta doubted its efficacy.

"I'm hungry." Louise plopped onto the sofa, seemingly unaware of its cold comfort.

"Stay here until I return." Henrietta used the tone she'd employed on wounded soldiers. Like them, Louise looked up at her wide-eyed and obeyed.

Swirling around, Henrietta quickly went to Dominic's study and knocked.

"Yes?"

She pushed the door open. The new steward looked up

from his seat across Dominic's desk. He seemed to be a studious type, spectacles perched on the brim of a well-structured nose. His tweed coat lent his slight build a conservative intelligence that she could appreciate.

"My lord," she said, gaze skittering to the enigmatic man sitting behind the desk. "I apologize for interrupting, but might I have a word with you?"

If he was surprised by her boldness, he did not show it. A curt nod, and he was walking toward her, tall and confident, that dimple present in his cheek, though she could not fathom why. She certainly had not been able to smile the entire afternoon.

She went into the hall and he followed. Disarmed by his nearness, she nevertheless held her ground. "Louise has returned."

He expelled a deep and hearty breath that was filled with relief. "Where is she?"

"I told her to stay in the study."

"We will go to her now."

She nodded, respect and a warmth welling within her at his obvious care for his niece.

Dominic kneaded the back of his neck. Stressed, no doubt, as being responsible often provoked the urge to commit to something or someone other than oneself. Still, her heart softened at his evident distress.

"I know you are but the governess—"

"I shall stand with you," she said firmly.

He nodded. "Give me a moment."

He was gone but two minutes, and then they walked to the drawing room. She could not help but be aware of his presence beside her. Strong and smelling of some exotic cologne that no doubt cost a month's salary. But she could not fault him for the expenditure, when the result was so very pleasing.

They found Louise sitting exactly where Henrietta had left her. On the couch, scowling. Her eyes flickered up to them. "I'm starving."

Henrietta drew in a deep breath, suddenly realizing that this would be so much more difficult than she had anticipated. She glanced up at Dominic and found strength in the fact that his jaw was firm, his mouth steady. Resolute.

"Louise, running away when you're upset and not coming home until all hours is worrisome to us," he said sternly.

Louise crossed her arms.

"I have spent the day—" Henrietta's voice broke. Horrified, she wet her lips and swallowed hard, all her well-planned words sticking in her throat. "What I mean to say is that your uncle and I have been extremely worried."

"He doesn't care." Louise looked pointedly at Dominic, her eyebrows forming tight little ves.

"You missed dinner," he said. "Tonight you shall have bread and water in your room. Tomorrow there will be extra lessons to make up for what you missed today. If you run off and miss dinner again, you will be confined to your room for a week. Is that understood?"

Louise shot to her feet. "You can't do this. I can do whatever I want." The high, shaky quality of her voice betrayed the challenge in her eyes.

Henrietta longed to go to her then, to wrap her in her arms and assure her. But this was a matter for her uncle, and suddenly she knew that her presence could only exacerbate this battle of wills.

"My lord, perhaps I should go?" she offered quietly, hopefully, and to her great relief, he dipped his head in agreement.

She brushed out of the room, her shoulders tight and straight. A most terrible consternation crippled her from within. On her way to her room, Jacks stopped her to give her a letter.

Mail from her uncle.

She gripped the rail on the way to her room, for the first time in several weeks her lungs protesting the exertion. Perhaps Uncle William's words would take her mind from her worries. From Louise and Dominic.

But the letter did not help.

Her uncle asked after her health. He shared news of a Mr. William Charles Wells, who had read his scientific paper on natural changes in humanity over the course of time.

He did not invite her to join him.

She prayed while readying for sleep, but her stomach drooped and even the hot tea she sent for, sprinkled with her own special blend of ginger, did not ease the knots within.

The feeling of disquiet continued. The small room she'd been given, rectangular and comfortable, was beside Louise's. A nanny's room, but suitable for a governess.

Practical and generous.

Why wasn't she happier?

Her mind replayed the day. What could she have done differently? Said? In the future, she did not wish to inspire the raw feelings she felt now. She liked thinking. She did not care to indulge in emotions.

The cool sheets hugged her body. Her pillow, feather-soft, framed her face as she stared at moonlight sluicing through her curtains to illuminate her quilted figure. The quietness did nothing to ease the hollow, freezing ache that pulsated beneath her ribs.

For perhaps the first time since she was fifteen, since

the night she watched her father disappear into that thick,
black billowing cloud of smoke that had been their home,
she felt utterly alone.

Chapter Eleven

"Dom. Dom." Someone shook him, prying him from his dreams. He moaned, shrugging off the offensive hand and curling back into his blankets.

"Dom, wake up."

The blankets that cocooned him were ripped off. He bolted up. Louise leaned over him, moonlight highlighting the fear in her wide eyes. She grabbed at his shirt, tugging him to the edge of the bed.

"What is it?" He shook his head, trying to clear the cobwebs, to make sense of his niece in his room. "What's wrong?"

"It's Henrietta." No tears on her face, but they clogged her voice, thickening the consonants. "She's screaming in her sleep, and I can't wake her up."

Dominic scrambled out of bed, his mind hardly able to process her words. They made no sense. That was not like Henrietta.

Louise handed him his night robe. He tied it quickly and rushed out of the room, grabbing a sconce to light their path. Louise had come to his room in the dark, a sure sign of her panic.

When they neared his niece's room, she beckoned him

in. Henrietta's door was only a few feet down, but rather than risking it locked and thus taking more time to reach her, he padded after his niece to their connecting door. No screams came from the room, just a soft sound, like that of a mewling kitten.

Louise put her finger to her mouth. The light from his lamp flickered across her strained features. They crept into Henrietta's room.

It took a moment to orient himself. He'd never been in this room before. Had not realized how small and ugly it was. Why, he could practically touch each wall if he stretched out both arms. His gaze shifted to the small form huddled on the narrow bed that could hardly be called a bed. It looked more like a cot.

Louise was already near Henrietta. "She's crying." And her voice sounded so forlorn that his chest compressed into a tight little space. He moved forward, gently pressing Louise to the side.

He bent over Henrietta. There were indeed silent tears streaking her cheeks. A steady stream. The rest of her— the proud and small nose, the rosebud lips—was relaxed in sleep. Whatever nightmare she'd suffered had passed and it seemed silly to wake her now. Just as he drew back though, she moaned, and then her lids squeezed into pained exclamations and her mouth opened on a silent scream.

Wordlessly he handed the lantern to Louise. He slid his hands over Miss Gordon's shoulders, turning her toward him.

"Henrietta," he whispered fiercely. "Wake up. Wake up, Henrietta."

Her head thrashed, and for the first time, he wondered if this is what others might feel if they saw him have a seizure. To witness someone else's duress, to be helpless against it, was torturous.

He continued the gentle shaking. "Henrietta. It's Dominic. Wake up."

Her body stiffened, for one terrible moment growing horribly still, as though she'd stopped breathing. And then she melted against him, a long shuddering breath escaping as she slowly awakened. Her eyes fluttered. Opened to reveal an empty despair.

"You had a nightmare," he said, his voice as scratchy as sandpaper. "Are you awake?"

She blinked. Nodded.

As though suddenly realizing the impropriety of their closeness, of her bare arms touching the thin cloth of his night robe, the heat of his body seeping into hers, she pulled away and drew the blankets to her chin.

"I was so worried." Louise rushed forward, throwing her body on the bed with little regard for personal space. Dominic was forced to shift position or be knocked over. "You were screaming."

From behind Louise's mussed hair, she offered a wobbling smile. "A bad dream. We all have them sometimes."

"Do you want to talk about the dream? Perhaps find the meaning behind it?" he asked.

"Meaning behind a dream?" Henrietta's eyebrows pulled together, and that familiar condescension she often donned sent a profound relief through him. If she could give a look like that, then surely she would overcome whatever had so disturbed her sleep.

His niece popped up from where she'd been lying against Henrietta's legs. "Let's have warm milk and tarts."

"In the middle of the night?" Now she was fully aware, pulling herself into a sitting position, and with the worry abating, Dominic became conscious of how exception-

ally lovely she looked with her gold-streaked hair floating in disarray about her face. "I hardly think that would
be good for your digestion."

"But it is eminently good for our constitutions," Dominic remarked, winking at Louise.

His niece hopped off the bed, an expression of glee
upon her face that was no longer little girl, but not quite
woman. "I can tell you where Cook keeps her secret stash."

And so it was that ten minutes later, Miss Henrietta
Gordon joined them in the kitchen. She'd thrown on a
dress, though Dominic was not sure how as he'd heard
they were quite cumbersome to put on by oneself. No
doubt the practical woman had found a way without a
maid. As she came in, he found himself exhaling with
relief because color had seeped into her lips and cheeks.
There was no longer that empty, fearful cast to her gaze
that had caused his stomach to quake.

She surveyed the array of sweets Louise spread out
on the servants' table. Her mouth made a small circle of
wonder. "You were not jesting."

"Of course not." Louise lifted her chin, giving Dominic
such a proud, knowing look that he at once felt a swelling
surge of pride followed quickly by a wave of shame. While
he'd been licking his wounds at his cottage, Louise had
been mourning the death of her parents alone.

Certainly he'd visited every so often, but those small
moments could not ease the immense loss she suffered.
How incredibly selfish he'd been. All the more reason to
ensure Louise's happiness and health before ceasing to
give in to Old John's blackmail.

Henrietta sidled into a chair between Dominic and Louise. She had put her hair up, but not well. Tendrils curled
against her cheeks, making her look softer and vulnerable. There was a great choking feeling in Dominic now.

A sense of being propelled toward a future he wasn't sure he wanted or needed.

"How is it that you know Cook's secret hiding places? And that she has not caught on?" Henrietta snagged a tart.

Louise smirked. "My father taught me how to pilfer."

"He always had a sweet tooth," Dominic said ruefully.

"What was he like as a child?" Louise popped a whole tart in her mouth.

Trying not to laugh at the unladylike unawareness she displayed, he took his own biscuit and nibbled a corner before answering. "Your father was responsible and kind. He helped all those who asked, but he had a weakness, Louise. A fatal flaw, if you will."

Her eyes widened, and Henrietta was surreptitiously shaking her head at him, trying to warn him not to say anything to hurt his niece's feelings.

Smothering a grin, he picked off a piece of cookie and twirled it between his fingertips. "Not only did Edmund sneak treats in the middle of the night, but I'd follow him. And inevitably your father would get frustrated with me. I was the little brother. The annoying twit who wouldn't leave him alone with his biscuits. And sometimes, he lost his temper with me."

Both ladies watched him warily, listening.

He broke off a piece of biscuit, twisting it between his thumb and forefinger. A puckish urge swept through him. As though in honor of his brother, the boy who had led forays into the woods with sticks, scampered up trees, the man who had faith enough in Dominic to leave him in charge of his daughter, he flicked the tiny biscuit ball at Louise.

Henrietta gasped as the crumb flew past her startled gaze and flopped against Louise's forehead before falling to the ground.

* * *

Half an hour later, Henrietta picked the last piece of evidence of their sweets war from the kitchen floor. Louise was sprawled on a long bench against the wall, fast asleep. Dominic worked at the other end of the room, awkwardly sweeping a corner that received the brunt of the ammunition.

"You made a mess, Miss Gordon." He straightened from over the broom, his dimple deep, as though he'd heard her thoughts.

"Only because my target kept moving."

"You blame the target and not your aim?" He set the broom against the wall and walked over.

"My aim is superb," she retorted, but she was laughing, too. "Did your brother really throw cookies at you?"

"Every time."

They sat at the table, facing outward, their backs resting against the surface. Louise slept on, her hands tucked beneath her head and her face as still and perfect as a trusting babe's.

"And did you two pick up after yourselves?"

His face pleated into a laughing scoff. "Cook did."

"The same cook?"

"Yes, she's been here as long as I can remember. Used to swat my hands with her spatulas. Edmund and I made a game of snatching and running. One of us distracted Cook while the other grabbed the sugary loot."

"What a perfectly lovely story." Henrietta looked down at her own hands. They were capable and steady.

"Did you never sneak into your kitchens at night?"

Though the question was innocent enough, it brought her back to the reason they were up in the middle of the night in the first place. A shudder rippled through her.

"That looks like a no." Dominic's low voice filtered

through her struggle to not remember. "Are you thinking of your dreams? Do you want to talk about them?"

"I don't wish to speak of them." Because they'd hurt. Because she could still feel the flames' heat licking her face, the raw-throated cries of soldiers as surgeons sawed off their legs.

"Do tell. I am not sleepy yet. Too many biscuits in my stomach." He winked at her "Louise was scared. If you talk about what bothered you, then perhaps you won't have the same dreams anymore. Perhaps I can offer advice."

"I do not wish to scare her further. I suppose you make a good point."

"Don't sound so reluctant to admit my finer qualities, Miss Gordon. Or should I say, Retta?"

She shot him a slit-eyed gaze, even though his use of the moniker threaded a surprising thrill through her emotions. "Very well. It's a recurrent dream. Though it was more severe tonight, more intense." She glanced at Louise's prone form, wondering what exactly had happened to upset the plucky girl.

"She said you were screaming in your sleep," said Dominic.

"The dream starts with the soldiers. One in particular. Adam. His leg had gangrene and it was spreading. He was the one who told me God loved me. That I could talk to God. He gave me his Bible." She swallowed hard. "We had to amputate the limb, but infection set in and he died. Sometimes I dream of him. I dream that he blames me. He is crying for his wife and two children, and he asks why I didn't stop the infection. Because I know how. Clean the wound. Use herbs and poultices to draw out impurities. But if the infection gets into the blood—" She choked, stopping.

"There was nothing you could do."

"For any of them. All those men…whole families. The wives followed their husbands. Made camp on the outskirts of the battlefield. There was a fire set in Newark. It was wartime, and there is nothing good that I remember from that time, but sometimes my mind forgets that it is over." She drew in a ragged sigh, staring at her clasped hands, digging her nails into her skin. "And then the dream inevitably turns to the night my parents died."

She looked up in time to see his eyes flicker, as though surprised. She smiled a rueful smile. "It is silly, is it not, to dream of something almost ten years past? Yet I do. My mind will not let me forget. My father loved my mother, too. They had what is called a love match. She wanted the same for me, but love is truly a matter of our humors. Our brains at work, creating emotions. Perhaps chemicals within that cause us to feel certain responses."

"But you speak of God's love, and He is not made of chemicals."

She blinked. "I have never thought of that."

His mouth curved. "Perhaps my brain is not so atrophied after all."

Finally, she could smile. The pressure lifted from her chest with that one sentence. "We shall give you the benefit of the doubt, my lord."

"Why do you suppose you have these dreams?"

"Why?" She shrugged. "Perhaps your altercation with Louise brought back memories of my own family. My old home is not far from here. An hour or so? I believe Lady Brandewyne and Uncle William grew up as neighbors."

A tickle curled at her neck. She reached up and realized her hair was falling out everywhere. One pin poked behind her ear. She pulled it and her hair cascaded over her shoulders and down the front of her pelisse. It was a particularly thick fabric that served perfectly when she'd been with her uncle, suitable for occasions for when she was called out suddenly in the middle of the night.

She dipped her fingers beneath her hair, lifting it to repin, and she noticed St. Raven staring at her strangely. An odd expression was in his eyes. When their gazes met, he looked quickly away, making a strange sound in his throat.

Frowning, she repinned her hair quickly. "Please say there is not a stray crumb in my hair."

"No." He cleared his throat. "Not at all. Your hair is just very long. Surprisingly so."

"Well, most women have long hair," she said primly. She rather liked her hair color, too. Perhaps it was vain, but the swirls of brown and gold reminded her of a caramel she'd once eaten in Paris. Her hair color was, perhaps, her only mark of beauty. "We should return to our rooms."

"Your childhood home is nearby, you said."

"Yes."

"Why don't we visit it tomorrow?"

"Whatever for?"

"Remembrance. It might be a good idea to see it as an adult, to banish those childhood fears."

"They are not fears." She heard the starch in her voice. And she smelled the smoke again, the fire at home and the fire at Newark mingling into one overarching terror. The loss of those she held dear. Her parents' graves were in the Morningside village cemetery. They had their own vault. "I have never, however, visited their mausoleum. That might be an important trip to make."

"It's set then. Tomorrow after we break our fast, we will depart for Morningside."

Henrietta nodded, quickly making her escape to her room, but uneasiness gnawed at her throughout the night, and sleep eluded her.

Chapter Twelve

There was no denying the heavy dread weighing on Henrietta's shoulders as they began their trip to Morningside Manor the next morning. They had decided to ride horses, after determining the fair weather would make for an enjoyable journey.

A cloudless cerulean sky accompanied their ride. Dominic had attached a lunch basket to his saddle and Louise rode ahead, sporadically sliding off her docile mare to collect wildflowers growing on the edges of the road. Her enthusiasm distracted Henrietta from the direction of her thoughts. Though she'd had no more nightmares, she still felt the thick, pungent stain of smoke coating her tongue, poisoning her day.

Memories were sliding through her, slippery and too quick to catch. She hoped visiting her parents' mausoleum might bring a type of comfort. Or at least a respite from bad dreams.

Beside her, Dominic's horse snuffled. He tossed his head. Her own mare responded with a whinny.

Dominic chuckled. "They are bored with our silence."

She patted her mare's chestnut flanks, appreciating the sleek hide beneath her fingertips, the way sensation grounded her to the present and made her forget that ashy taste in her mouth. "Nonsense. They are animals. They're simply responding to external stimuli. A fly, perhaps."

"Where is your imagination?"

"In my brain, where it belongs," she responded pertly. Perhaps this trip would not be so onerous after all. "I am interested in seeing the village after the cemetery. My supply of chamomile is running low, and I'd like to get more feverfew."

"You're demanding for a governess."

"It's temporary."

"Your demands?"

"Don't sound so hopeful." She shot him a grin. "The position."

"Ah, yes. Being a governess does not suit you."

She drew her horse to the left, as it kept gravitating toward St. Raven's. "No, that is not it at all. I enjoy teaching Louise."

"Bossing her about."

"Really, my lord, do you want to have a conversation or are you going to persist in sniping at me the entire trip."

He chuckled, an easy roll of laughter. "I am only returning the favor."

"I don't snipe at you." She touched the horse with her heels, determined to leave the earl behind.

He sped up, drawing his mount close to hers. "Don't be so prissy, Retta. I'm jesting. Tell me more about your herbs, if you want."

"Prissy? Retta?" She pressed her lips together to give him the impression she was highly irritated, when in fact, for the oddest second, her stomach flipped and she felt unaccountably pleased by his teasing tone. They had grown even closer, somehow.

He quit his teasing to ask her about herbs, and as she

spoke, warming to her subject, she remembered how fulfilling it felt to fix people's hurts. Before she knew it, they were cresting the hill that led to Morningside Manor. Dominic had listened so well, and asked so many intelligent questions, that she'd forgotten herself and monopolized the conversation.

Louise pounded over, her small mare's dark mane streaming in shining wisps. Her broad grin betrayed her excitement. "Is this where you grew up? Why, it's lovely. The most lovely, flowery home I've ever seen. There is ivy growing up the walls, Henrietta!"

Before they could respond, she whirled her horse around and galloped the rest of the way up the hill, then disappeared over its top.

"I guess that means my cousin rebuilt."

"Your cousin? William Gordon did not inherit?"

She shook her head, slowing her horse as they neared the top. A bitter unwillingness to see her former home choked her. "He is the third son. My father was the oldest. The second son inherited, but I believe he died several years ago, leaving my cousin as owner."

"Perhaps we should pay a call."

"No, no, I would rather not. That is no longer my world."

They were getting closer now. Closer to seeing the place she tried to never think of. The childhood she'd deliberately forgotten until memories took her dreams hostage.

Dominic said, "Do you not find it unfair that your uncle pulled you from what could have been a life of wealth and comfort? He thrust you into a life of war, a life not fit for a lady of your stature." Though he spoke gently, Henrietta felt the sting of his opinion.

She loosened her grip on the reins, which were digging into her palms. Remembering brought more pain. They reached the top of the hill, and there was Morningside Manor.

Rebuilt.

Splendid in the morning wash of sunlight, gleaming with good health and care. Louise had been right. There were several colorful gardens visible from here, planted in careful symmetry around the rectangular structure of the house. A catch of breath was trapped in her throat and for a long second, she was certain her heart forgot to beat.

"I expected rubble," she said quietly. Her horse stomped, impatient to keep moving, but she did not want to go any closer. Louise sat at the base of the hill while her mare snacked on the succulent grass.

"Why?"

"I suppose that moment in my life is frozen in my memory. I left and never came back."

"But you knew your uncle would inherit. You must have known they'd rebuild."

"I suppose I did not think too closely about it. I threw myself into studying the human body, various diseases, how to heal people. The past remained shut away, a painful time I refused to dwell on." She could not look at him, for a betraying sting pricked her eyelids. She needed a moment to compose herself, to concede that the world had moved on while she remained ensnared by the past.

She inhaled, dismayed that it was a shaky, unsure breath. "My aunt and uncle tried to take me in. But I was fifteen. I was being groomed to enter society, to make an advantageous marriage, and I was angry. Furious that my parents had been taken from me. Uncle William came for the funeral. While the others were weeping and having fits of vapors and multiple glasses of cognac, he was stoic. He stood at the grave strong and in control." She blinked and, once sure her eyes were dry, looked over at Dominic. His somberness encouraged her to continue. "I admired his fortitude. I watched him, and I did not cry, either. We had a chance to speak and I found that a gargantuan curiosity lived inside of him, the same that breathed within me. He was a university-trained physician who expanded his knowledge by performing surgeries. He did not care that gentlemen are not to work. He was breaking societal molds. Doing important things with his life. And he was so kind. It is in his eyes, Dominic, a great and charitable kindness that reminded me of my father. And so I chose to go with him."

"I am surprised your guardians agreed."

"They did not, at first. There was a great fuss involved. My aunt had no daughters and was looking forward to giving me a come-out."

"Most young ladies are determined to marry." A sour note tinged his tone.

"That is true. But, you see, I had already developed an interest in learning from my father. He was a natural teacher. My mother enjoyed botany, as well. I eventually achieved my goal of going with Uncle William when I pointed out that my parents, titled as they were, did not have a great deal of wealth. Therefore, taking into account my plainness and my lack of dowry, it was determined that my odds of catching a husband of rank were low. It would probably take several years of expensive Seasons, clothes, tutoring in the fine arts of being a well-mannered debutante… You see my point. Then I proceeded to behave monstrously. I made my aunt's life miserable. She finally gave me to Uncle William." She noted Dominic's look of surprise with a confirming nod. "Yes, I was worse than Louise. Older. More manipulative and determined to have my way."

"I have only seen you behave in a straightforward manner."

"Uncle William and my relationship with God have changed me." She proffered what felt like a rueful smile. "Though, as I am planning to join my uncle, unbeknownst to him, perhaps I have not completely ceased my manipulative maneuverings." They shared a smile then, and she found her heart skipping, lightening. Warmth not caused by the sunlight suffused her being.

How very easy it was to speak to Dominic. He made her feel both comfortable and comforted.

Dominic brought his horse closer, leaning forward until she could feel the heat of his face against hers.

"Your aunt and uncle were very wrong about one thing," he said in a husky, low voice that put tremors in her belly.

"What?" she asked in a shallow, breathless voice that sounded unfamiliar to her ears.

He grinned, the lines fanning out from the corners of his eyes, unbearably attractive. "You are not plain."

Dominic could not take his eyes from the woman riding in front of him. Radiant. That was the word that came to mind. Effervescent, even. And the irony was that she had no idea, or perhaps she did not even care. She called herself plain.

If one did not speak to her, one might make such an assumption. But he remembered the first time he'd seen her, hovering over him, eyes alight, alive…with warmth. Compassion. Dark with intelligence, and because she'd been so close, he'd noticed her lips.

Despite the pain he'd been in, those lips had made a quite remarkable impression on him.

They rode past the estate now, not venturing closer.

Louise and Henrietta were ahead of him, discussing flowers and herbs. He gripped the reins, urging his mount to pick up pace. He should not have said such a thing to Henrietta about her looks. She was the governess and not even a permanent one, at that.

He hoped she stayed a few years, at least. Long enough to prepare Louise for society, or until his niece was ready to enter a finishing school.

He read the longing in her eyes to practice medicine again. Any flirtation would be temporary, at best, and though it amused him to put color in her cheeks, he needed to exercise more self-control. There was also the matter of his illness.

He was in no position to indulge in any romances. Not with Barbara's constant desire to take Louise and Old John's threats to expose his epilepsy. He was to make another payment soon. A nuisance, and everything in him protested the acquiescence to the spineless blackmailers.

He pulled up alongside the ladies. "Where are we headed, as Morningside Manor is now behind us?"

"The cemetery," said Louise. "I picked flowers for Henrietta's parents."

But when they reached the spot of their burial, and dismounted, there were already flowers at the mausoleum door. He caught the shock flitting across Henrietta's face. Masking it, she dropped to her knees, hands clasped.

"Someone has brought my parents fresh flowers."

Louise slipped her hand into Dominic's. "Does that mean they are missed?"

"Yes," he answered. "And cared for. Are you sure you do not want to make a call on your cousin?"

"The Season has started, and I doubt anyone is home." She stood, shaking debris from her skirts.

"Take a second alone." Dominic steered Louise toward

the horses. Well he recalled visiting the graves of his family. It was a private moment, for reflection, for remembrance. But as they waited with their horses, he found that the wan complexion and sober set of Henrietta's lips bothered him.

She did not take long and when she walked back to them, a telltale sheen dusted her eyelashes.

"Let's eat," said Louise, who had been suspiciously quiet this time. She, too, felt the sadness of the visit. They stopped to picnic near a stream. The trees offered shade, but the meal was quick. He could see the distraction in Henrietta as she ate.

"The village should have an herb shop," he said as they packed up. "We will inquire about who leaves the flowers."

"Someone who loved my parents," said Henrietta.

"Agreed."

The ride to the village did not take long. It was a quaint little town with various shops and an inn, just as he expected. They left their horses at the livery to be fed and watered for the return ride to St. Raven. As they neared the herb shop, Dominic spotted a familiar figure.

The apothecary, striding toward them with a leer, prompted Dominic to pause outside the door. Instead of going inside with the ladies, he crossed the street, hoping his blackmailer would follow him.

Old John met him on the corner of the walkway. He spoke before Dominic. "I've been waiting."

"You'll have your money."

Old John cackled, rubbing his hands together. "It'll be double this time, for your tardiness."

Dominic's jaw hardened. "It is not due until tomorrow."

"We changed our minds."

Never negotiate with a blackmailer. It's not that he

didn't understand that no good would come of this situation, it was simply that at the moment he didn't feel he had any other choice.

Old John was eyeing him, licking his lips.

When Dominic still didn't speak, he said, "It's a simple matter to send a small note to your sister detailing your sickness. I'm sure she'd be happy to get her hands on yer estate. Not to mention the girl."

"You'll have your money," he said tersely. "Did you follow us here?"

"Nay, we apothecaries trade herbs. In fact, I was headed there now. I've heard yer new governess deals in medicine."

He didn't like the gleam in the old man's eyes. "Leave now and you shall have your double this afternoon."

"Ye've not much to bargain with, but I'll give ye that for now."

Dominic strode past him, heading to the shop to join the ladies. They were at the counter paying for their goods when he arrived.

"Allow me," he said over Henrietta's protests.

Then they left and no sooner were they riding home, Louise in front as usual, than Henrietta turned to him. "Out with it," she said in a crisp tone.

"Out with what?" He patted his horse's neck, avoiding her face.

"You have been sulky and taciturn since we left the village. What happened?"

"It's not your concern."

"Not my concern?" A sharp edge entered her tone. "You have seen me at my most vulnerable, and I have seen you at yours. I do believe it is my concern."

"You're my employee."

"I am not just an employee, and well you know it."

Dominic nudged his horse to move a bit faster. Telling her about the blackmail would only draw them closer, but it was unwise. He didn't wish to grow closer to Henrietta. He had a disease to cure and a child to successfully raise. Besides, she might try to fix the problem and that could lead to Barbara discovering his epilepsy.

Which would mean doctors and doubts about his sanity and more problems than he wished to think about.

"That is all you are, Henrietta."

"Balderdash."

He raised his brow at her then. Her face was flushed and her eyes sparked.

"There is no need for you to be upset," he said, trying to smooth her obviously rumpled feathers.

"No need? I hardly think you are one to speak to me of what I may or may not need. You hardly know me."

"I know that you excel as a governess. I know that eventually you will join your uncle and exceed society's expectations of a woman practicing medicine. I know that you needed to visit your old home to heal the wounds of your past."

She sputtered, shaking her head. "I am not discussing anything further with you, Lord St. Raven. I shall ride with my charge." She cantered past him. "Where I belong."

Her back was ramrod-straight as she joined Louise. Dominic sighed, rubbing the back of his neck. He didn't want to hurt or anger her. His intentions had been to help.

Her reaction was confirmation that he did not need to facilitate any more closeness between them. After this trip, he was done interacting with her in any way other than what was expected of their positions.

Chapter Thirteen

Admitting wrongdoing gnawed at Henrietta's sense of pride, and yet the next day she found herself paused outside Dominic's office, her fist poised to knock.

After their trip yesterday, she'd sequestered herself in her room. Though she had been repeatedly invited to dine with Dominic and Louise, such a thing was really not appropriate for a governess and she always declined. Last night no invitation was sent.

She had been relieved, as she had much to think about.

To soothe her mind, she had reorganized her medicine box and relabeled the herb jars.

And now, before going to visit Mrs. Smith to check on her arm, she knew she should speak to Dominic. Thank him for taking her to see Morningside. But oh, how it grated to know he'd been right.

She rapped on the door, the sting of contact smarting her knuckles.

"Come in." He sounded preoccupied.

Straightening her shoulders, she pushed the door open and walked in. He sat at his desk, bent over papers, his hair a wild mass of blackness that looked more becoming to a pirate than an earl.

Such a fanciful thought for one not inured to fancy. She mentally shook away the image of a pirate, though it remained stubborn, especially when he looked up from his desk. The way his hair hung about his face, framing the sharp cheekbones and focused expression. Nonsensical fancy. That was all.

She strode in. "I'm here to thank you, my lord."

"You are?" He leaned back in his chair, beckoning her to come closer with a lazy, long-fingered gesture. "By all means, have a seat."

"It shall not take long." She drew a long, fortifying breath. The arrogant look upon his face almost changed her mind. "You were right to insist I visit Morningside. I found it most informative."

"Informative."

"Helpful," she hedged. What was he getting at? Staring at her so, as if expecting some other answer.

"Did you feel anything?"

"Of course I felt," she said quickly, a hot tightness compressing her breastbone. Though he did not sound accusative, the burn of his words seared her. "What are you wanting me to say? I've come to thank you."

He smiled then, a half-hearted thing that did not reach his eyes, which she suddenly saw were fatigued.

"You do not look well," she said.

He tapped his plume against the desk, then pushed back his chair and stood. "I am tired. It was a long night. Is there anything else?"

"Oh, no. Simply my thanks." She paused. "Did you have another attack?"

A long silence before he inclined his head. "Last night. They leave me exhausted."

"Are you still planning to leave for your home in the north?"

"After I sift through these papers. The steward has ideas regarding farming techniques. They have merit, and I suppose I should also thank you, Miss Gordon. If not for your interference, the estate would still be languishing."

"One must not ignore responsibilities."

"Indeed."

"I have a suggestion, my lord."

"Why am I not surprised?"

"I promised to help you, but I believe our best opportunities lay in London."

He stroked his chin, eyeing her. "What is it about London?"

"There are societies that meet to discuss medical advances. They will have updated knowledge. And there are bookstores where I might acquire modern literature on the subject. The books I have are old. Possibly inaccurate." She shifted on her feet. She did not want to disclose what they said about epilepsy.

That it was brought about by sin and evil. That those who had it should be locked up in asylums.

"You would help me find a cure?"

She hesitated. "I'm not sure there is a cure, but perhaps there are ways to lessen the frequency of attacks. Epilepsy has been a feared illness, but I do not believe it should impede on your life. With knowledge, you might reestablish your previous lifestyle."

"No, that was a different life. But I am interested in what you say. It would require some planning." He grimaced. "There is the possibility of a run-in with my sister."

"The one who wants Louise to attend school outside of England?"

"She thinks it would be best." His brow furrowed. "I do not."

"Louise loves you but she is a twelve-year-old girl in need of a firm hand and guidance. I believe you are capable of meeting her needs, but you will need to believe so, as well. Running off to your northern estate will accomplish nothing."

"I see," he said in a crisp tone.

"Louise would also benefit from a trip to London," she added, hoping to ease the furrow that had wedged itself in his brow. "There is so much to do there, and it will broaden her educational experiences."

"Point taken. What is in your hands?"

"Oh, this?" She held up the jar of ointment. "It is for Mrs. Smith's arm. I'm on my way to check her progress. Louise is waiting in the stables for me. You really should speak with the village apothecary. He did a terrible job treating her. It's quite the travesty."

His eyebrows lowered, making him look less charming and more like a pirate once again.

She quickly added, "At least supply him with new medical textbooks. In fact, I should like to meet the man." And give him a piece of her well-trained mind. Dominic had no need to know about that, however.

"He won't be serving the village much longer." Dominic came around the desk. "I shall accompany you to Mrs. Smith's. The fresh air shall do me good, and I believe she was the one with the roof in need of repair."

"That is correct, my lord."

He passed her, leaving an aromatic trail of cologne. "Let's join my niece, shall we?"

"Yes," she murmured, following him out the door and across the bright lawn. Another sun-swept morning.

"How is it that you learned so much about herbs and remedies?" he asked as they walked.

"A few days ago I would have said I learned it all with

Uncle William, but now, I remember my mother cultivated many gardens. She instilled a love for science within me."

Their footsteps whispered across the grass. She hugged her reticule and ointment jar to herself as the memory of digging in the dirt, planting, lingered in her mind. How very long ago it had been. Another lifetime, a different girl.

"How is Louise doing with her studies?"

"She is curious and bright. Absolutely fine."

Dominic shook his head, his hands tucked neatly into his pockets. "How is it that she ran off every other governess? She's almost like a different child."

"You're here," Henrietta pointed out. "As much as I'd like to believe I've made a difference, I truly think she needs you, and your presence calms her."

He seemed uncomfortable with that answer and said little else. They greeted Louise, who was hopping about in a way that alarmed Henrietta more than it did the horses. They watched her, their ears pointed forward, casually shuffling their hooves.

Soon they were off, Louise galloping ahead, laughing. Henrietta couldn't help smiling. She and Dominic rode in a companionable silence. They arrived at Mrs. Smith's. To Henrietta's relief, the rash was healing nicely, and the roof had been repaired.

As they were preparing to leave, Mrs. Smith cleared her throat. Quite loudly.

She gestured for Henrietta. Dominic was helping Louise adjust her stirrups. Henrietta walked back to the door frame, where the tenant stood, twisting her fingers in her skirts.

"I'm sorry, miss, but I feel I should tell you. Though I know it's not my place." Mrs. Smith's eyes flickered past Henrietta to where Dominic helped Louise mount. "My friend Jane has a terrible cough. I remembered what you said about the apothecary. It's not going away, and she's been on his medicines for almost a month. I'm worried."

"I will pay her a visit. Where does she live?"

Mrs. Smith gave directions. Henrietta hurried outside. "Dominic, I must check another tenant."

He wheeled his horse around. "Another?"

"Yes, you two may go on without me, if you'd like. That mound of paperwork on your desk requires finishing, I'm sure."

His face twisted. "It does. Louise?"

"I'm hungry."

"Then it is settled," said Henrietta. "I shan't be long."

The two rode away. Large and small, swaying with the same agile grace in their saddles. For a second sadness invaded her. She'd grown quite attached. Perhaps too much so.

Steeling her spine against any further melancholy, she steered her horse in the direction of Jane's house. Coughs could be quite dangerous. At least she had her medical bag, with a few jars and tinctures. Logical thinking had urged her to bring it. When she reached the cottage, a smaller version of Mrs. Smith's, she tethered her horse and then made her way up the uneven walkway. Spare bits of grass and weeds poked up between the stones. A broken shutter leaned at a crooked angle against the window.

She rapped on the door, but no one answered. "Jane?" No answer. Stepping to the side, she peered through a dirt-stained window. Visibility proved ambiguous.

More knocking on the door. Mrs. Smith had seemed very concerned. Past experience had taught Henrietta to be patient. A sick person often took longer to answer a call. Her reliance on experience proved helpful when at last the door creaked open.

A haggard woman peeked out, her blond hair pulled into a messy bun and her eyes listless with fatigue. Henrietta noted the strain around the woman's mouth and the sunken skin beneath her eyes.

"Mrs. Smith sent me. I am Miss Gordon, a trained physician's assistant. I've come to check on you."

Jane opened the door wider but before she could speak, a deep, rattling cough shook her body.

Henrietta had heard that sound before. It came before death.

She pushed the door open. Jane finished coughing and removed the cloth from her lips. Crimson streaks stained the ivory rag. A bad sign.

Henrietta scanned the room. "Are you taking medicine for your cough?"

Jane nodded. "By the stove."

Finding the glass bottle, Henrietta opened it and smelled it. Laudanum? "This is for your cough?"

"The doctor said it would relax my lungs."

"And he gave you nothing else to help?"

Jane shook her head.

Sighing, Henrietta walked to a hard chair near a wall. "Please come and sit. I shall listen to your heart and lungs to determine the severity of your case."

"Will this cost?"

"No, not at all. Ideally, you should be using a compress every day to loosen mucus. There are certain ointments to assist your breathing." She pulled her chair near Jane. First she rapped on Jane's chest and listened carefully. She did so several times, noting the changes in sound.

"I need to listen more closely." She waited while Jane removed her outer garments, down to the chemise. Then she pressed her ear against the woman's chest, over the right lung. Her skin was hot through the fabric.

Henrietta moved her head to different areas, listening intently, verifying the unfortunate prognosis.

Riles.

The rattling sound of the woman's lungs was indicative of consumption. Anyone trained in medicine could have made the diagnosis sooner, as the cough sounded advanced. She straightened, trying hard not to show the alarm that raced through her.

Even if the apothecary did not know enough of scientific analysis, surely in his years of practicing he had seen "the white agony." Another term for consumption. He should have referred Jane to a sanitarium, not given her a bottle of laudanum.

Because of him, Jane not only grew worse, but she had also possibly spread the disease throughout the village. Jaw tight, she helped Jane put her clothes back on. The thin, rough fabric fueled her rage.

She would have to tell Jane the news, recommend that she leave for a sanitarium and then alert the village.

Dominic studied the most recent reports on an acre of land to the south of his property devoted to corn crops. They did not seem to be faring well. He flopped his head down on the desk, closing his eyes.

The last thing he wanted was to change how his brother had run the estate. But if bad harvests kept affecting farming… He groaned. The desk was cool against his cheek.

"Ah, excuse me, my lord?" It was Jacks.

Wonderful. Time to behave like an earl again. He had no idea how Henrietta suffered through responsibility on a daily basis. He lifted his head, beckoning his valet in.

"My lord, I apologizing for disturbing you, but there seems to be a…situation that perhaps you may need to resolve." The strain in Jacks's voice was a bucket of cold water dumped over Dominic's head.

He assumed a more earl-like position, which included squared shoulders and a concerned expression. Most likely they had run out of flour again. *That* had been an uncomfortable experience. "What is the problem?"

His valet, though, did not act as he had during that incident. In fact, he looked distinctly pained, even going so far as to pull his collar away from his neck. "In the village, my lord."

"In the village…"

Jacks visibly swallowed. "It's the governess. She is infuriated with the apothecary and inspecting his shop."

Dominic shoved to his feet. "What do you mean, inspecting his shop?"

"It—it was told to me by a servant who has come from town that Miss Gordon is there. She is, well…livid. Not the behavior one expects from a governess." A bit of starch ironed Jacks's voice now. Servants did not like uppity servants, and though a governess ranged a bit higher than the working class, she didn't quite make gentry. Certainly not peerage.

The censure in Jacks's tone bothered Dominic, though he could not say why.

He rounded the desk. "Get me a horse."

All the way to the village, he brooded. The closer he got, the more annoyed he grew. Henrietta's interference with Old John could cause massive problems. The tendons at the back of his neck tightened with every beat of his horse's hooves.

Inspecting.

Why would she be inspecting Old John's store? It made no sense.

She had gone to see the other tenant. Obviously something had happened to send her into town. To gather more medicine, he presumed. But from the look on Jacks's face, there was more to the story. More than he was willing to say in front of his employer.

Dominic dropped his horse at the livery. He stalked to Old John's store. A crowd had gathered outside. The sun pummeled Dominic, and his stride slackened as he neared. The villagers talked amongst themselves, but when they saw him, their voices dropped to whispers. They parted, creating a path. No one addressed him, but everyone dipped into a bow or curtsy.

He offered a tight nod and moved through the path they made for him, clomped up the wooden stairs and went into the store.

More people were packed inside, though when they noticed his presence they attempted to give him space to enter. Eyes averted, the people in the room fell silent, but for one voice. One loud, distinctly feminine and condemning voice.

"You quack. You have as good as killed that woman and exposed this entire town to infection."

"Excuse me," he said to those around him. Unfortunately, the room was so small they could not make any more room for him. He scanned above their heads, his height a blessing.

Henrietta had not noticed him. He thought that might be her gold-streaked mane of hair at the far end of the room. An answering murmur came, perhaps Old John's rebuttal. Dominic applied a bit more force and gained an inch into the room.

"Ignorance is no excuse, sir." Henrietta's indignant words rose above the hushed whispers. The authority that resonated in those words did not surprise Dominic, but he could not have her scaring the villagers. He did not know these people. He had made no effort to learn about them, and he could count on one hand the number of times he had rode through the village.

But he knew Old John.

He could not allow Henrietta to browbeat him or disparage him, as she was so clearly bent on doing. Even if she was right, even if she had seen past the man's facade when no one else had. He finally squeezed to the counter, where his childhood apothecary hunched against the wall, his white hair framing an alarmed expression.

Henrietta's back was to him and the closer he drew, the more he noticed the rigid set of her shoulders, the palms on her hips. They faced each other like duelists at dawn.

He finally reached her and, as though sensing him, she spun. The look on her face was fierce, her eyes bright and strong, her ivory skin framed by soft curls that drew attention to the curve of her lips.

"Finally, you are here. This man—" she lifted her finger and pointed at Old John "—should be forced to leave the village at once."

Dominic, affection fading quickly, tilted his head. "Miss Gordon, I see you have met our apothecary."

"He does not deserve that title."

"I think you should return to my estate at once. We will discuss your opinion there."

Her eyes flashed, dark and brilliant. "Not until you rid this town of this false practitioner of medicine."

"You are to leave this store."

She made no move to follow his orders.

He leaned closer, not enough to flaunt convention, but close enough to smell the clean scent of her skin. "Do you defy me, Miss Gordon?"

A speculative silence fell about the room as everyone awaited her response.

Chapter Fourteen

Henrietta's breath caught in her throat, quivery and rapid, as her chest seized. The green in Dominic's eyes this morning reminded her of burnished emerald, smoky with challenge. Out of the corner of her eye, the quack cowered.

But in the room, everyone listened. And that was enough to remind Henrietta that though she was right, that this cowardly man who handed out advice without knowledge deserved to be banished from the village, she was also Dominic's employee.

He could dismiss her and she had not quite saved enough money to travel to Wales. Exhaling an impatient breath, she surrendered to his smoldering look.

Shooting the apothecary a scathing glare, she walked around Dominic and threaded her way through the watchers. By their expressions, they had no idea what to think or believe.

She went out and waited for Dominic. She did not pace the walkway, but merely stood silent against a post. A few meters away, a woman watched her. Wrinkles whittled her skin, the carvings of grief.

Henrietta offered the woman a smile, which the woman responded to by moving forward.

"Miss..." Her voice faltered.

"I am Miss Gordon, his lordship's niece's governess. I am also a trained physician's assistant." She tilted her head. "Are you in need of care?"

The woman glanced around, but the crowd had dispersed and no one would hear their conversation. Just as well, since the woman wore a covert expression. She came closer, her voice dropping to a whisper.

"He killed my daughter."

Henrietta did not startle. Practicing medicine was just that. Practicing. Terrible tragedies occurred and most often, the practitioner was blamed. That was not to make light of this woman's obvious pain. "What happened?"

"I came to him for feverfew, to lower her fever. He gave me the wrong thing. Laudanum. I only knew after she died. I laid my head against her deadness and smelled the opium on her skin. Then I tasted what was left in the bottle." The woman's face warped, wringing out her grief in dry twists.

"I am so very sorry," Henrietta said quietly. "When did this happen?"

"Last year."

"How old was she?"

"Lettie was twelve." The woman stepped back. "That man is no healer." She spun around and marched away. A second later, the door to the apothecary's shop swung open.

"Why are you still here?" Dominic emerged, brow furrowed and clearly displeasured by her presence.

"You told me to leave the store. I did." She crossed her arms. The apothecary, that terrible person, stood behind Dominic. Hiding, no doubt. "This is important. This man does not belong in your town, serving up deadly concoctions."

"I see you met Mrs. Lowery."

"She told me what you did."

"Wait a second." Dominic held up a hand. "This is not the place."

"I beg to differ, my lord." Henrietta fixed a hard glare on the apothecary, her stomach roiling, her heart racing. "That could have been Louise who died. Laudanum? Is that your regular prescription for everything?"

The old man's eyebrows drew together. He did not look cowed by her words. "I gave Lettie a mixture of feverfew and laudanum. The girl's fever spiked. There was nothing I could do."

"A likely story." But doubt took root. Grief often provoked strange perceptions. "Whatever happened with Lettie does not excuse what you have done to Jane." She turned to Dominic, ignoring the dismay on his face. After all, being an earl meant more than wealth and privilege. "It is your responsibility to address this misuse of medicine."

Dominic expelled a breath in a way that suggested annoyance.

She glared at him. "Your village apothecary gave laudanum to a woman who quite obviously has consumption. Not only that, but she has probably spread the infection. She should be sent to a sanitarium. Her lungs sound as though it is an advanced case. Did you even listen to her lungs?" She directed that last bit to the apothecary, whose blasé expression only increased her irritation.

"That would be unseemly," he replied.

Archaic nincompoop. The muscles in her neck were drawn as tight as a corset. "You do not listen to the sound of your patient's cough?"

"I often put my ear against a man's chest, but what you

are suggesting carries a level of impropriety for a woman. It is my practice to avoid such things."

"You are a fraud, sir. To put social etiquette above a science that saves lives."

"Consumption is not curable."

She squared her shoulders. "But it is containable, and you have not done your part."

Dominic moved between the invisible artillery flying between her and the apothecary. "That is quite enough, Miss Gordon. Go back to the estate and see to Louise. I will address this with you this evening."

"Very well." She shot the apothecary one last, furious look before going to collect her horse.

It wasn't until after the dinner hour that Dominic summoned her. She'd been able to calm herself somewhat by itemizing her concerns by importance. If she didn't think too hard about the apothecary's ineptitude, she could actually eat her food, a meal that was served to her cold. Again.

Evidently the new maids were not being properly put to use.

That went on her list. Even if his parents had spent no time preparing him for earldom, due to his being a second son, that no longer excused his neglect.

She went to his study with a list of items to discuss.

As usual, his greeting for her to enter sounded distracted and glum. He sat behind the desk, studying a mound of papers. She expected him to look up and appear concerned. To perhaps have grown a few more gray hairs the way she felt she had this afternoon.

Or maybe a new line upon his face to replace that irksome dimple.

But no, when he straightened, it was with a charming

grin and spiraling crinkles at the corner of his eyes. The lamplight caught his hair in a shining mass of ebony.

How very unfair that he was so unaffected by this afternoon's tumult. She squared her shoulders, her list clutched within her right hand. Smoothing her hair with her left, an altogether vain move and yet comforting in the order it suggested, she seated herself and placed the paper on the desk.

Dominic reached for it, but she slid it toward herself.

"Is that your resignation?" The crinkles flattened. He pulled back his hand.

Containing her surprise, she shook her head. "No, my lord, unless you feel I should tender one?"

He regarded her, the crescent in his cheek deepening. "I hardly find such a dramatic move necessary, and today has been filled with enough theatrics without adding that to your list." He nodded at the paper.

She pursed her lips. "There are only three or four concerns, but they are important. I thought if I wrote them down, you might find it easier to fix them."

"You do not find yourself to be presumptuous?" He steepled his fingers. The green in his eyes was deeper tonight. An inane observation, but present nonetheless.

"Is it presumptuous to see a problem and suggest a solution?"

"I asked first."

"Very well. I don't find myself to be presumptuous. I'm tired of eating cold food. Despite your new maids, it is being delivered to my room cold and tasteless."

Dominic frowned, and the tilt of his lips did nothing to detract from his handsome features. "Our food was served hot."

"Perhaps you could speak to your staff, then." Shrugging off the uncomfortable thought that perhaps the servants disliked her, she continued. "It is also necessary to update Louise's collection of books. They are outdated by at least fifty years."

"That is not surprising."

At her lifted eyebrow, he shrugged. "My brother and his wife were not interested in furthering their education beyond farming and Seasonal activities in London. The books he kept are incomplete." He shook his head. "But that is not your business."

The comment should not have stung, and yet it did. She ignored it to broach the final item on her list. "My final concern has to do with the apothecary."

He heaved a giant sigh that to a less hardier personality may have induced pity. She was not swayed by his lack of desire to argue the subject.

"It was you who said we would speak of it this evening," she said in a firm voice.

"And you never shy away from tackling difficult discussions, do you, Miss Gordon?"

She shook her head.

"Very well." He fixed her with a stare as firm as her voice had been. "Today you publicly insulted him and flaunted my authority. You are to apologize."

The shock on Henrietta's face was almost comical. Dominic had no doubt that the lady had never been told to apologize for anything in her life. From what he'd seen, she had been indulged a little too much. That brain of hers had stunted other aspects of her personality, namely her humility.

He waited while she sputtered.

Finally she said, "I certainly will not apologize."

"Why?" Perhaps he should not be surprised, but he was. "Your behavior was unacceptable."

"I beg your pardon?"

"No, you should be begging mine." Any humor that may have been tempting Dominic to laugh fled beneath the knowledge that she truly did not see how inappropriate she'd been.

"No. No, absolutely not." She set her jaw in a prissy jut.

Dominic shuffled the papers on his desk, mostly to look busy while he considered a new approach. Dismissing her was out of the question, but he couldn't have her jaunting into the village and stirring up strife. She had inspired him to do more with the estate, to ignore the fear of failure and the commitment involved, but she was not in charge.

"Very well," he said finally. "I will consider the matters you've brought before me. In the meantime, you are not to practice medicine or provide any medical assistance without my permission first."

"That's not acceptable."

"Your actions today were borne of emotion and anger. They were not professional and helped no one. You undermined me and what I'm trying to accomplish as the earl here."

She was watching him with a blank face now. Discomfited by that indefinable look, he continued, "As the master of this house, it is not unacceptable for me to demand your obedience."

"I simply find it odd that a man who has shunned his responsibilities now finds them so very important. Enough so to keep his people from the proper care, all to protect a fraudulent physician. A man hardly skilled enough to be called an apothecary." There was a starkness in her eyes that he wasn't sure how to erase.

He groaned. One word from an angry Old John, and Barbara would swoop down with her greedy husband and take Louise. Maybe even the estate. He wouldn't put it past his brother-in-law.

"Medicine is a serious pursuit. He has demonstrated a lack of respect for the practice." She crossed her legs, placing her hands on her knees as though assuming a position of authority. Which he may have found amusing and slightly endearing if he was not so surprised by her complete revulsion toward Old John. "I have no problems running my diagnoses by you, but never think I shall stop serving those who need my skill and knowledge. I shan't. And that is all there is to it."

Strong words, but the tone was not combative. Rather, it was an acceptance of who she was, why she existed. Once again, an admirable trait that he wished he could emulate. He had never had purpose. Until now.

They would never be just earl and governess. They had learned too much about each other now. And he cared for her. Drawing a deep breath, he realized it was time to tell her the truth about Old John.

"Your strength of character and fortitude is admirable. Regardless of your actions today, I hold every confidence in your skills." He paused. "There is something you should know. Old John has a friend who wrote and told him I'm suffering from epileptic attacks. They are blackmailing me."

She gasped. "I do hope you are not giving in to them."

"I had to, temporarily."

She was shaking her head. "This will not do."

"For Louise," he said roughly. "If they tell Barbara or even spread rumors, then she will insist on taking Louise and perhaps even the estate. I have no doubt that she will have me institutionalized."

"You ignored the estate and left Louise alone, so what

does it matter if you lose these things?" Her voice was gentle, her logic impeccable.

"Do you want me to be locked away? And I am doing my best to rectify my past mistakes. I know that Louise wants me in her life. I just hope to be all that she needs."

"I understand. What can I do to help?"

"Stop annoying Old John until I can figure out a way to solve this." He cleared his throat. "My sister has invited me to a house party a fortnight from now. It will be in London. You will both go with me."

"Excellent news, my lord." She smiled kindly. "We shall have much to explore and learn while there."

"Yes." For the last week, since he'd hired his steward and since he'd realized how much Louise wanted him there, he'd hardly thought of the parties he was missing. There were a few widows he used to attend events with, but since his accident, he had not heard from them.

"I had planned to tell Old John that I will no longer bow to his blackmail demands. Now that he has been publicly attacked, I will need to do so sooner. If the villagers don't run him out first."

"When is the next payment?"

"I sent one today. I have some time to figure out how to stop them without ruining Louise's future."

Henrietta waved a hand. "Who cares what that twit says? No one with a modicum of sense would give him credence. Even the threat of an asylum is unlikely."

"Do you think so?"

"There is a chance of institutionalization," she amended, "but thankfully you know me. And I happen to know several powerful physicians. I will not let you be put away."

His brow rose. "Strong words."

"Well, I'm certainly not going to waste time uttering

weak ones." She grinned then. "While in London, I suppose you will be able to take up hobnobbing with your dandy friends."

"Dandy friends?" An unexpected laugh erupted. "Have you seen how they dress?"

"You have a very white, elegant cravat," she said defensively.

"My naive Miss Gordon, you know little of society and fashion."

"And neither do I wish to," she said pertly.

"Yet you must learn, if you are to prepare Louise for entrance."

"Perhaps I do not wish to prepare her for a shallow lifestyle."

"You believe me to be superficial?"

"That is not what I said." Henrietta's lips pursed.

Dominic's back stiffened. Of course, it was how she saw him. He had never seen the need to live in a purposeful way. No longer did he wish to use his ailment as an excuse.

Still, her low opinion rankled. He felt as though he had become debased in her eyes.

Blood rushed through his head. Muscles tensing, he leaned closer, fixing his gaze upon her. "If that is how you feel, then perhaps this is not the right position for you after all."

"Of course it's not," she quickly responded.

Stunned by her acquiescence, he tapped his fingers against the desk. "You disrespected me today."

"Are we back to that again?"

He was annoyed, so yes. "I expected more from you."

"I demand honesty and justice," she choked out. "I shall not apologize for confronting that man."

"Will you apologize for undermining me?" A bold

question, but he found himself curious. He had not liked her dismissal of his station. Her lack of respect. An odd feeling, as he'd never cared in the past for others' opinions. But hers counted.

She wet her lips, her tongue a pale pink slip of movement against lips a shade darker than her rose-tinted cheeks. "May I think about it?"

"Think about an apology?"

"Yes." Her voice was thin, and suddenly Dominic saw the youth in her eyes. She was a woman thrust into unknown circumstances, doing her best to thrive in a world she no longer belonged to. How well he knew the feeling.

Patience and grace. He could afford to give those.

Inclining his head, he accepted her request. "Very well. Please let Louise know that in a fortnight we shall be traveling to London."

"I shall do so." She swept upward, the tight curl of her fingers against her skirts the only evidence of her distress. "Will we be visiting a library?"

"I don't see why not."

A smiled curved her lips then, and Dominic felt a sure and traitorous skip to his pulse. When she left, he stared after the door, the rapid beats of his heart a nonstop hammer in his chest.

He had told himself he would not allow anything beyond professionalism, and yet, in the few seconds it had taken to tell her about Old John's blackmail, his feelings had slipped into a place of trust.

He trusted Henrietta. Not only with Louise, but also with his secrets.

He was sliding into something he had not anticipated, and he did not dare to think of where he might end up.

Chapter Fifteen

Henrietta grabbed the jar of chamomile and shook it until her forearms ached. She moved on to the next jar, until all of her tinctures had been shaken. Only a few more weeks and they'd be ready to mix into ointments, balms and other remedies.

"Do you have to shake them every day?" Louise sat propped on a stool, her legs swinging.

"If you want to do it right, yes." Henrietta lined the jars neatly on the shelf. Cook had let Henrietta use the small room off the side of the kitchen as a place to mix and store her herbs. Many recipes required weeks of sitting in airtight jars before being ready for use.

"Dom said we shall be visiting London soon."

"Yes, I meant to inform you of that," Henrietta murmured, touching the feverfew she'd laid out on a cloth for drying. The plant bent beneath her fingertip, suggesting more time needed for adequate dryness. It had been several days since she'd seen the earl, and she was glad for it. Never had she felt so unsteady as when she'd left his office.

Apologize.

She did not want to. His challenge echoed within, stirring emotions she'd rather ignore. While she admired the way he'd seized control and demanded the apology, being on the receiving end of his authoritativeness rankled.

"Do you think I shall be able to attend a ball?" The uncertain waver in Louise's voice pulled Henrietta from her thoughts. She crossed the room and sat down next to her.

"You are too young, as of yet, but perhaps in a few years. Your aunt may have a room above the ballroom, where you can watch the attendees."

"Will you sit with me, if she does?"

Henrietta's heart twisted at the somber loneliness in Louise's voice. "I shall do my best," she said quietly. "Shall we go search out new blossoms? Perhaps we will find a few caterpillars before they've all gone into metamorphosis."

They headed to the gardens, which thanks to the added staff, appeared more manicured than when Henrietta had first arrived. Despite the changes, a lush wildness still remained. It was to the wildness that she and Louise traipsed in search of caterpillars.

"We will look for a guide to insects when in London," she said, peering beneath a fuzzy green leaf. No caterpillar, but the striations on the leaf reminded her of veins in a human heart. "Look, Louise."

The girl pattered over, dropping to her knees and dipping her head to peer at the underside of the foliage. Henrietta, on her knees also and propped on one hand, motioned Louise to adopt the same pose. "Do you see these lines here?" She drew her finger gently across the skin of the leaf, and Louise followed her movement. "When on the field, I met a surgeon who had previously performed…" She paused. The subject might not be suitable for a young girl. "That is to say, he had some experience with studying human hearts, and he showed me one. It was quite remarkable."

"Where was the person the heart belonged to?"

Henrietta grimaced, edging out from beneath the plant while wracking her mind for an acceptable answer.

"Yes, Miss Gordon, where exactly is that person?"

She stood, brushing dirt off her petticoat whilst formulating a response. Louise shuffled out as well, and then jumped to her feet.

"Dom," she cried, throwing her arms around him with little heed to the soil clinging to the folds of her dress. "I am so happy to see you."

"As I am to see you," he said, his voice lowering in a gruff way that touched Henrietta.

How very much his love for Louise reminded her of Uncle William. She brushed the dirt from her skirts while the two chatted. She blinked because her eyes stung a bit at the remembrance of her uncle.

She should write him again. Find out exactly where he'd be in two months' time. By her calculations, she should have enough saved by then to join him.

"Could I speak to you, Henrietta?"

"You're supposed to call her Retta." Louise crossed her arms, but she smiled as she spoke.

"Of course. Now?" A bout of nerves jangled within. She wet her lips.

"Louise, could you please ask Cook for a few tarts? I wish to join you on your…is it a caterpillar hunt or a discussion of human hearts?"

"Both," they replied in unison.

And then they all laughed, glittering chuckles in a flower-scented garden, and something deep inside Henrietta loosened. Like the lid on her herbs, kept tightly sealed until ready for opening. Was this what it was to feel like family?

She stuffed away the thought, for it brought to the surface both terror and longing.

Their laughter faded, and Louise ran off to find Cook. Which left Henrietta and Dominic in a dappled spot of sunlight. A tight band of emotion encircled her chest, pressuring her to speak, to break the silent camaraderie, but she pressed her lips together.

She had said quite enough at their last meeting.

And yet not enough. She owed him an apology, at least, but the words would not cross her lips.

"I have heard from my sister."

Not what she had expected to hear. Her tension seeped away. "Is that good or bad?"

He pushed his fingers through his hair. "It's unfortunate. She wants me to bring Louise to London for a visit."

"Which we are planning anyway."

"Yes, but I was not planning on seeing Barbara."

"Why?"

"Ah, the straightforwardness of your mind. It is one of the very first things I noticed about you."

A curl of pleasure unfurled within. "And what were the others?"

He squinted against the sunlight, smiling. "Your voice. Your hair. Your lips, especially."

Unbidden, she touched her mouth.

As though remembering himself, he cleared his throat. "I wanted to ask you to keep an eye on me during any visits we have with her. If you notice any oddness in my visage, or if I go into a seizure, I will need your help."

"I promised I would help you," she said gently. "I meant it."

"Thank you." He paused. "I have not been to London since the accident."

"I see. All will be well, my lord. I shall be praying wholeheartedly."

He inclined his head, and her heart squeezed painfully. Already she felt too much for him. What would happen when she left? She could only foresee the pain of parting, and she felt powerless to stop it.

Dominic was never so glad for Henrietta's presence as when they arrived at his sister's house. In a way he had not anticipated, having a governess sufficiently diverted Barbara's attention from chastising him.

After a two-day ride from St. Raven, in which he'd spent more time than he liked losing to Louise at *Wit*, he was exhausted. To be fair, he had not honed rhyming in years, while she admitted to practicing before their London trip so that she could best him. A few times he had wondered how Miss Gordon might fare at wordplay.

She had the intelligence, but did she have the imagination? Either way, he had no doubt she'd make them laugh. The perplexing lady had ridden in the other carriage with a female servant and it had been disconcerting to realize he missed her acidic take on his humor. Nevertheless, he and Louise kept themselves occupied and before he knew it, their carriage was rolling down the well-kept streets of Mayfair.

Despite the hour being before noon, servants bustled in the streets. Very few of the peerage were to be seen. Most still lay in their beds, recovering from the merriment of the night before. Resting for more tonight.

It was a well-laid rhythm that had also been his life until the accident. He had attended university, went on the requisite Grand Tour and then spent his days gallivanting about without a thought or a responsibility. He'd collected an appreciation for the aesthetic qualities of other cultures and histories.

He'd even gone so far as to commission a portrait, which hung in his house at the other side of Mayfair.

Their carriages pulled up to Barbara's home a little before noon. It was a fine-looking townhome. She'd married well. A viscount, if Dominic recalled, though he had not paid particular attention to the match. Edmund had arranged the relationship.

A familiar clutch of grief gripped him and for a moment he did not realize that his valet held open the carriage door. Louise exited first. Her yip of delight trailed her, and as he stepped from the carriage, he saw Henrietta doing the same from the other.

Their eyes met. She looked attractive in a pale yellow muslin and quiet bonnet. Her reticule hung from her wrist and had anyone not known her true situation, she might've been called a lady.

He gave instructions to his drivers to take the carriages and servants to his own London house. No doubt Barbara would send him and Louise home in a stylish curricle later. Bracing himself for his sister's wagging tongue, he went up the steps and came to a halt in the hallway. Louise stood at Barbara's side, listening in rapt attention as Henrietta described a medical procedure that involved… gruesome details.

His sister's wide eyes and complete stillness lent Dominic a sense of worry.

Barbara waited for a pause in Henrietta's speech before turning to him. "St. Raven, darling brother. An introduction, please?"

Ah. That look. It usually made him cringe because it was inevitably followed by questions about his life. The most notable being, when did he plan to marry? That had been her preaccident ritual, at least.

He swept Barbara an overdone bow designed to spark her irritation. "Good evening to you, too." Louise giggled behind a hand. "Shall I present the ever lovely Miss Stanford? She hails from the verdant region of—"

"Cease your antics." Barbara held up a hand. In the months since he'd seen her last, she'd grown more stuffy. "The governess, I presume."

"Ah, yes, Miss Gordon. Meet my sister, Lady Winthrop."

Henrietta performed a wobbly curtsy.

Barbara pulled a jewel-encrusted chained quizzing glass from her pocket and put it to her eye. Presumably to examine Henrietta more closely, but the appendage made her look ten years older. And so very pretentious. "Is there a reason, Miss Gordon, why you are standing in my hallway rather than in the servants' hall?"

Henrietta's face suffused immediately with color. Louise's wiggling stilled and a tense silence ensued.

How often Barbara had employed that tone with him. He truly disliked it. He had thought to be relieved with her attention focused on Henrietta, but sympathy overrode his own survival instincts. That and the knowledge that the intelligence of his governess, combined with her world experiences, would not allow her to suffer his sister's superiority complex for long.

He could not predict what Henrietta would say, but undoubtedly, it would be atypical for someone of her station.

"She goes with me," Louise said, stealing her aunt's attention and Dominic's thoughts. "I need her."

Barbara lowered her glass. "Need?" She glanced around, ascertaining that the servants were not visible or within earshot.

Louise nodded vigorously, looking too worried. He

Dear Reader,

IT'S A FACT: if you answer 4 quick questions, we'll send you **4 FREE REWARDS!**

I'm not kidding you. As a leading publisher of women's fiction, we value your opinions... and your time. That's why we are prepared to **reward** you handsomely for completing our mini-survey. In fact, we have 4 Free Rewards for you, including 2 free books and 2 free gifts.

As you may have guessed, that's why our mini-survey is called **"4 for 4".** Answer 4 questions and get 4 Free Rewards. It's that simple!

Thank you for participating in our survey,

Pam Powers

stepped forward, placing his hand on her shoulder. "I did not instruct Miss Gordon where to go as she often accompanies us and provides educational commentary. She is well-traveled."

Barbara's eyes flickered. She leaned forward and said quietly, "She is the governess, Dominic."

He inclined his head. "Miss Gordon, one of Lady Winthrop's maids shall show you below stairs. We will be leaving for my townhome this evening. I shall arrange a carriage to take you there sooner so that you might prepare a schoolroom."

A maid appeared and, without words, the two left. Barbara linked her arm to Dominic's and led him toward the parlor. "I have recently acquired a barouche. It is quite comfortable and charming. Louise, would you enjoy a ride after some refreshments? There is much to see. All the ladies in their finery shall be out."

"That sounds interesting," his niece said wanly. A perplexed air hung about her, as though she could not process that Henrietta was indeed of a different class than her family. His jaw clenched. Never had he paid an overt amount of attention to how the servantry was treated, but he found that Barbara's dismissal of Henrietta irritated him.

Barbara tugged on his arm, slowing their walk until they stopped outside the parlor. Louise had already gone in to investigate. "Do you have feelings for the governess?"

Startled, Dominic pulled his arm from hers.

"Don't look so put out," she said with censure. "You have behaved beyond the pale in the past. I do not need to remind you of your antics, I'm sure. I have no idea why Edmund left you in charge of Louise. She needs stability. Propriety. What do you know of this Miss Gordon?"

"I know that she is highly educated and provides Louise with all that she needs. Stay out of this, Barbara."

She harrumphed, sounding like a dowager rather than a twenty-four-year-old viscountess. "It is my duty to make sure all is as it should be. Do not think I won't consult a higher authority, should you prove unfit."

"Is this because you have not provided an heir?"

Barbara gasped, looking quickly about to make sure no one had heard his reference. "That has nothing to do with it." But two bright spots of color stained her cheeks, and Dominic knew he was right.

"Everything will be fine," he said. But her threat hung over him the rest of the day. When he stopped paying Old John, she would discover the truth. If her husband agreed that he was not a fit guardian, then Dominic was in trouble.

Thankfully he had Henrietta as a governess for a little while.

But he would need to make plans, and quickly, before Louise's life was forced into another, unwelcome change.

Chapter Sixteen

Henrietta enjoyed teasing Dominic about being a dandy, but quite unexpectedly she discovered that he was not truly one.

Friday started out regularly enough for a governess, she supposed. Ignored by the staff. Left to her own devices. Which suited her perfectly.

She planned lessons in the morning because Dominic did not wake up until noon, and then he took Louise out, leaving Henrietta to explore London on her own.

After quite a bit of inquiry, in which she discovered that most servants did not like to read, she found a wonderful little shop in Covent Garden on Tavistock Street filled with book lovers. Though the store did not have any medical texts about epilepsy, the owner directed her to a few gentlemen who specialized in that sort of knowledge.

She returned to Dominic's house with two books and a clearer understanding of London's streets. The maid she'd brought along was only too glad to be home and disappeared immediately. And so it was that Dominic found her in the library that afternoon, bent over an especially interesting commentary on surgical practices throughout the world.

"Reading about rogues and maidens in distress?" He settled in the chair across from her, his cologne a distracting scent.

Sighing, she looked up from her studies. "If you are referring to those novels in which the heroine always needs rescuing, I do not indulge in that drivel. I am, in fact, trying to find out more about your epi—" She cut herself off as he held up a finger, signaling to keep silent.

"Secrets should not be spoken aloud," he said, but his eyes were sparkling.

She closed the book. He evidently was in one of his lighthearted teasing moods, which for some unfathomable reason made her feel more lighthearted, too. Even though she'd just been reading a most gruesome account of a surgeon removing the wrong leg because he had not looked beneath the sheet before using the saw.

"Is Louise available for lessons? She has not mastered her reading."

"My spitfire of a niece is shopping with Barbara today. As for tonight, there is a dinner party. Barbara had a cancellation and has asked that you fill in to keep our numbers even." He held up a finger. "Now, now, don't shake your head at me."

"I have nothing to wear."

"Barbara has already taken care of that. It's simply to keep the numbers even. You eat, converse and then it will be over."

Henrietta pressed her lips together, contemplating. She knew that it was not uncommon for a hostess to seek evenly numbered guests, but she did not have to like it. Furthermore, to tell him no would be to discredit him in front of his sister.

She could not possibly do such a thing.

And that was how she discovered the fashion trend of

wearing elaborate and expensive clothing inspired by Beau Brummell, one of London's most expensively dressed men and arbiter of all things stylish.

Lady Winthrop had sat her between an elderly man with alert eyes and a soft-faced man with a cravat so snowy white and impeccable that she felt she must excuse Dominic for his own cravat sensitivities. Henrietta promptly decided that she'd try to engage the older man in conversation. Style, after all, was not her forte.

During the second round of food, the dandy talked to her. At first she did not realize he was speaking to her, but soon his voice intruded and she was forced by good manners to look at him.

"Madam, I must tell you how much I admire the cut of your gown."

"Thank you, but it is borrowed."

His hand flew to his neck cloth. His eyes widened in what she could only imagine was horror. Out of the corner of her eye, she saw Dominic smirking at them. Setting her jaw, she forked another mouthful of butter-soaked vegetables into her mouth.

"You have uttered words that are unusually frank, Miss...?"

She swallowed. "Miss Gordon. I am simply the governess, here to even out the numbers."

"An honest woman," he murmured.

She eyed him, wondering in which direction he planned to direct conversation and if she should develop a sudden megrim. But she did not want to miss dessert.

It became clear, very quickly, that Mr. Hodges was wry and amusing, his personality as rumpled and interesting as his clothing was not. Every so often she felt Dominic's eyes upon her, like a hot spot in the middle of her back, but when she looked at him, he'd merely dip his head in acknowledgment.

Mr. Hodges regaled her with tales of his travels with the East India Company when he was younger, and she laughed when he described an unfortunate fiasco with a monkey.

"My uncle has a pet monkey," she said. "He takes Cheepers with us everywhere."

Mr. Hodges's finely plucked blond eyebrow rose. "Indeed? Where is your uncle now?"

And so it was that they began the most intriguing conversation on medical advances, technology and the vagaries of pet monkeys. Their engagement lasted through dessert and into the drawing room, where they immediately found an alcove to chat about telescopes.

A young lady played a rousing melody upon the pianoforte and several card tables had been set up. Dominic stood at the opposite of the room. She gave him a tiny finger wave for his eyebrows were lowered and his lips flat.

She turned to Mr. Hodges, who watched her in a strange way. He was very attentive, even going so far as to bring her a drink. "It is my opinion that if an instrument can be designed to search out the stars and make them clearer, then surely we as a society must find a way to look inside the human body. Current microscopes are not sufficient. They must be improved."

"Have you ever read the book *Micrographia*?" he asked.

"Unfortunately not."

"Stunning illustrations. I shall lend you a copy."

"That is most kind of you." She could not help her widening smile. "I shall enjoy such a book immensely."

"Miss Gordon. Mr. Hodges." Dominic appeared, bowing and scowling, though it seemed as though he was trying to hide his ill humor beneath a tight grimace of a smile.

"St. Raven. It's been ages, man. Where have you been hiding?"

"Inherited an earldom and realized it was time to grow up and be responsible."

"How utterly boring," Mr. Hodges drawled.

Barbara sauntered over just then, the lift of her jaw indicating displeasure. Henrietta bit back a grin. She was not so inured to societal snobbery that she didn't recognize when her time was up.

"Miss Gordon, it is customary for the governess to retire to her room after dinner. You are no longer needed."

"Ah, the lovely Lady Winthrop. What a delightful dinner party. I am in absolutely awe of your splendid table." Mr. Hodges spoke in a rather foppish way that made Henrietta rethink her initial pique with Dominic's superficial humor. His could not compare to this silliness.

A woman with shining brunette ringlets that cascaded over perfect skin glided over.

"Do introduce me, Lord St. Raven?" She studied Henrietta, a calculating gleam in her eye and a possessive lean in her position toward Dominic.

Henrietta shifted, suddenly feeling her first nerves, for while Mr. Hodges felt harmless enough, the way both ladies looked at her rather made her feel like their meal for the night.

"This is his governess." Barbara tittered. "Miss Gordon," she added as an afterthought.

"I see." The lady cut her chin to the side, dismissing Henrietta as one would a servant.

And that was what she was, but she did not like the feeling at all. As a woman working with her uncle, she had been treated like this often. Slighted. She stiffened her shoulders, prepared to advise the snobby lady that if she was using arsenic to attain such a perfect complexion, then she should beware of the chemical's toxicity.

Dominic spoke, however, surprising her.

"Miss Gordon is not a mere governess. She has assisted the physician Mr. William Gordon in his practice for many years."

"Mr. Gordon?" Barbara turned an astonished gaze to Henrietta, as though just seeing her. "You are related?"

"He is my uncle."

"She is only governessing as a favor. Louise took a shine to her when she stayed with Lady Brandewyne. An old family friend," he added for good measure.

Henrietta relaxed when Barbara's features softened. The woman beside her, who had not been introduced, pinched her lips together.

"You were raised as a lady, then?"

"My parents died before my Season," Henrietta said shortly. "Thus, my gentility was lost with my wealth and my home and my family."

"What a varied experience you've had," Mr. Hodges pronounced gaily. "You've gone from riches to rags, from ladyhood to physicianhood. A romantic tragedy fit for a Byron poem." He sighed in such a comical way that all members of the party laughed.

"Miss Gordon has provided excellent medical advice to many of my tenants. She is certainly an asset to my estate," said Dominic, and her heart warmed at his praise.

"Certainly an unconventional governess." Barbara gave her one last, tight-lipped look and, taking the other woman's arm, wandered off.

"Well, then, I should hobnob with other beautiful women before people begin talking about us." Mr. Hodges granted her a long, exaggerated wink before spinning around to thread his way to the other side of the room.

"Interesting man." She sipped her drink. Maybe it was time to leave. Lady Winthrop had made it clear that she didn't belong. No matter who her parents had been.

"He's a true dandy."

"Indeed?"

"You have made fun of my admittedly dashing cravats, but I can assure you that Mr. Hodges spent at least two hours on his toilette. And his clothing? Eight hundred pounds a year, at the minimum."

It took all her willpower to keep her jaw from unhinging at that fact. "Are you sure you're not spouting out unverified information? Otherwise known as gossip."

"My dear Retta, I only repeat information from the verified source of Lady Hupperdink, a bastion of the beau monde and keeper of all our misdeeds. She is often found at Almack's, gathering new information to share with worthy listeners."

"You are quite ridiculous, my lord." She fought her smile and her blush. He had called her "dear Retta." It was deliciously inappropriate, but she had no desire to correct him. She scanned the room. "Is Lady Hupperdink the one with the hat?"

"Ah, yes, her hats. She makes a statement with them, don't you think?"

Henrietta squinted. Was that a *nest* perched upon her brim?

"Real bird feathers, I'm told." Dominic's eyes crinkled in suppressed mirth, and a hot shudder rippled through her. How very handsome and elegant he looked tonight. Eyes like shining emeralds and his jaw a clean, firm line that suggested strength.

She must ignore this feeling moving through her, gathering momentum. She simply must.

There was nothing to be gained in having an attraction to this earl.

Nothing but heartbreak.

Henrietta spent the next day roaming London with Louise. Their maid lagged behind them, carrying their bags of trinkets. Or rather, Louise's. Her aunt had given her pin money, which she was determined to spend.

The sheer waste of it bothered Henrietta, but she kept her mouth closed. After all, if Mr. Hodges spent eight hundred pounds a year on clothing…the very idea flabbergasted her. While traipsing down Piccadilly Street, Louise talking about Lady Winthrop's upcoming ball and Henrietta partially listening, they passed a window where she saw books.

Books everywhere.

And people reading.

She jerked to a stop, surprising Louise into silence. "We are going in here."

Before her young charge could protest, she marched into number 187 Piccadilly Street. Better known as Hatchards, a store she had often heard of in her uncle's circles. A renowned place of learning and education.

The scents of leather, paper and ink welcomed her.

"What is this?" Louise spoke in a whisper, as aware as Henrietta of the sanctity of such a bookstore. Men lounged in the corners, their deep conversations hushed and sacred lullabies.

"A bookstore." One that might carry information about epilepsy.

Though she wanted to spend hours within the confines of this happy and safe place, the hour was growing late and Dominic expected them home. She spoke with a man at the counter, who found her a dusty book of rare medical conditions. Without bothering to glance through it, she bought it.

"Why are you buying that?" asked Louise as they walked to their carriage.

"Research. Books are a veritable fount of information."

"Is it because of Dom's illness?"

Henrietta stuttered to a stop, causing a few glares from passing ladies in flouncy dresses and overwrought hats. The green of Louise's eyes glittered up at her. Knowing. Challenging.

"What do you know of that?" She began walking again, aware of the maid behind them, and wondered if she could hear their conversation.

"I saw him once, when he did not know. I was quite terrified."

"Why did you not say something?"

She shrugged. "He seemed fine afterward, just tired. I felt it better left unmentioned."

"His illness is best kept private for now." She clutched the book to her chest. "I hope to find a cure for him."

Louise's eyes narrowed. They reached the carriage, and the footman opened the door for them. The girl slid in first, shoulders sharp-edged squares against the velvet backdrop of an earl's carriage. Henrietta followed, nerves twisting.

The maid did not join them, sitting up with the coachman instead. One more difference in stations, Henrietta noted. The carriage jostled to a start.

"Does it bother you that I want to help your uncle?" she asked Louise.

The girl shrugged, a mulish expression creeping upon

her face. Was there to be a tense silence the entire ride? She hoped not. There'd been great strides made with Louise. She seemed happier and Henrietta did not want to see that end.

"I just don't want him to die," she blurted out.

Henrietta blinked. That had not been what she expected to hear. She set the book on the seat beside her and leaned forward, holding Louise's worried eyes with a calm expression. "Your uncle has very little chance of dying from his illness so long as it does not strike him unawares."

Louise blanched.

Perhaps that had not been quite the right thing to say. Taking the girl's hand, small and tiny in hers, she gently squeezed. "We shall look out for him. If he looks pale or faint, we must make sure he lies down somewhere safe. The nature of his illness is a loss of bodily control. It can be very scary, but it will pass quickly and he will be fine again." She forced a soft smile. "This must be kept secret because his illness is rare and misunderstood."

"I understand." Louise pulled her hand away, frowning. "Aunt Barbara is having a ball in two days' time. She said I might watch from an upper room that is hidden from view. Will you join me?"

"Of course," she said with more assertion than she felt.

"I want to keep an eye on Uncle Dominic. You know all the women want to marry him now."

"Because he's an earl?"

Louise nodded sagely. "I have come to a conclusion."

Henrietta raised her eyebrows, even as Louise's tone warned her that she might not like what was coming next.

"Uncle Dominic does not want to be married. It is up to us to protect him from fortune hunters."

"And how do you suggest we do such a thing?" Especially when she did not plan to be here much longer.

"It is simple." Louise grinned a puckish smile laden with intent. "We sabotage."

Chapter Seventeen

Sabotage.

Barbara's words echoed in Dominic's ears.

He scanned his sister's crowded ballroom with a long, lazy perusal. She had outdone herself this Season, heaping within the room a maddening crush of bored peerage and flittering debutantes. He had been introduced to so many he'd lost count. Their names escaped him, his memory filled instead with eager eyes and white dresses.

All eager to wed an earl.

Word had spread quickly of his new wealth and holdings. Since he'd been out of London, he'd forgotten the predaceous nature of society. He felt it now. Each gaze a talon tugging him toward the altar.

"Sabotage," he said aloud.

"Yes." Barbara stood next to him, her posture neatly positioned to denote a gracious and benevolent host. "My maid told me this morning of Louise's plan. Really, Dominic, what has gotten into that girl? Marriage is the best possible choice for you. You can add funds to your coffer. Lord Winthrop tells me that profits from farming are on the downswing."

"Your husband is right about the crops, but I'll be fine,"

he replied absently, his gaze roving the room. "I've investments beyond the estate. How did your maid hear of Louise's shenanigans?"

"She was discussing them with that governess of yours." Barbara sniffed. "Why don't you send Louise to that school I told you about?"

"Your concern is noted," he said drily. "I suppose your husband will watch the estate for me?"

"Do not make it sound as though he is a greedy relative."

"Forgive me." He rubbed the back of his neck, suddenly eager to leave the crush of her ballroom. "I'll speak to Louise."

He moved to exit, but his sister's hand on his arm stayed him.

"There is no need to leave. Our niece is in a bedroom upstairs, overlooking the ballroom. When we constructed it, we wished to have a place to watch unknown."

"That is very forward thinking of you."

"Yes, Lord Winthrop is an intelligent and experienced man." She made no indication that she'd heard his sarcasm. He barely refrained from wrinkling his nose. Lord Winthrop was a stuffy bore thirty years his sister's senior and wealthy enough to create a ballroom large enough for London's elite.

Dominic ran his fingers through his hair. Months ago he would have enjoyed the dancing and flirtations. The promise of nothing more serious than a smile and a dance.

His perspective had changed.

"I'll check on her, at the least."

"Do remind her that sabotaging your marital prospects is not only unladylike, but her attempts to thwart the natural order of things will not succeed." She pointed upward, to a balcony he had not noticed jutting out above the ballroom entrance. "Don't forget we have a day party this week. We've been invited to Lord Waverly's country estate. It is only an hour's journey south of London. I've accepted on your behalf, as he has an eligible daughter."

He dipped his head in acknowledgment of her words, if not acceptance, and spun to leave. He found the room easily enough. A quick jaunt up a circular staircase, veer to the left and a tap on the closed door.

Before anyone could answer, he opened it.

Louise turned from the balcony, her surprise quickly changing to delight. "You came!"

"You expected a visit?"

Her face took on a secretive cast. Lips a furtive line and eyes averted.

"Louise has been scheming."

Dominic pivoted at the sound of Henrietta's voice. She sat on the edge of the bed, her face cloaked in darkness. There was one candelabra lit, its flickering flames dancing shadows in the room. Light from the ballroom only spilled in so far.

"That is what I've been told." He injected censure into his voice.

"All those silly women trying to interfere with our life." Louise skipped forward, placing her hand on his arm. "You understand, don't you?"

"How exactly are you planning to stop them?" He patted the careful upsweep of her hair. "Spreading nasty rumors of my vicious temper? Or perhaps that my fortune is a ruse."

"I was thinking of ripping up any calling cards and perhaps engaging in a tantrum or two. Strewing cookies across the parlor furniture." She shrugged. "Any number of things to convince them you're not a good marital prospect."

A sound issued from the dark confines where Henrietta sat. Something that sounded curiously close to a snort.

"And did you make sure that your aunt's maid would hear of your plans?"

"I might have." She passed a censorious glance toward Henrietta. "She refuses to help me. I was forced to resort to more obvious methods."

For a moment, he was taken aback. Louise sounded like an adult. Unsettled, he allowed his gaze to fall on Henrietta. "Perhaps it is time for Louise to return home? A reminder that she is but a child?"

Her harrumph was so dramatic and heartfelt that it coaxed his lips into a wide curve.

Strains of a waltz began, and Louise rushed to the balcony window. "Oh, Dom, look at them all dancing! How romantic. I should like to learn to waltz." She grasped imaginary hands and weaved back and forth. "He will be taller than me, of course, and so very handsome. Perhaps he will wear a long, black mustachio and swirl about in a pirate's coat."

She spun around, locking a forceful look on Dominic so intense he felt quite frozen by it. "You must dance with Henrietta." Upon seeing his surprise, she crossed her arms. "Please. I want to see how it is done."

Henrietta was shaking her head. Dominic could see the movement dusting the air.

Now that Louise had said something, however, he realized how much he'd enjoy sharing a dance with his prideful and not quite proper governess. He held out his hand.

There was hesitation. It was almost as though he could feel her waiting, denying herself what she might enjoy. "Come now, Retta, we have danced before."

That was apparently all she needed to hear. She stood and stepped toward him, emerging from the shadowed bedside. His breath locked in his throat. Her hair had been curled up and the candlelight played against the caramel colors. A flush softened her features and light glistened in the chocolate depths of her eyes.

Her dress was one he'd never seen before. A pale rose with lace and flowers and…he could not find his thoughts. His hand was still out.

She placed hers upon his. Warm skin against his own. Louise watched them with a strange expression, but the music flowed and he did not take the time to analyze the look.

He could only be aware of the woman coming toward him, slight and graceful, with a message he could not decipher dancing deep in her gaze.

Then she was to him. He smoothed one hand down to her waist, pulling her against him. The other hand curled around hers, trapping her so that her upturned face silently asked questions to which he could not answer.

The music, a blend of violins and piano, pumped through his blood, carrying the beat of his heart until he couldn't think. He only felt this woman in his arms, the way her steps haltingly matched his.

The scent of roses drifted from her hair, teasing him, begging him to draw her even closer. They looped around the room, her skirts swishing against his legs, her fingers digging into his shoulders.

And she did not speak, but there were words in her eyes. They locked gazes. He dipped his head against hers, dimly hearing Louise's clapping in the background, the squeal of her excitement joining the song. Heat from Henrietta's cheek brushed against his own, and he heard her faint intake of breath as he moved them across the floor.

His nerves thrummed. He had danced with countless

women. In countless countries. Never had he felt this connection, this drawing. He wanted to kiss her.

Absolutely, unaccountably unacceptable.

But he would think about that later. He would grind these feelings to ashes and sweep them from his life. He could not make the promises she deserved to hear when his future was unknown.

The strains of the waltz were dying down, fading away, and he brought her to a halt in the middle of the room. How could such dark eyes glisten at him, swimming with emotions and thoughts, asking him his in return. Her lips parted, soft and rosy.

"Oh, that was so lovely, like watching an artist painting on a canvas." Louise's trilling voice wedged between them.

Henrietta removed her hand from his. She backed up, and he slid his palm slowly away from her waist. Too slowly, for she gave him a castigating glare that told him she knew exactly what he was doing and that she did not approve.

Casting him into the box of flirt again.

He belonged there. It was for the best.

Henrietta could never know of these feelings springing within him, unfurling and blooming. She must never realize, and if he had to play the part of superficial to keep her from ever seeing him as anyone better than he was, so be it.

"Miss Gordon, you have a caller."

She looked up from the book she'd bought. The pictures were in-depth and well done, but so far she'd found nothing on epilepsy, nor how to treat it. Not for the first time, it occurred to her that Uncle William might know something of the disease.

She set the book to the side and stood, smoothing her skirts. Dominic's butler wore a long face and bored eyes. She gave him a quick nod. "In the parlor?"

"In the hall." With one long, disparaging look, he left.

Of course, he would find it beneath him to deliver a message to a mere governess. Clenching her jaw, she hurried out of her room and down to the main area of Dominic's house.

The gilded door frames and large windows brought to her attention how exceptionally lovely and lush his home was. What would it be like to live here for the rest of her life?

Goose pimples skittered up her arms as she remembered their waltz.

No, she told herself firmly, descending the staircase.

Flirting was second nature to a man like Dominic. It meant nothing. Though, she must admit that perhaps she owed him an apology. After meeting so many people during the dinner, she had realized that the beau monde of London was much worse than him. Even Mr. Hodges, for all his good humor, struck her as unreliable.

As she neared the bottom of the stairs, she focused on the figure awaiting her. A serious, square-shouldered man with a physician's cane and elaborate top hat. At first she thought it was Uncle William, but then she realized it was Mr. Moore.

One of her uncle's dear friends.

"Mr. Moore, how do you do?" She curtsied, and he responded with a gentlemanly bow.

"Very well. I had heard you were in town and thought a walk about Hyde Park might be just the thing." Thick gray eyebrows wiggled over gentle blue eyes. This man had sporadically been a part of her life as far back as to even when her parents had been alive.

"What a lovely surprise." She hesitated. "I am governessing, at the moment, and will need to ask permission." How that grated, but it could not be helped.

"What is this talk of permission?"

She spun around. Dominic strode into the hall, the lighthearted quirk on his lips setting her heart aflutter. As soon as that betraying physical response occurred, she struggled to contain it. She pasted a stern look upon her face, denying the smile that edged her lips.

She had fought very hard to not think of their dancing, of the hopes trembling on the precipice of her emotions. He could not just stride in here with his long legs and fancy-free demeanor and bring it all back. She refused to allow him the power.

"Is that why you're scowling?" he asked, eyes twinkling. "You need not frown at me so, Miss Gordon."

Mr. Moore inclined his head in greeting. "You must be Lord St. Raven. I am an old friend of Miss Gordon's. We have studied many a medical mystery together, with her uncle. While in town, I thought it good to take a stroll about Hyde Park."

Dominic pulled out his watch fob and made a show of reading its time. Henrietta's toes danced beneath her skirts. Was he being obtuse on purpose?

"Louise is practicing the pianoforte at her aunt's this morning. Miss Gordon can be spared a few hours, if she wishes." There was laughter in his voice.

Did Mr. Moore hear it? A hot wash of heat doused her. How very humiliating to have once been free to do as she pleased, to discuss the greatest medical advances in the world with minds of great scope, and now to be reduced to an employee who must have permission to take a walk.

Galling and unwelcome and all her uncle's fault.

It was as if Dominic knew how she strained against this societal cage, and he laughed at her.

Sparing him a haughty glance, she turned to Mr. Moore. "I would love a turn about Hyde Park." She swooped her skirts in a flouncing statement and exited the door he held open for her.

She peeked behind her once, just a quick look to see if Dominic still laughed at her. A shudder rippled through her when she saw him in the doorway, his smile gone, his eyes a dark, impenetrable mask.

A fanciful thought.

But the image invaded her conversations with Mr. Moore. Even as he expounded upon an herb discovered in the Outback, or Down Under, as he said many called it.

"That is a land of convicts, is it not?" She tried forcing interest. Her bonnet kept the sun off her face, but it was a hot London summer day. Close to noon and the street was filled with people of various sorts, of varying incomes and classes.

"There is violence. I've letters describing angry aboriginals and former British convicts seizing control of the colony. Our military has been working on restoring order." Mr. Moore paused. "But enough of that. How is it that you are a governess? You should be with your uncle. You are one of the best herbalists I've ever met."

She explained the entire thing, then, ending on how she'd decided to join her uncle without his permission, asked him to not divulge her current employment status.

"I will not say a word, my dear. Are you sure it is wise?"

She began to blurt out that practicing medicine was all she wanted, but stopped. A memory of tea with Dominic and Louise bombarded her. The cool breeze, the warm laughter. That feeling of belonging that had been absent since her uncle left her. And something more. An intangible spice that could not be identified, something that had been missing in her life.

Drawing a deep breath, she said, "I cannot stay a governess. Practicing medicine is all I know."

Mr. Moore grazed her arm, enough to stop her, but not enough to cause notice from passerby. His kindly eyes roved her face, concerned. "I saw Mr. Gordon only a fortnight ago in Wales. He confided in me, and it is time for me to confess to you, that he asked me to call on you. To ascertain your happiness."

Unexpectedly, her eyes watered. She blinked rapidly, willing her tear ducts under control. She would not be in this position if he had not abandoned her.

"He told me," continued Mr. Moore, "that he has hopes you'll marry."

"Marriage is not conducive to the study and practice of medicine."

"It could be."

"Are you married, Mr. Moore?"

His face crinkled for a second, and perhaps she may not have seen that brief ripple of pain if she had not been studying him so intently.

"There was someone. Years ago." He looked down the street in front of them as though peering at the past. "The youngest daughter of a vicar."

They continued walking, the sounds of their shoes lost in the clatter of passing carriages.

"I did not marry. I chose medicine and learning over creating a family."

"A difficult choice," murmured Henrietta. She never wished to face the wrenching tug between mind and heart. What a terrible, terrible situation to find oneself in. "You are happy, though, are you not? Why, if you'd stayed with her, think of all the education you might have missed. The medical community would have suffered greatly by your absence."

He chuckled. "You flatter, my dear."

"I read your paper on leeches. It is why I refuse to use them."

He made a commiserating sound, but there was a frown upon his face. "I cannot help but wonder what became of her."

The longing in his voice, perhaps unbeknownst to him, carved holes in Henrietta's certainty that a man of his caliber would not regret leaving a lowly and possibly uneducated vicar's daughter for a far greater calling. She blinked against the sunlight.

"It is fortuitous that you chose to see me today. Even though Uncle William put you up to it. I am researching epilepsy, but there is very little information to be found. What can you tell me of it?"

"There have been studies published in France. I shall find them and send them to you. I do have a friend studying the pathology of the disease. What is your interest in it? I do not think herbs can bring relief." He studied her.

She ignored the question for another. "If one was discovered to have epilepsy, would there be a danger of incarceration?"

"I should think so, depending on the family and rank of the individual."

"A member of the peerage?"

"Ah, one who can afford the costs of a hospital. I daresay that if a peer was found to be suffering seizures, there are many who would wish to consign that person to an asylum. But a title can get one out of all sorts of predicaments."

Dominic would be happy to hear that, she thought.

He needn't worry about being locked up after all, and he could have Old John arrested or, at the very least, run out of the village.

A great relief trembled within. She would tell him as soon as possible.

Chapter Eighteen

Dominic grabbed the edge of his seat as the carriage rocked to a stop. Opposite him, Louise braced her feet on the floor and lobbed a toothy smile. "Are we home?"

He peered out his window at the darkening skyline. "Almost to London, I think."

They had spent the day at Lord Waverly's estate. Louise and Henrietta had been in a different group somewhere on the property, while Dominic stayed with Barbara and her husband. It had been quite boring and he'd dodged several eager mothers wishing to introduce him to their daughters.

His footman opened the door, revealing a stout man with a creased face beside him. He doffed his hat. "Yer pardon, my lord, but there's been an accident. Do ye by any chance have Miss Gordon with you?"

He climbed out. "In the other carriage."

"I'm here." She was already charging toward them, that determined, no-nonsense expression on her face as dear to him as her doe-eyed, pink-lipped response to waltzing with him.

A band tightened around his chest.

The man who'd stopped them tipped his hat to her. "Joseph O'Gregory, blacksmith in the village of Craven, just over the hill. There's been word from the Waverly estate that you've a doctor with you—" he tipped his head to Dominic "—my lord."

"I went into a nearby village to purchase a few items and happened to see a man in need of medicine for his cataracts," she said shortly, by way of explanation. "Go on, please. Time is of the essence." Despite her small stature, there was an innate pride in her form, in her expression, that bespoke knowledge and skill. No one seeing her now would think her less than she was.

"My nephew fell off a roof. His leg be twisted funny, and he can't walk. Passed out, he is." The man pressed his cap against his heart. His gaze bored into Henrietta and his hands gripped the cap so hard his knuckles were pale-boned spheres against the rough fabric. "Can ye fix him?"

"I shall certainly do my best." She did not even glance at Dominic, but motioned for the man to leave. "Ride ahead and I will follow. Put him on a flat stretcher of sorts and carry him into a house. A clean house. Try not to jostle him. Tell someone to wait at the village edge to show us where to go." With a flip of skirts, she rushed back to her carriage. Presumably to tell *his* driver where to take her.

He hurried to his own carriage, heart pumping strange beats within his chest.

She had not asked permission.

As an earl, most people looked to him for guidance. Even when he had not been earl, his position as second son often lent him an authority that the nonpeerage responded to.

"Follow them closely," he told his driver, before opening the carriage door himself and getting in.

"What's wrong?" asked Louise.

"Nothing that can't be fixed, I hope." He rapped the carriage ceiling to signal he was ready, and they started off.

It took only ten minutes before they reached the village. Less than five more and they were in front of a small, well-tended cottage. Henrietta had beat them there. He heard the quiet timbre of her voice through the open windows of the house.

"You will continue home," he told Louise.

"But—"

He gave her a no-nonsense look, and for once she capitulated. A pouting capitulation, but a small victory, nonetheless. Satisfied that she'd stay put, he gave his driver instructions to take her back to the estate.

He ducked into the little house. It was surprisingly full.

"I'll need everyone but his parents to leave," Henrietta said in a loud and clear voice. Murmurs ensued, but the look she gave almost made Dominic want to turn and run himself. A chuckle rolled in his throat and he ruthlessly shoved it away.

He stepped to the side, allowing everyone to exit.

"You may leave, as well." She was bent over the patient, who remained oblivious to his surroundings. A blanket covered his lower half.

"I shall stay and assist." One glance at the white-faced parents assured him that she would need his help. They were too shocked to be of much use.

Henrietta looked up, her pupils large and dominating her irises. Two bright spots of color stained her cheeks. An escaped tendril cupped her jaw. "Very well, if you've the stomach for it."

She straightened, pulling the sheet down to expose ripped and bloody clothes that shrouded a leg jutting at a sickening angle.

He nodded, forcing back the instinctive need to flinch.

That queasy feeling was still with him when they finally made it home four hours later. Eyes heavy with sleep, he yawned as the carriage pulled into the drive. He had ridden up with Bates to protect Henrietta's reputation. He lowered himself to the ground. He didn't envy his driver's position, and it occurred to him how spoiled he had lived the last few years.

He'd never considered what a servant's life entailed, or even cared.

He squeaked the door open and found Henrietta sleeping on the seat, her cheek resting against her hands, her lips soft with sleep. A catch of breath buried itself in his throat.

Her eyes fluttered, opening in a slow movement. "We are home?"

"Yes, we're home." His voice cracked, but he didn't think she noticed.

What was worse than falling for a woman determined to leave? A woman with her own goals and dreams?

Even if she didn't have those, he could not trust himself to be responsible for a family. His body did what it wanted, when it wanted. What if he had a seizure in public? Worse still was the threat hanging over him from the apothecary. Until he established a plan for what he was going to do with Louise, he was trapped.

No, he should not have danced with Henrietta. He should not have flirted with her. Perhaps he should not have hired her, but he could not regret such a move when it protected Louise and helped further Henrietta's dreams.

After all, at the time he had none of his own.

Now he was dreaming of a life that could never be.

When Henrietta awoke the next morning, one idea was clear in her mind. She had to speak with Dominic. She dressed hurriedly, ate quickly and set Louise down for a math lesson. While her pupil figured sums, she went downstairs.

Her heart pounded in her chest—quick, rhythmic movements that matched her footsteps. She paused outside Dominic's door, steeled herself and knocked.

His faint reply encouraged her to open the door. How often she saw him bent over the desk. Surely the man she'd first met at Lady Brandewyne's had changed. Perhaps due to her meddling? Pride filled her, but quickly seeped away when she remembered her reason for being here.

She had nothing to be prideful about.

It had been a slow reckoning, but last night had sealed the feeling for her. Watching Dominic be so serious, so alert to what she needed done, had shown her how he cared. Perhaps he had lived a superficial lifestyle in the past, but that had been his way of avoiding failure.

Not only that, but the dinner at his sister's had also proven that he was simply a product of conditioning. He had been told it was okay to behave in the manner he had. Now that he knew differently, he changed accordingly.

She squared her shoulders, walked to him and sat in that familiar and uncomfortable chair again. She was not here about his shortcomings. She was here about hers.

He looked up, his signature dimple present. "You may put your list of items for me to fix on the desk."

"Your townhouse is run more efficiently than your estate, therefore I have no list."

"To what do I owe the pleasure of your presence then?"

"I have been thinking—"

"As you often do," he said, dimple deepening.

A hot flush zipped through her. Suddenly she was remembering their waltz, the placement of his hand on hers, the steadiness of his gaze as he guided her through the steps. Her pulse thrummed. "You were right."

Oh, how difficult to speak those words. They pushed through lips frozen with pride and self-worth.

His eyebrows shot up. He leaned back into his chair, tapping one long finger against the paperwork on his desk.

"It is to my sorrow that I must confess that I acted like a priggish, overinflated buffoon."

"You're being a bit hard on yourself."

There was a delicious purr to the rasp of his voice that only worsened the heat flooding through her. She shifted on her seat, interlocking her fingers to keep from fidgeting.

"I am seeing myself as you must have seen me." She hesitated, swallowing hard. "The thing is, my lord, I have never had to apologize for anything. My uncle valued my input and often praised me for my perspicacity. We worked together in perfect harmony, and it was not until I contracted rheumatic fever that our partnership crumbled."

"I see." He steepled his fingers beneath his chin. The dimple eased, but she detected a sparkle in his eyes that gave her pause. "To which instance are you referring to regarding your buffoonish behavior then?"

"Whatever do you mean, 'which instance'?"

He shrugged, and now she was certain that he was laughing at her, because it seemed that his shrug had a bit of wiggle to it. As though containing the most improper urge to laugh.

"I wish I could find the humor that is so easily available to you," she said testily, "but alas, I am too overcome with mortification over my behavior."

"Behavior that I remain unclear on."

She released a long-suffering sigh. "Very well, I shall spell it out. I am *not* referring to my opinion of your quack apothecary."

That got a reaction. Only a frown, but for a man like

St. Raven, it indicated deep displeasure. It was wrong, but she felt a smidge of satisfaction that she could upset him when he was finding such great joy in teasing her.

"My opinion of you has changed," she continued primly. "I was wrong to have judged you as a superficial coward hiding from responsibilities. As a careless flirt. You are so much more than that. A good man who must deal with a strange malady while juggling new responsibilities. You are kind and helpful. It is not your fault that you grew up thinking you could live however you like without consequence."

His gaze flickered. "Do you have any idea how arrogant you sound?"

"Arrogant? I'm trying to apologize." Her voice almost quavered. She managed to put a bit of iron into it. "I judged you wrongly."

"No, you judged correctly. I was exactly who you thought I was, and if you think I'm different now, it is because I am."

Stymied, she could only stare. How fierce he looked. Even, dare she think it, stern.

"I will be honest, Henrietta. I had hoped you planned to apologize about your behavior at my estate." Though humbleness flavored his voice, his emerald eyes cut sharp.

She drew back, his words unexpected. "I was right to behave so. We both know that man is not a good person."

"He certainly is not. Yet, you are filled with pride. Doesn't the Bible admonish us against that?"

Her mouth dropped open even as a terrible schism of pain invaded her. "I hardly expect you to be an expert in such matters."

Oh, how could she have been entertaining tender feelings toward this egotistical, rude man. She folded her arms, pressing them in a snug little circle about her body.

"You have already decided who I am. Why don't you just tell me who you are." He bit off the words.

"For two months more I am a governess."

"Only two months?" He sounded shocked, which rang a little alarm at the back of her mind. She continued, ignoring it. "After that, assistant to a renowned physician."

"Who has no idea of what you're planning."

"That is not relevant to this conversation."

He dipped his head in a mocking manner. "By all means, then, what is relevant?"

They locked eyes, and though she burned at his censure, there was now a little voice inside insisting that she listen to him. That she take a clear view of herself and how she treated others. She had marched through the village like a soldier instead of going to him and trusting him with the problem. She had emasculated his authority to the people who relied on him for income and protection. Realization dawned.

They needed to have confidence in him the same way a patient should trust his or her physician.

"You are very right." Cheeks on fire, she looked down at her hands, which were still clasped and beginning to cramp. She released them, stretching her fingers before looking up at him. She expected to see triumph. Instead, he looked tired. Handsome, but weary. "It was not my place to confront your apothecary. Nor to make a spectacle in the village. I should have come to you with my concerns, and I am very sorry for rushing off like a hotheaded fool."

Perhaps this was how it felt to be humbled. A curious mix of pain and relief, much like the sensation in lancing a boil. Perhaps one could get used to being wrong. Or at least admitting to it.

As though hearing her thoughts, Dominic edged closer

to his desk, quirking a smile in her direction. "Was that so hard?"

"Yes," she said in a tone that was almost petulant, but not quite. Because she had never been petulant in her life, and she was not about to start now.

"Your honesty is refreshing." He rose from his desk, walking over to a small table on the other side of the room, where a pile of papers was stacked. "Admittedly, your actions were inappropriate to the situation, yet I cannot help but admire your resolve and bravery."

"Bravery?" Unexpected words, and reassuring. "I do not presume to know what you mean."

"That's a first."

"I beg your pardon?"

"Haven't you already? One beg per week is quite enough, Miss Gordon."

He was flirting with her now, resorting to his previous persona. He took a folded paper from the stack. Vellum, she saw as he neared, sealed with an expensive wax seal. "You don't care what others think. Your sense of justice is impressive. That is very brave of you." He held out the paper. "This came for you."

She took it, recognizing at once her uncle's initials in the scarlet seal. The stiff vellum beneath the pads of her fingers reminded her of his life. Strong. Rich. Unique.

That was the life she wanted, wasn't it?

But it was hard to think clearly with Dominic standing so close, shaping her thoughts with his opinions, as atrocious as she sometimes found them to be. He wore that expensive cologne, too. A scent she should chide him for due to its obvious cost. The luxury he took for granted. She could not bring herself to criticize him, though, not after last night.

"I saw you," she blurted out.

"Saw me?" A tiny crinkled appeared in his brow, a ripple in his laughing exterior.

"Yes." She pressed the vellum to her bosom. Reading it could wait. "You gave money to that man's family."

His brow lifted. The crinkle deepened. "And?"

"I thought I had you figured out, but you keep surprising me."

"My goal in life, madam." He swept her a large, entirely ridiculous bow reminiscent of Mr. Hodges.

Despite herself, she smiled. "Very well. I have apologized and we have reached an impasse, if you will?"

"I shall let you decide which words to use, as you are the governess." His gaze cut to the letter in her hands. "Only two months," he murmured. "How much longer do you suppose before I'll need to put word out for a new one?"

"A new what?" Louise bopped into the room, a heavy book in one hand and a tart in the other. "I finished my math. Whatever is the purpose? You know that I shall not be doing sums. I will have a steward for that. Or a housekeeper. Or someone who enjoys trying to fit numbers together like a puzzle. A mismatched puzzle."

"Every lady of breeding must know basic sums. If you plan to run your own household—"

"But what if I don't?"

Henrietta looked at Dominic, trying to ascertain if he intended her to answer the girl. She would be the worst example, she supposed. She didn't run households or manage daily tasks. She had no desire to do such a thing.

"You don't want to get married?" she asked carefully.

"Of course I'm getting married. It will be terribly romantic." Unexpectedly, she began spinning around the two of them in a silly, young-girl way that brought memories to the forefront. Once upon a time, Henrietta had dreamed of having a love like the one her parents had shared.

"But I shan't be keeping his house," continued Louise. "We will be having adventures, discovering new species. Drinking tea in exotic places like those that exist in *Arabian Nights*."

Henrietta held up her hands in mock surrender. "I did not put these ideas into her head, my lord."

"We shall blame fiction." Dominic was laughing, though. "Just do not let your Aunt Barbara hear you speak thus. It will send her into a fit of apoplexy. I believe she already has a standing order for your first Season, and a list of prospective grooms."

"Psssh." Louise's eyes were alight. "It will be our secret. Just between Dom and Retta and Lou."

Henrietta groaned at the nicknames. "It is time for another lesson. This conversation is senseless."

"I find it rather entertaining, and there is sense in that." Dominic sat on the edge of his desk. Very un-earl-like.

"It is not useful."

"Surely there is a part of the brain that requires entertainment for growth and stimulation? We are not designed to be automatons."

"Oh, very well." She didn't have time to argue with him, and he made a good point. It was just so very hard to indulge in senseless entertainment when she could see no practical value to it. "According to some fringe scientists, laughter is a medicine in and of itself."

"The Bible says that, does it not?"

Henrietta nodded, then said to Louise, "We must finish your lessons before our tea."

"But what are we getting that's new?" She plunked on one of the chairs, ignoring Henrietta in favor of nibbling on her tart. "And I want to go to Gunter's for ices this afternoon."

"We shall check your sums first."

"And the new item? What is it? A puppy perhaps?"

Dominic made a sound in the back of his throat. "A what?"

"There is the most adorable mongrel in the park and it follows me about every day. I bring him ham, of course."

"No, most definitely not an animal," said Dominic, his voice panicked. He shot Henrietta a pleading look, but she only shrugged.

A puppy was not a bad idea. "The idea has merit, my lord."

Louise jumped and clapped her hands. "I can't wait. I love new things."

"Well, that is not what your uncle and I were discussing. When you get a new governess you will need—"

"What?" She stopped jumping. The book dropped from her hands to the ground.

"Yes, I cannot stay forever."

"But…" Her gaze whipped between them. "Governesses do stay. They stay until they're no longer needed. I have been good." There was emotion building on her face, the same kind Henrietta had seen before, right before Louise ran away.

A hard lump settled in her throat. "You must have known this was temporary?"

Dominic was suspiciously quiet. She didn't dare look at him. If she took her gaze from Louise's bright, shocked eyes, she felt certain the tenuous, invisible thread between them would snap.

It was a fanciful notion that could not be upheld by scientific theory, nor by logic, but nevertheless, her heart pumped hard and desperate beats against her sternum. She did not want to disappoint Louise.

She did not want to hurt her.

Yet the vellum letter remained clutched in her hand, its sharp corner digging into her palm, a painful reminder that her life could not remain as it was now.

"Louise…" Dominic's voice trailed off.

Startled at the sudden intrusion of his voice in the voided silence, she looked at him. And then Louise ran. Her footsteps echoed as she raced out of the study and into the hall, then the front door slammed.

Pulse racing like a jackrabbit in her throat, Henrietta sprung forward. Louise could not roam London alone. Too many pickpockets, thieves, murderers. It wasn't safe.

This was her fault.

And only she could fix it.

Chapter Nineteen

Dominic hurried after Henrietta. She was already out of the house.

"Jacks," he yelled, swiping his cane from the corner of the room, where he kept it for London walks. Obsidian-black, it looked the epitome of a gentleman's accessory, but the polished handle hid a sharp point. He'd bought it in Turkey, after a band of ruffians had nearly killed him and his friends during his Grand Tour. He set his top hat upon his head.

"I'm going out," he told the valet. "If Louise or Miss Gordon return, see that they do not leave this house until I come back."

He stepped out into blinding sunlight. Walking to find them would be best. Right or left? Where would Louise go? Hyde Park? Gunter's?

He'd try Gunter's first, since she'd mentioned wanting ices. Barbara may have given her pin money that she hadn't spent yet. He strode quickly, passing others out for leisure walks. He ignored most of their looks to avoid conversation.

By the time he reached Gunter's, he was in need of an ice himself. The day was hot, bothersome. He had almost rounded the lawn where customers brought out blankets to sit in the sunshine while enjoying their treats, when a high trill stopped him.

"Oh, my lord, my lord, so very good to see you." A woman he did not recognize fluttered in front of him. The type he used to ignore quite easily. In fact, every instinct demanded he run. And fast.

A better man did not run from irksome women. He nodded, returned the greeting.

"Have you met Miss Penelope? My second daughter, just out for the Season." The woman batted strangely long eyelashes at him while pushing a wisp of a girl in front of her. He wracked his brain, searching for some memory of the mother's name. Any idea to which family they belonged.

Most likely friends of Barbara's. Since the girl was not speaking and it seemed the mother was waiting for him to say something, he inclined his head. "Lovely day for ices."

"Yes, yes," the mother gushed. Miss Penelope, bride-to-be no thanks to her mother, said nothing. She had pale blue eyes. Striking on their own, but bland with no personality present.

He thought of Henrietta's chocolate eyes then, while the ice began melting and the mother melted and the daughter remained speechless.

Henrietta would not endure a conversation about weather. She would be bored. She would be moving or looking or thinking.

These two obviously expected something he had no intention offering. His card, perhaps. A promise to call. A marriage proposal.

He drew out his watch fob. "Ah, look at the time. I must be off. Farewell, ladies." He pivoted and walked straight out of the park. Thankfully no one else tried to stop him.

The entire walk home he brooded. He had not felt so on edge since he was a young man.

No matter how much Henrietta made him laugh, he also blamed her for her demands, expecting more than he felt capable of giving. And yet he had risen to the challenge.

But for what? She planned to leave. Not just him. But also Louise. He had not thought of how her abandonment would affect his niece. On the walk home, it was all he thought of. Well, almost all. He also thought much of his own self. He had come to rely on Henrietta's wit, sharp comments and truthfulness.

Where was Louise? A terrible, sharp-edged worry cut into his senses, propelling his legs forward. He had to ask Henrietta to stay.

For Louise's sake.

The idea relieved the tension snaking across his chest. Barbara would eventually leave him alone about the school, if Louise had Henrietta. And if Old John decided to open his mouth about Dominic's epilepsy, Henrietta had said it wouldn't matter.

If she stayed, she could practice medicine on his estate. He would give her leeway to go to conventions and symposiums, should she so wish. She would have her coveted independence and an income apart from anything she might make with medicine.

He stopped by Barbara's, but Louise was not there. The household still slept, the butler told him, looking cross and disapproving, as all butlers were wont to do. He supposed they taught them that at butler school. Dominic left a note for Barbara to call on him later that day.

Amazing how finding a solution made everything better.

He did not see Louise at the park. Neither did he encounter any men of ill repute attempting to rob him. He had not had reason to use his special cane in years. In the past, pugilism offered a release from stresses, as well as a fine form of entertainment. Since inheriting his estate, he had not engaged in any pugilistic bouts.

Perhaps it was time.

And so it was, ideas and plans racing through his mind, that he arrived home. Jacks immediately informed him that both ladies had arrived. He said so in a low voice, his head dipping.

Dominic handed him the cane and his top hat. "Is there a problem?"

Jacks eyes flickered. "Perhaps you should see for yourself."

That was when Dominic heard giggles. And then another sound, so out of place and foreign that for a second, he felt like an interloper. As if he'd entered the wrong house.

Jacks was disguising a smirk now, and failing utterly at it.

"Is there a dog in my house?" Dominic pointed up. Without waiting for an answer, he sprinted up the stairs, following the sounds to a room next to the old nursery.

Dogs. He had never liked them since not one, but two, had bitten him as a child. Granted, they were starving mutts that had wandered onto the estate and his brother had mercilessly chased the poor beasts each time.

Still, his memories of dog encounters did not serve to endear him to the women who had brought one into his home. At least Louise was safe, which brought an immeasurable relief.

He pushed open the door.

The sight that greeted him did nothing good for a mood that was quickly disintegrating into annoyance. Deep annoyance. Did they think him easily duped? A soft sap who allowed anything and everything? Mouth grim, he leaned against the door frame, crossing his feet and arms and waiting for acknowledgement.

Which did not come.

Henrietta and Louise giggled and grabbed for an *animal*, which repeatedly escaped their grasps and yipped its way across the room, leaving mud trails and bubbles. They scrabbled after him, their skirts dark with water, their hair coming undone.

He did not want to laugh. He really didn't. What he wouldn't give for one of those miniaturists to be here at this moment to capture the ludicrousness of the scene in oil.

"I've got him," Louise proclaimed, tackling the animal and hefting him up. But as she stood, her foot slipped out from beneath her and she fell on top of Henrietta, whose face was buried in her arms. Her laughs filled the room, and at his niece's added weight, the laughter collapsed into breathy giggles.

The thing ran in circles around them, its tail whipping back and forth in unmanageable swipes.

"What is the meaning of this?"

The girls' laughter cut off. Even the dog stopped moving.

Despite the bubbles on Henrietta's cheeks and a stubborn one clinging to her forehead, he easily read the guilty look that crossed her face. She scrambled to her feet.

"I can explain," she said in a higher voice than usual.

"You had better."

"I didn't run off, Dom." Louise didn't bother standing. Obviously she had no concern for repercussions. He didn't know if that made her braver or just foolish. The more he looked at the room, and the mongrel who had decided to clean himself on a rug that Dom knew for a fact he'd bought in Italy, the more irritated he became.

"I went to the back of the house. Through the servant's entrance."

"You are not a servant."

"Retta found me and explained everything. We took a walk and Smiles found us. He was starving, Dom. Why, look at his ribs? They are jutting out." She crossed her arms in an eerily fashion reminiscent of his own stance. "I couldn't leave him there, not when he so obviously needs a home. It is beastly for you to even suggest such a thing."

"I said nothing."

"It is in your eyes."

Dominic looked at Henrietta, who remained unnaturally quiet. Perhaps she realized how completely she had overstepped her bounds.

Henrietta was trying very hard not to laugh.

She donned her most serious look, fighting the twitch of her lips and refusing to meet Dominic's glare since the chastisement in it only made her want to giggle more.

His boot tapped the floor. Perhaps he was waiting for Louise to say more? She dared not even peek. To see such astonishment upon a man who prided himself on his nonchalance only increased the amusement flipping her stomach.

She cleared her throat. It still tickled with giggles. She stood slowly, shaking her skirts of clinging bubbles. "Smiles is a sweet addition to your home. He will provide Louise with an outlet for her energy, as well as a way to learn responsibility. It is my suggestion that she be the one to feed the animal. Care for him."

He straightened off the door frame. His arms crossed his chest. He legs spread in what Henrietta considered a warlike stance. Surely he was not truly angry. For the first time, it crossed her mind that he might be.

She had never seen Dominic angry. Annoyed, perhaps. Miffed. Put out and stubborn.

But angry?

She examined the jut of his jaw, moving on to the squint about his eyes. The movement of his jugular, very faint but discernible, caught her attention. Perhaps she could count the beats and detect whether or not his heightened heartbeat proved his anger?

"Are you very angry, Dom?"

Or she could ask, just as Louise had just done.

"No, not angry. I have not decided whether you will be able to keep this dog, Louise. You are a young lady of twelve and it's time for your tantrums to stop."

Looking suitably chastened, Louise dropped her chin. "I know."

"Very well. Clean this mess and dry off that dog. Miss Gordon?"

His use of her name brought her head up. "Yes?"

"My office, if you please." He spun on his heel and left.

Any thoughts of laughing faded. How haughty and arrogant he sounded. It made her bristle a bit, though on second thought, perhaps they should have washed the dog in the garden.

Smiles had fallen asleep near the bed. He let out a little doggy snore, and both Henrietta and Louise looked at each other and smiled.

"Go," Louise said. "Dom is miffed and better for you to be reprimanded now. I shall take care of my shaggy mongrel."

Henrietta nodded. She made her way to Dom's office. Louise had accepted the fact that she was going to leave too easily. It bothered her, but she could not pinpoint why.

The office door was open. Dominic stood near the window, peering out at the busy streets, hands clasped behind his back, shoulders straight and proud.

A lump rose in Henrietta's throat.

"When are you leaving?" he asked, his tone subdued, his voice low and husky.

She thought of her uncle's letter wedged beneath her pillows. "I was not able to read Uncle William's letter yet."

"What do you think it says?" He turned then, moving away from the window, putting himself into a shadowed part of the room.

It was fanciful of her, but for a moment, a quiver of doom darted within her. She could not see his face.

Wetting her lips, she put her palms up. "Hopefully that he wants me back. That he will provide funds for me to join him."

"You saw how upset Louise became."

"Yes." She wiped her palms on her skirts, but it didn't help as they had not dried yet from Smiles's bath. She felt soggy, suddenly. Unkempt and unsure. It was a foreign, vain feeling that she did not appreciate. "You are concerned she will revert when I leave."

"How little you understand of human emotion, Miss Gordon."

"And what exactly do you mean by that?"

"What I said."

Now her temper was rising, drowning any sense of self as she understood that he was insulting her. Not her intelligence, but her humanity. "You think me cold?"

"No." He left the shadows so quickly she did not process what he was on about until he stood in front of her, his gaze narrowed so tightly on her face that a shiver passed through her.

"Then what, pray tell, prompts you to so rudely accuse me of—"

"Of being logical and kind and utterly blind?"

How had he gotten so close? Her breath suspended and all she could see was the stone emerald of his eyes, and all she could smell was the cologne that invaded her thoughts at the most inopportune times. He dragged his gaze down her face. Her lips tingled. Her muscles clenched and a slow, viscous heat spread through her.

"I can see you very clearly," she murmured. How had she never noticed the fullness of his lips before. Awareness skittered up her spine.

She had never before kissed a man. Never before even been tempted to. Was this what it felt like then, to want to press your lips against another's, to feel the rasp of his cheek against your own?

Her uncle's letter sat upstairs, unopened, containing secrets she longed to read. This might be her only chance to try out a kiss. Her only chance to feel what others spoke about in hushed voices, in the pages of those tiny novels about dim-witted heroines and dashing heroes.

In the Song of Solomon.

Heat cascaded through her. She knew what she wanted. And Henrietta Gordon did not let anything keep her from her goals. Let alone societal strictures.

She closed the gap between them, and put her lips upon his.

Her mind wanted to process the feelings, to categorize each sensation and label it for future reference, but when his arms went around her, when he pulled her tight against him, her mind stopped working.

Her arms slid up around his neck and any thoughts fled as her body and emotions took over. A sweet ache flowered in her heart.

She stopped the kiss, pulling away, feeling the coldness of her parting but unable to articulate why. His cravat hung crookedly and his face had lost that stony look that so alarmed her.

He was the first to speak.

"Just like a woman. Using tried and true methods to quiet me."

She couldn't respond. Her heart was beating entirely too fast. Surely that could not be normal. And her stomach… flip-flopping. Her fingers trembling. Is this what kissing did to someone? Or was it the fact that after she left to join her uncle, she might never see Dominic again?

It was a terrifying thought.

Dominic touched her cheek, his finger a gentle, warm pressure. "Don't look so upset. Please."

The plea in his voice hooked her, drawing her gaze to his eyes, which were intent and serious. His hand dropped, and she let out a shuddering sigh.

"What I meant earlier," he said, "is that Louise will miss you, if you leave."

And will you miss me? The words almost left her mouth, but she reined them in. She squared her shoulders. She willed the butterflies and nerves to still. They did not listen.

"I will miss her, too."

His eyes darkened. "It occurred to me, today, that perhaps we could work out a mutually beneficial arrangement. One that even Louise would appreciate."

Her thoughts halted. What was he saying? Surely he was not going to propose matrimony. She bit her lip, hard. The sting kept her grounded. "And what would that be?"

"You stay as governess until she no longer needs you. I will give you leave to attend various medical symposiums and to treat my tenants."

She blinked. Her neck hurt from the strain of remaining utterly still. She must be practical about this. He had not said what she expected, and why had she expected more? Because he was an accomplished flirt? Because he seemed to care for her opinions and trusted her?

It had been a foolish moment.

She gave him what she hoped was a pragmatic smile. "Your offer is fair and would certainly make Louise happy." She paused, weighing her next words. "It would be unwise for this to happen again."

He tipped his head. In agreement, perhaps?

"May I have time to carefully consider your offer?" she asked.

"Of course." He dipped his head, and her throat seized with emotion. How handsome he looked, with that dark lock of hair falling over his eyes. When he lifted his head, his eyes crinkled in their customary way. "Do not take too long, Henrietta, for I am an impatient man."

Chapter Twenty

They left London the following day. Dominic amused himself by besting Louise at cards, but when the two-day trip ended, he was relieved. He'd been away from the estate too long.

They rolled into the drive, and he immediately called for his steward. While he waited, he perused the papers on his desk.

He had not seen Henrietta. She'd been sent ahead, with a different carriage. He supposed she was on the estate somewhere, puttering about. Their kiss seared his memory.

It changed things.

He could not kiss her again. One loose-lipped servant who saw them would be all it took to decimate Henrietta's reputation.

The responsibility for her welfare weighed on him. Suppose she decided to stay as a governess? He'd been trying to be a better man for Louise's sake. Perhaps even an attempt to please God, who was becoming more real to him every day.

He should not have allowed the kiss. He'd seen that look

on her face. That open curiosity, the analytical wonder. He smacked the desk with his fist.

He had to stop thinking about her. Shooting to his feet, he rounded the desk.

"Where is the steward?" he barked.

The butler scooted into the room and neatly bowed, then said, "He made a trip to the village, my lord."

"Ready my horse."

A good solid ride should cure him of this angst, this ill-founded irritation.

"Dom?" Louise stood at the top of the stairwell. "What is wrong?"

I kissed your governess, and any honorable man would marry her. But he could not utter such a thing to his niece. He refused to marry. Not with blackmail and disease hanging over his head. He needed to find a cure so that he could live a normal life. Bitterness coated his mouth.

Beside Louise, the dog whined.

"I'm fine," Dominic said abruptly.

"If you see her, tell her I am home and ready for lessons. Cook said she went to the village because her herbs died."

Dominic gave his niece a curt nod, then left the house. If he waited for the steward to get home, he might avoid seeing Henrietta. That kiss...it wasn't as if he'd never kissed anyone else. But he cared for Henrietta. He admired her.

He spurred his horse forward. By the time he reached the village, his thoughts had calmed. He found his steward at the livery. After inspecting the horses and asking after Mr. Smith's family, which had just increased by one, he and his steward spent over an hour touring the estate and the farms.

As Dominic had suspected, the crops were not doing

well. He approved his steward's request to introduce a new method of farming. After all, if he didn't do something, he'd have to find another source of income for the estate.

His own investments had done rather well, but he wanted to keep the incomes separate.

"Who is over there?" Mr. Phelps pointed to the next cottage, which sat on the crest of a hill. Two figures stood near one horse.

"Let's see." Dominic pointed his horse in that direction, and they rode over.

They arrived to see Henrietta mounting her horse.

"My lord." The cottage's mistress dropped into a deep curtsy.

"We are riding the estate. Is all well here?"

"Oh, yes." The space between the woman's freckles filled with pink. "It is so good of you to allow Miss Gordon to help us."

"It was nothing," said Henrietta. "I am happy to be of service."

"Are you sure I cannot offer you something in return?"

"Quite sure."

"Miss Gordon is in my employ. I shall see that she is properly recompensed." He hated how stiff his voice sounded, but seeing her again was doing uncomfortable things to his composure. Her hair curled in wisps about her flushed face. Vibrancy shone from her features, and with a start of annoyance, he realized Phelps was staring at her.

"Very good, my lord." The woman looked at Henrietta. "I change the bandage twice a day?"

"Yes, and I shall be back in a few days' time to check the stitches."

"I thank ye. More than you know."

"You were smart to seek help immediately."

"If you hadn't been there—"

"But I was," Henrietta said in a soft, soothing voice. "Do not hesitate to send word to the manor should you need something."

They rode back to the estate together.

"Miss Gordon, this is Phelps, my steward." Dominic did not miss the interested perusal Phelps gave her. Of course they were close in social stations. Phelps was probably at the age where he was looking for a wife.

Frowning, he listened as they engaged in small talk.

When they reached the stables, he sent Phelps on a meaningless quest to search out an invoice in his office. He turned to Henrietta, who was removing her riding gloves with a bemused look on her face.

"Your steward seems quite knowledgeable."

"He is." Dominic shoved his hands in his pockets and leaned back on his heels. "We should talk about that kiss."

"There is nothing to say." She tucked her gloves in her reticule. "If you'll excuse me, I must attend to Louise now."

"You stitched that woman?"

"You know that I did."

"And how did you hear of her wounds?"

A flicker of unease crossed her face. "A villager came to the house."

"I was uncouth to have kissed you."

Her brow rose. Such a fine, delicately drawn brow, little owning to the tough resilience of the woman before him. "As I recall, I kissed you first."

"Many women would be demanding marriage," he said carefully.

She laughed then, a pleasurable trickle of sound that smoothed away some of the worry he felt. "It is just a kiss, my lord. You must calm any sense of duty you feel."

At that, he grinned. "Am I right in believing that you are now telling me to shirk my duty?"

"Nonsense. This estate is your duty. Watching over and loving and protecting Louise is your duty. *I* am not your duty."

He should be relieved. The uncomfortable pressure in his chest persisted, however. Patting his horse one last time, he gave the reins to a stable boy. "I will walk you back," he told Henrietta.

They left the stables, stepping out into the afternoon's muted sunlight. Summer heat had not yet arrived and a cool breeze brushed past them in welcome. His house, tall, imposing, waited ahead of them, its Elizabethan structure reminiscent of days past.

Henrietta walked with her head up, eyes forward. He soaked in the sight of her curved lips.

"You are happy," he remarked.

"Yes, I was just thinking…"

"Of?" he prompted. Nosy, he knew, but he saw no reason not to pry.

Pink stained her cheeks and she kept walking. "I do not wish to upset you, but I opened the letter from my uncle."

"I see. He wants you to join him." His gut tightened as he awaited her response.

She shook her head. "Not quite."

He laughed, but it was without mirth. "I fail to understand why you were smiling, then."

"I should have opened the letter before we left London, but I am smiling because when he wrote it, he was preparing to leave for Bethlehem Hospital. They've a few cases they want his advice about." She stopped, pivoting to look up at him. The sunlight hit her, highlighting the gold-streaked hair that peeked out from beneath her bonnet. Her lips were a soft pink, like the color of the sunrise on clouds.

"You are smiling because he shall be at the hospital?" He tried to collect his scattered thoughts, but it was hard to concentrate when she looked like this, alight and happy. No pretense of boredom that he'd seen so often affected by the women of the *ton*.

"Because he is near us." Her dark eyes searched his face, begging him to understand. And he was trying, but remembrance of their kiss kept distracting him. "I have been saving to travel to Wales, but now he is only a two days' trip back to London. If I leave soon…that is what I hoped to speak to you about."

"Leaving?" His brain was mush.

"Yes, I can leave so much sooner. The funds I have been saving are more than enough to travel to London now."

The expression on Dominic's face increased Henrietta's frustration. He looked blank, as though he didn't understand what she was saying.

"I realize that I have not answered your generous offer. It is with some regret that I must decline a permanent position as governess." The sun beat against the back of her neck, hot and unyielding.

Dominic's gaze narrowed. The way the light hit his eyes made them glow like phosphorescent emeralds. She became aware of the sounds of bustling servants and whickering horses around them. Would they hear their conversation?

"It is not as though I do not appreciate all that you have done for me," she said quickly, conscious of an uncomfortable ache in the pit of her stomach. "I have a week or so to prepare, and to give you time to hire a new governess."

"Do you suppose that will be time enough for Louise to recover?"

"I am not abandoning her. She is welcome to visit while I'm in London. Perhaps she will want to write me, and we shall communicate that way."

"Barbara wants to send her to a school on the Continent."

"You will be able to find another governess before then."

"You have not found a cure for what ails me?"

"I have some letters of inquiry out. Mr. Moore is also doing a spot of research for me." She paused. "You must not let your illness keep you from caring for Louise. She needs you."

"I will not," he said roughly. "What if Old John makes it known—"

"No one is going to show up and cart you off to Bedlam," she replied, but her stomach sank at the look on his face.

"Does your uncle know you're coming?" His voice sounded as hard as the stone his eyes mimicked.

She resisted the urge to shift her feet, but the pain in her stomach deepened and spread. "No, I'm surprising him."

"And if he turns you away?"

"He would not." She bit her lip, hating the doubt blossoming inside. It wasn't as though she hadn't already considered it, but surely he would not turn her away. She couldn't stay with Dominic any longer. After that kiss, a memory that corroded her thinking, her plans, she knew she had to leave.

Marriage had no place in her life and neither did romance.

Dominic uttered a hearty sigh, and she wished there

were crinkles at his eyes. Something to show he wasn't completely disappointed in her.

She squared her shoulders. And why should she care? She had only met the man two months ago.

"Henrietta…" Dominic paused, as though subjecting his next words to analysis. Completely unlike him. "This has nothing to do with the moment we shared, does it?"

"Of course not," she said with a bit too much vehemence. She drew a strong breath, willing her pulse to slow and her hands to steady. "You hired me with the intent of steering Louise in the right direction while providing me the ability to follow my life goals. I never intended to become a governess for the duration of Louise's school years."

The sun's heat created an almost unbearable burden. Her eyes burned and sweat trickled down her back. "I am not abandoning her and I am not running off because of a tiny little kiss."

At that, his lips quirked into a harsh grin. "Trust me, there was nothing tiny about that kiss."

"If you say so," she said stiffly. "Either way, I'm joining my uncle. I'm called to medicine, to helping others and treating their ills. Not—" she waved a hand "—this."

"This?" His mouth flattened.

"You know…making money. Living off the labor of others. Wearing expensive clothing. God has a higher plan for me." Her mouth was running away with her. This never happened. She swallowed hard, but it didn't take the coarse rebuke of her words from her mouth.

"And here I thought that maybe God might want me to take me responsibilities as an earl seriously. As an uncle, even. You are saying that what I do is frivolousness." He stepped forward, closing the space between them.

If anyone saw, they could misconstrue this situation. She moved backward.

"Quite arrogant, Miss Gordon, and perhaps the first time I've ever heard you sound exactly like a privileged member of the *ton*."

"I must get inside. This heat is overwhelming."

His brows crinkled. "It is not hot. Perhaps your guilt stains your conscience and makes you oversensitive."

"I feel guilty about nothing," she retorted.

"Do not come running back to us when your uncle refuses you," he said darkly, his eyes pinpointing her into feeling like a tiny, terrible speck of humankind.

"He will not refuse me." She would not allow it. Not if she had to follow him about like Smiles after Louise's tarts.

He ran a hand through his hair, mussing it even more. She wanted to smooth it down, to give it order. She could not, however. It was bad enough they had stood talking alone for so long in broad daylight, but to touch him could forever tatter her reputation.

"You must not tell anyone about our kiss," she said.

If possible, his face darkened even more, became stormy and irritated. How well she read his emotions, when she had never before bothered to be attuned to how someone felt. Feelings were not facts. They did not bring a solution. They only muddied a situation.

"Very well," he answered.

She blinked, her legs turning weak and sorrow invading her senses.

His jaw jutted upward. He backed away from her. "I shall write you a letter of recommendation on the chance that your uncle turns you away."

She forced her head to nod, her lips to say thank you,

but as he walked away, his figure wrinkled and blurred. For the best, she told herself.

If only she could believe that.

Chapter Twenty-One

Dominic slapped his palm against his desk. Too many bills, not enough income. Another, more insistent demand from Old John. That missed payment must have upset the crook. Dominic penned a terse reply, sealed it and set it in the basket for outgoing mail.

Pressure weighted down his shoulders, even though just this afternoon his steward had assured him that in time, their new methods and machines would produce a greater harvest.

He sighed, resting his head on his knuckles.

Henrietta's two week absence hurt.

The dog, mangy little mutt, scampered into his office, sliding on his hairy paws. He jumped on Dominic's leg, yipping. He patted his head. The dog yapped louder.

Sighing, Dominic pushed to his feet. This had happened almost every day since Henrietta had left for London. Two letters from Henrietta had arrived in that time, both for Louise.

He had gone over everything in his head a million times, and could not see a different path. Henrietta had been determined to go. She didn't think they were worth staying for. Who was he to argue with God's calling?

Yet, he wanted to argue. An immense sense of help-lessness grasped him. He pushed to his feet, following Smiles out of the office. Smart pup. He was leading him to a crying Louise.

Anger surged. His jaw pulsed with pain, and he realized he was clenching it. He strode after the dog, who swished and slid all over the shining hallway floors.

He was struck with how much had changed since he'd decided to become responsible. To care. It was painful and inconvenient, just as he'd always suspected it would be.

The dog careened around the corner and he hurried after him.

He found Louise hunched on a bench in the garden. Beneath a rose trellis. Henrietta often smelled like roses. Ruthlessly, he pushed away the memory. She was gone from their lives now. It was for the best.

"I'm here to rescue you from your daily cry." He sat beside her, patting her back and feeling less awkward than he had felt previous days. A week of back patting helped with that.

She straightened, and he realized she held a letter in her hand. No, an invitation embossed with gold filigree.

His eyes narrowed. "What are you doing with my mail?"

"I saw it on the tray and took it."

Not a tear in her eye, but she sounded perky and an un-natural brightness lit her green irises.

"Where is your governess?"

"She's taking tea in her room. A megrim took hold." She said the last with entirely too much satisfaction, and a matching smirk.

At least she hadn't run this one off. Then again, the woman had just arrived yesterday.

He took the invitation from her and read it. "I hardly

know Lord Astley. I've seen him a bit during sessions in the House, but that's all."

"I also received a letter from Henrietta." Louise kicked her legs up, stretching them out beneath the sunshine. Her shoes, he noticed, were more scuffed than he expected to see on a twelve-year-old girl.

Was he supposed to buy her a new wardrobe? Perhaps, but he had no idea how to go about it. He could ask Barbara, but it would only give her leave to press about taking Louise for the remainder of her life. He'd just had a letter from his sister yesterday, asking him if he really felt fit to raise Louise.

"Louise." He cleared his throat. "There is something I've been meaning to talk to you about."

"Can we discuss it later? I've a much more important matter at hand."

He noted her mussed hair, the flush on her cheeks. Tawny freckles sprinkled in haphazard fashion across her nose. Anathema to any young lady entering her Season. Had she freckles when she first came to live with him? He could not remember.

"Oh, Dom, that frown looks positively atrocious on you." She laid her head on his shoulder. The imprint of her trust. He owed her more than he was able to give. "Are you thinking of Henrietta?"

"No," he choked out.

"Well, you should be," she said in a scolding voice. She straightened, turning her body to face him. She grabbed his chin and moved it so that he was forced to look into her eyes. "Henrietta hasn't joined her uncle yet. He had to leave for the south of England on sudden business. She is staying with Lady Brandewyne, who is in town for the Season."

He pulled away, rubbing his chin. "That was a little too forceful, even for you, Lou."

Her eyes sparkled. "Finally you are learning to use the name I prefer. Now, Dom, I have made a plan."

He groaned, but within, a tiny spark had alighted. "Your plans alarm me."

"That is most unkind." She stood and swirled around, then with a dramatic flourish, pulled another letter from her pocket. "This came four days ago. From Lady Brandewyne."

"To you?" he asked skeptically.

"Not quite. To us." She pressed the letter into his hand. "I shall summarize it for you. Henrietta mopes about the house and lacks any drive. She has gone to a few balls but failed to catch anyone's eye, but that of Mr. Hodges. Who from all accounts is a good man with immaculate fashion sense." She paused. "He follows Beau Brummell, you see."

"Then he shall be broke in no time," he said drily.

"They are great friends," Louise persisted, waving the letter through the air as though brandishing a switching stick at him. "In fact, he has called on Henrietta several times. They have gone to plays—"

"Alone?"

"No, silly. All together. Lady Brandewyne approves of him." Louise began to pace. "But, I ask you, dear Dom, if this is best for Henrietta? Who is this strange man?"

"I know him."

"What does he want with our lovely doctor friend," she continued as if she had not heard him. "We should investigate his intentions. Make sure they are honorable."

"Honorable?" He scrambled to follow her reasoning, while a forbidding discomfort kinked his neck.

Her eyebrows crunched together and she put her hands

on her hips. Her foot tapped the cobblestone. "Honestly, do you not understand what I'm saying?"

He must have looked somewhat befuddled because she threw her arms up in exasperation. She miraculously kept hold of the letter.

"Men," she said in a voice that sounded just like Barbara's. "I shall spell it out plainly for you then. This Mr. Hodges is courting Henrietta, and we must ascertain if he will make a proper husband."

The discomfort spread to his shoulders. He rubbed his chin, eyeing the child who had suddenly blossomed into a young, clear-thinking lady before him. "Henrietta does not want to marry."

"Oh, you silly, silly thing." Louise tsked. "Women are susceptible to wooing, and according to Lady Brandewyne, this Mr. Hodges thinks very admirably of her unconventional skills. It is doubtful he will try to restrain her from doctoring. If anything, he is encouraging her. Thus ensnaring her in his malicious web of romantic intentions."

Mouth dry, Dominic nodded. "What is your plan, imp?"

Balls were such tedious enterprises.

Henrietta smoothed her silk skirt, glancing about the room for Mr. Hodges. He had said he would be here tonight to get the ointment she'd made for him. She was certain his trouble sleeping was due to his lifestyle and food choices, but he refused to listen.

So she'd concocted a lavender liniment for his feet.

People swirled about, and she caught sight of Lady Brandewyne in the corner. The lady smiled at her, and Henrietta reciprocated.

She pushed her way through the crowd to the refreshment table. It had been almost a fortnight of boredom and loneliness. She missed Louise's chatter and Dominic's flirtatious grins. Sometimes doing the right thing involved pain, she told herself. She sipped her drink, struggling to believe that she was right to leave.

If only Uncle William had been in London when she'd arrived, but he'd been called suddenly to southern England for a consult.

She would see him tomorrow, though. Lady Brandewyne had confirmed that her uncle planned to teach a symposium at six in the evening. Henrietta would be there, bags packed and ready to begin her life again.

She pushed away memories of Dominic and Louise. She could not bear to think of them right now.

"Miss Gordon, have you the medicine I need?" Mr. Hodges sidled up to her, his crisp outfit and perfectly coiffed hair in keeping with all of Brummell's guidelines. Rules Henrietta had recently become overly aware of, thanks to Mr. Hodges and his obsessive love of fashion.

"Indeed, I do. And will you stop drinking hot chocolate in the middle of the night?"

"Never."

They laughed as she dug the small jar from her reticule. "Then do not expect too much from this."

Mr. Hodges took the jar and then paused, his gaze shifting past her. "My lord," he said smartly, and bowed before leaving.

Henrietta turned to find Dominic standing behind her, his clothing impeccably tailored. He looked every ounce an earl. She curtsied, her mind in a flurry, her heart pounding hard and rapid beats. Why was he here? Had something happened to Louise?

He wore a glower almost as dark as his hair.

She found her voice. "My lord, how good to see you."

"And you," he said, sounding very stiff and formal.

She contained her wince. "How do you fare?"

"I heard that you are staying with Lady Brandewyne," he said, completely ignoring her question.

She dropped any pretense of lightheartedness as it was obvious he had some sort of purpose for coming here. Most likely to beg her to governess again. "Not much longer. My uncle comes into town tomorrow."

"Does he know that you are coming to see him yet?"

"Really, Dominic. We've discussed this." She fanned herself, looking away from his eyes that saw too much. That challenged her. She would not entertain the thought that Uncle William might turn her away. She'd begged Lady Brandewyne not to say anything to him, and she had to believe the lady kept her word.

Still, a nefarious heat cut through her body.

"You are risking all," he said softly. His breath feathered across the back of her neck, eliciting a shiver.

How had he moved so close? She stepped nearer to the punch bowl. Just to get more, she assured herself, not to escape his cologne or compelling presence. "I'm risking nothing. I'm merely returning to the life I've always known and loved."

"Would you be interested in a new life?"

His words trickled to her, low and gentle. Promising. "What kind of life?"

But he did not answer, for Lady Brandewyne had spotted them. "My dear Lord St. Raven, how good of you to come to my ball. I've missed your adorable face. I see you've found Miss Gordon. Do not try to steal her back, young man." She tittered, then rapped him on the arm with her fan.

The music started, but she grasped both of them by the elbows and rather forcibly steered them to the other side of the room, where it was quieter. A game of whist had been set up in the adjoining room, but Lady Brandewyne plopped down in a chair near the opening, tugging them down with her.

"It is quite a crush, is it not?" She fanned herself, releasing a self-satisfied sigh that shook her frame.

Henrietta exchanged a look with Dominic, who was not bothering to hide his amusement.

"Fit for the prince himself." The earl's gallant tone prompted a smirk to Henrietta's face.

"That's exactly what I thought. What a marvelous thing if he simply showed up, resplendent in the finest silks from Paris."

Henrietta rose an eyebrow. "The Prince Regent wears French clothing?"

"We all do." Lady Brandewyne eyed Henrietta pointedly. "Perhaps not you."

She had no response to that, seeing as she couldn't care less who made her clothing.

"Now, my dears," the lady said, patting their knees simultaneously, "I have a favor to ask of you."

Immediate stomach clench. She forced a smile. "Yes?"

"I'm asking it of St. Raven, really. You see, I'm having a bit of carriage trouble, and my head has been aching." She put a hand to her brow, as if to emphasize the pain. "Would you be so kind as to escort Miss Gordon to her uncle's symposium tomorrow? I believe you own an open carriage, do you not?"

"Oh, no, I can't impose," Henrietta blurted out. Just the thought of being alone with him hurt. How could she move on with her life if she allowed her feelings to tether her to a life that just wasn't going to fulfill her? "I shall take a hackney."

"Nonsense." Dominic's grin faded. "I'd be happy to escort her. What time shall I arrive?"

"Five o'clock sharp." She clapped her hands. "This is a huge help, my lord. My thanks to you."

Henrietta grimaced. So now she was to endure an evening with his lordship, forcing herself to forget all his finer qualities while attempting to woo her uncle into letting her join him.

Chapter Twenty-Two

Dr. William Gordon saw them at once.

Dominic folded his body into a small, uncomfortable chair while noting exactly when the esteemed doctor's gaze lit upon them. He was older than Dominic had expected, with silver hair and leathery skin that denoted his time spent outside. He did not carry the falsity of London physicians, nor did he wear their customary hat and use their customary cane.

Dominic watched him closely, intrigued. They were early, but the man did not come down to greet them.

The symposium had only been about ten minutes from Lady Brandewyne's. Henrietta had been nervous the entire trip, twitching and fiddling with her skirts. Prattling on about surgical methods and how her uncle wanted to overcome the barbarity of amputations on the field.

He had simply soaked in the sound of her voice, that husky flavored drink that poured in a flawless flow of melodic syllables. A fortnight without Henrietta. He still could not fathom how he had borne the boredom.

Already she had made him laugh with her concrete opinions and her resistance to his invariable charms. That brought to mind the reason they were here. He was not

sure how he'd gotten roped into this event, except that refusing Lady Brandewyne was akin to agreeing to ongoing
torture. Her ladyship did not readily take no for an answer.

As though hearing his thoughts, Henrietta leaned
over. "I'm surprised how easily you capitulated to Lady
Brandewyne."

Rustles ensued as more people arrived and took their
seats.

"She is a fearsome lady when she does not get her way.
I told her no once."

Henrietta gave him an approving smile. "Well, once
is something."

"I was ten," he continued, "and never have I been so
terrified. She pinched me by the ear and marched me to
her carriage. The entire way back to my estate she did
not cease talking. And then for thirty minutes more the
tirade continued. So not only did my earlobe ache from
the trauma she inflicted, but my brain has never recovered
from the sound of her voice when thwarted."

Henrietta laughed. Several people turned to glare at her
but she paid them no heed. "And what were you doing at
her estate in the first place?"

"I snuck in." He gave her a grin that brought pink to
her cheeks, which in turn brought a strong sense of satisfaction to him. "She threw huge parties for her children
several times a year. My brother was always invited, as he
was their age. I was too young, they said. So I took matters into my own hands."

"How very enterprising."

At that moment, her uncle began speaking. Dominic
yawned and suffered through the boring lecture. All because of a woman. He could have just dropped her off, but
he had a sneaking suspicion that things weren't going to
go well with her uncle. Henrietta had been supportive of

him. At the very least, he should be at her side when her uncle told her no.

A sharp nudge in his arm jolted him.

"Wake up," Henrietta snapped. "It's over."

Indeed, people began clapping. Dominic stretched, then yawned. "Did you learn anything new?"

"No."

"Don't look so smug, Miss Gordon." He winked at her, and that lovely rose flush suffused her cheeks again. He did not think he would ever tire of seeing that shade on her. "One should never presume to know everything."

"I have attended this symposium before, and he taught nothing I have not already heard." Her attention shifted to the front.

Dominic watched through hooded eyes. He had not decided yet what he thought of this man who dragged his niece away from society, exposing her to war and disease, and then abandoned her on a friend's doorstep to be wed off.

Eventually the doctor was left alone, his admirers and fellow physicians seeping away with their spectacles and tweed coats and auspicious hats. The old Dominic might have smirked at them, making fun at their assumed intellectual superiority.

He had changed. Perhaps they were different than him, and certainly more boring, but that did not mean he should not show them the respect due to their position. He had learned that, being an earl. The importance of deference to those in different circumstances.

Henrietta stood to her feet, walking quickly to her uncle. Interesting that she'd waited for others to leave, even though she had not seen her uncle in months. She adored him. Why would she exercise such caution?

He unfolded himself, stretching again and ignoring the

dirty look Henrietta gave him. Perhaps it was time to meet this enigmatic fountain of virtue. Determine for himself if he was as worthy of Henrietta's devotion as she believed.

The introductions were quick.

"Lady Brandewyne has told me of your unfortunate circumstances." Mr. Gordon looked over his spectacles. "I know the vagaries of raising a young girl into womanhood. How are you faring?"

Dominic held very still, determining how to best respond. "It has been challenging, certainly, but Henrietta was a huge help."

"Henrietta?"

"Yes, she is a natural teacher." Too late he realized he'd referred to her by her given name, rather than as Miss Gordon.

Mr. Gordon was trying to hide his surprise, but Dominic saw an alertness enter his face. "You two must see each other often."

"She was my niece's governess."

"Governess, you say." Mr. Gordon's eyes widened. He swiveled to her. "You didn't mention that you had taken a position in your letters."

This was quite intriguing. So her uncle did not know? He lifted his eyebrows at her, noting the tightened lips and flashing look in her eyes.

"Yes, that is what I've come to speak to you about." She wet her lips, and Dominic felt a surge of amusement. It was a rare thing indeed to see Henrietta Gordon fidgeting.

"I have been waiting quite a bit of time, you see, for you to send for me."

Mr. Gordon was regarding her with a soberness that reflected his intellectual meanderings. "I was quite clear that I expect you to marry."

A quick flash of surprise blinked across her face. She

hid it beneath a stiff smile. "Your expectations were clear, but they are not what I want for my life."

Mr. Gordon shot a glance at Dominic, as if questioning his part in all this. In fact, he felt as if he was an interloper suddenly, listening in on a conversation best said in private.

"I think I shall excuse myself," he said, avoiding looking at Henrietta. "You will take her back to Lady Brandewyne's?"

"Ah, yes, Lady Brandewyne. I had quite forgotten that she has invited us all to supper. Come, we shall discuss your future there." He grasped Henrietta's shoulder, and Dominic realized that they had not hugged nor exchanged endearments when first seeing each other.

Henrietta's chin lifted but surprisingly, she did not disagree. How very unlike her.

"You, too, my lad." Mr. Gordon gestured to Dominic. "She instructed that I insist you join us."

He stifled his groan. Though he wanted to be near Henrietta, the thought of wading through a long, drawn-out dinner made his skin crawl. He gave an acquiescent nod, however, and followed them out the door.

She had been duped.

Henrietta sat through dinner, her jaw aching from clenching it so tightly. How very difficult to hold back expressing her opinions, or from just leaving, but she hadn't seen Louise in so long and the girl was clinging to her.

She and Dominic were the only reasons Henrietta tempered her behavior.

The dinner had started out pleasantly enough, although she had already been fighting an annoyance at the way Uncle William cut her off at the symposium. Nevertheless, when she saw that Louise was at the house, her annoyance simmered beneath a great joy at seeing the girl.

She'd brought Smiles and so they spent some time playing in the garden with the dog. Henrietta hadn't realized how much she missed hugs until Louise gave her the first one. A huge, lung-popping embrace that unexpectedly made her throat clutch.

Then they sat down to dinner.

And indulged in the most inane conversations centering around marriage.

"I think every woman ought to get married," Louise said, before popping a delicate piece of Chateaubriand into her mouth.

"Manners," said Henrietta automatically. "Otherwise you shall eat in your room as usual."

"You are so strict, Retta." But she grinned while she said it and picked up her fork.

"Retta?" Uncle William's head tilted.

"Oh, yes, it's my pet name for Henrietta. Doesn't she just look like a Retta?"

"No," the adults said in unison.

Louise's face fell. "I think it makes her sound quite beautiful."

"Beauty is a mere positioning of symmetry of the facial bones and features." Henrietta picked at her food, which was growing cold. She was not one to lose appetite, but the way her uncle was avoiding her was distressing, to say the least.

The rest of the meal passed, and she contributed little to the conversation. When it was over, she excused herself, received another jubilant hug from Louise and wound her way outside.

Or rather, to the small garden behind Lady Brandewyne's townhome.

She had not been sitting long before Dominic came out. She smelled him first, that familiar, rich scent. Then he moved out of the shadowed doorway and into the moonlight. The blue-hued light caressed his face, avoiding his eyes, turning them into dark holes in his face.

He settled beside her, maintaining an appropriate distance.

"Is all well, my lord?" What other reason could he have for coming out here, joining her in the dark.

"Well enough. Your uncle and Lady Brandewyne have retired for the evening. Louise is in her room, spying on us." He pointed behind them, to a window on the second floor.

Surely enough, Louise's face was a white moon against the window. She gave no indication that she noticed their perusal.

Henrietta chuckled, hands clasped in her lap. "She will challenge you greatly."

"Will? She already does. Are you saying it gets worse?"

"Perhaps not. She has a strong mind, though. You should respect her independence."

She heard his indrawn breath, as though preparing to say something deep and meaningful. At the moment, she did not want to hear it.

She held up a hand. "There is no need to have a discussion."

"Presumptuous again, my dear governess."

"I am not your dear anything." Would he never stop flirting? She sighed.

"Very well. I merely meant to tell you how lovely you looked this evening. A new gown?"

She wrinkled her nose at him. "From the clothing Lady Brandewyne bought months ago. It was stagnating in her closet."

He shifted, and in that movement, she felt a change in his demeanor. He was going to go ahead and say something she would not like. She braced herself. This day had gone from terrible to worse than terrible, but she wasn't going to let that stop her. Tomorrow she'd confront her uncle. Make him see reason. After all, no good could come of him allowing his emotions to make his decisions.

"Henrietta…"

"Yes?" She willed herself to patience.

"I noticed when you saw your uncle, that he did not greet you in a warm manner."

She had not expected this comment. More along the lines of "Henrietta, you should have told your uncle that you took a governess position."

"I don't understand your meaning." She positioned her body to face him, searching his eyes, noting that they were no longer dark shadowed orbs, but glinting moon-kissed emeralds.

"He saw us when we came in. He gave no recognition."

She fluttered her fingers through the aromatic night air. "Oh, that is nothing. One cannot give in to familial affection at a professional event."

"You deserved a greeting."

"Are you chastising my uncle?" Her skin prickled. The scents of honeysuckle and lilac drifted on the breeze. They were not as comforting as one read in poems. "You are out of line, St. Raven."

"I'm not chastising him," he said softly, as soft as the aromas teasing her senses. "I was surprised. It made me wonder how often you've been touched or shown affection."

Henrietta bristled. "Not every family is like yours. We show affection in a different way. An intellectual way."

Even to her ears, the words sounded snobbish and elitist, but she could not take them back, for they were true. Her uncle had always stressed the importance of mental connection, of the exchanging of ideas and thoughts and facts. Her parents had been similar. She did not remember if her mother and father had ever hugged her. No recollection of physical expressions of love existed, but she had the faintest sense that her mother had sometimes smelled of violets, her father of tobacco.

Her breath tugged within her throat as she fought to calm herself. "It is inappropriate for you to be out here with me. You will start rumors. Why are you insinuating…what are you insinuating?"

He grimaced. "I suppose I don't know. It bothered me, somehow. I wanted to make sure you were happy."

"I'm fine. Happiness is the least of my concerns." She bolted up. What did he know? He had just now began the long process of respectability. Uncharitable thoughts ached to burst through her lips in accusation. She withheld them. He did not deserve vitriol. Though her blood strummed with the temptation to be unkind, to blame him for her frustration.

She stood up, feeling her nails digging into her palms, her toes curling into the stone path. Slippers were another complaint of society. In the Americas, she'd owned sturdy boots.

"Are you angry?" he asked. He made no attempt to stand.

"Not at you. At myself. Perhaps my uncle." She drew a ragged breath. "It is no matter. Tomorrow I will speak to him before Mr. Hodges arrives."

"Hodges?" Dominic's head jerked up in a startling manner.

"Yes, you remember him?"

"I know exactly who he is."

"There is no need to sound so caustic, sir. Mr. Hodges is an acquaintance who is accompanying me to an soiree tomorrow evening." Was it her imagination or had Dominic's shape stiffened? The darkened shadows made it impossible to know for sure.

"He's courting you."

"Not at all." She crossed her arms, eyeing him more closely. "I do hope you will not be joining everyone else in their misplaced notions about marriage."

"Why are you so against it?"

"Me?" She put her hand to her heart. "Marriage is a perfectly acceptable endeavor for most, but can you imagine a married doctor?"

"There are no female physicians in England, that I know of."

She detected a thread of amusement in his voice that annoyed her to no end. "Very well, I shall tell you a secret, St. Raven. But if you dare tell…"

"I would not. You know that."

She nodded. "Here it is then—I have been in contact with a renowned physician in Italy. He is my secondary plan."

This time she was sure his posture changed. She moved a tad bit to the left, forcing him to follow her with his gaze, forcing his face to move into moonlight. She could sit down, she supposed, but she rather liked being taller than him for once.

"Italy?" He sounded choked.

"Yes, they are much more progressive than England regarding females in the medical field. It is simply the next step should my uncle refuse me. Which he won't," she added unnecessarily.

"I suppose I won't be seeing you again then."

She shrugged, an easy, careless movement that belied

the sharp pain daggering through her heart. Would she never see him again? After all the time they'd spent together, the secrets they shared, the emotional closeness? She swallowed hard.

"I am sure we will see each other at least once more."

Chapter Twenty-Three

Dominic saw Henrietta sooner than she expected.

He scanned the room, tension resonating through his body, making his movements tight and quick as he moved past flowing couples, shimmering dresses and obsidian top hats. She was here. He had seen her earlier, talking with a countess whose name he had forgotten.

Thankfully he had not seen her with Hodges.

He threaded his way to the wall. Even at an evening soiree, the *ton* enjoyed dressing their best. He imagined Henrietta's caramel tresses pulled up, a few curls languishing against her pale, smooth neck. Was she dancing the waltz with someone else?

The reason he was here, of course.

He had spent the night tossing and turning, annoyed at the thought of Hodges wooing her into marriage. He did not truly believe she could be wooed, but nevertheless, he did not sleep well.

There. In a corner surrounded by older people. Henrietta's face was alight as she spoke, her hands moving with her mouth. She wore a pale green silk dress and her hair was just as he imagined it would be. Grinning, he strode over to join the group.

"Ah, St. Raven. Good to see you." Lord Bruckley, an elderly acquaintance who sponsored a society for steam research, shook his hand. "Miss Gordon here has just been sharing some of the advances being made in medical schools on the Continent."

"Fascinating." He eyed her, noting the overly flushed cheeks, the bright eyes and perhaps a tiny line of strain about her mouth. Had her uncle refused her then? "There is a nice breeze on the balcony. Perhaps Miss Gordon is in need of air?"

Not his finest maneuver. It was abrupt and the surprised expressions of those in the circle showed it, but anything less direct and he was sure Henrietta wouldn't pick up on it.

She nodded quickly. "Perhaps some punch. I'm feeling a tad peckish."

They made their salutations and he led her to a balcony door. She slid her arm through his, reminding him of her small stature, of how frail she had looked when he first met her. It was no wonder her uncle wanted her safe in London. It was easy to forget her size when dealing with her personality.

They stepped onto the terrace, which was enclosed by a wrought-iron balcony that overlooked a garden filled with hanging lamps of varying colors. From this vantage point they could see guests wandering the shadowed pathways. No one looked up at them, and due to the positioning of the balcony, he felt alone with her.

He wasn't alone, though. The ballroom was right behind them and her reputation would not suffer.

She pulled her arm from his and looked out over the gardens. "Will you be getting me a drink?"

"Stay here." He went quickly to the punch table, the strangest feeling within that she would disappear while he was gone. That he would never see her again. And that just would not do.

Thankfully she was still on the balcony when he returned. His chest loosened a little. He handed her the punch, which she accepted with an almost smile.

She stared out at people below. It wasn't quite dark, but there was a dusky quality to the air, combined with lamplight, and it put her profile in soft repose.

"I did not expect you here tonight."

He leaned on the balcony rail. "You expected Mr. Hodges."

She cut her gaze to him. "I came without him. I am not interested in him courting me, and have made it clear to him, but that is not pertinent."

"It is to me." He cleared his throat. "Did you speak to your uncle?"

"You are prying."

"I care about you, Henrietta, and wish to see you happy."

"As I already told you, happiness is not my goal. However, I shall be fulfilled when I travel to the Continent. I've been corresponding with the well-reputed physician who hired me. He's finding a residence."

"And this is what you want?"

"I wanted to help Uncle William." Her eyes flashed at him. "It is unlike you to be so interested in plans that have no bearing on your own life."

"Perhaps I wish them to."

Her mouth tightened imperceptibly. "What are you saying?"

His pulled at his cravat. It had shrunk. "I have come to realize, in days past, that Louise and I truly miss your presence."

"Is the other governess not adequate?"

How he longed to take her hands in his, to press them against his chest. But such a touch was unacceptable between them. He gripped the rail instead, fighting for self-control. "This is not about adequacy. Do you not see?"

"I'm flummoxed, my lord. You followed me out into the garden last night to insult my uncle, and now you are here saying…what? I do not follow."

"You shall have a raise," he said quickly. "Come back, be our governess and you will have more than enough money to practice and learn medicine."

"You have already offered this to me," she said quietly.

"Reconsider." He hated that he sounded as if he was begging.

Her mouth pursed. She looked down at her punch, as though it held answers. His own breathing was shallow. He had not had a seizure for several weeks. He prayed another did not descend. Not now, not during this.

"Dominic, I…" She lifted her eyes, and in them he saw rare emotion.

"What are you afraid of?"

She shook her head. "It is not so simple. I do not desire to be a governess. To be isolated. Neither servantry nor peerage. A governess's lot is a hard one, fraught with stigma and difficulty. It ends in poverty, very oftentimes."

"I wouldn't let that happen to you."

"But you are asking me to give up my dreams for what? A position that ladies fallen on hard times must resort to?"

Frustration boiled within him. "Do you feel nothing for us, then?"

Her brow furrowed. "Of course I do. You are offering me a position, though. A position anyone can do."

"Not the way you do, Henrietta."

"Hogwash."

He took a steadying breath, trying to calm his temper.

She had a point. He was not offering anything extraordinary. He simply wanted her in his life. The thought of never seeing her again…it was a vise around his chest, cutting off his air, strangling his lungs.

He had nothing else to offer.

But as he looked at her, noting the slim, aquiline nose, the direct eyes, the graceful curve of her fingers around the cup, it came to him that there was indeed something else he could offer. Something infinitely more appealing, something permanent and strong.

Something that terrified him beyond comprehension.

If he didn't have epilepsy, if institutionalization or even death were not right around the corner, then perhaps he would feel differently. Perhaps he would not fear offering such a solution.

It would get rid of Hodges for good. He felt then a curious twinge of satisfaction at the thought that the man would no longer be able to court Henrietta if she was a taken woman.

"That smirk on your face is positively frightening," she remarked, pulling him from his thoughts and back to the present.

No woman had ever said that to him. He squinted at her, not sure he'd heard correctly.

"Oh, yes, you heard me. I'm certain that it's beyond the scope of your imagination to think a woman could ever find you anything but attractive, but there it is. A strange and frightening smirk." She took a sip of her punch, her eyes never leaving his face. "Would you care to share your thoughts, for I am growing bored and I still have no idea what brought you to this soiree."

"Hodges," he blurted out.

"Hodges? He is a funny fellow. Harmless."

"Yes, well, if he was courting you, I felt I should know. As your friend," he added.

"My friend."

"Yes. Yes, I suppose you could call me such."

She blinked, a flicker of some emotion he could not name passing across her face. "I do not think I've ever had a friend."

The look on her face paused his next words. Sorrow etched her features.

"I will be your friend," he said quietly.

But she was hardening before his eyes, drawing back.

Panic filled him. He, the unconscionable flirt in his younger years, emptied of words. Henrietta was different than those in his past. She expected more from him than flattery, gifts. She saw more. He dug within, searching for the right sentence, the one that would make her look at him and never want to leave.

It was illogical, impractical to do such a silly thing, yet in this moment, he realized it was why he had come tonight.

"The reason I'm here is because I cannot imagine a life without you present. It has been terrible. Louise cries every day." He exhaled deeply, realizing suddenly that perhaps he loved Henrietta. He didn't know for sure, though, as he had never been in love before. "Is there any way you will consider staying?"

Henrietta gripped her punch, wishing to be anywhere but here. The way Dominic gazed at her, imploring, made pain spike through her entire body. She longed to run away from him, from the fear he inspired. She had thought of them every day while with Lady Brandewyne. Memories kept her up at night, hopes and dreams colliding with her new reality.

They had felt almost like a family.

Any way? Marriage, love. Those might sway her. But he had not spoken of either, and her goal of working in the medical profession had been with her for too long. Considering another role was contrary to all she'd taught herself to believe. A giant rock of emotion lumped in her throat.

"You have probably guessed that Uncle William refuses to take me with him," she said. Strains of music filtered out to the balcony, the muted music of a world she didn't belong to.

Dominic nodded. There was a strange wildness to his face, to the contours of his handsome features. She wanted to smooth it away. To assure him that all would be well.

She could not, of course.

"This position with the doctor, it is groundbreaking, really. He believes me to be quite educated, which I am."

"Don't go," Dominic rasped.

"The ticket has been bought."

"So soon?"

"Uncle William insisted I stay with Lady Brandewyne. I went and bought the ticket shortly thereafter."

"He wants you to stay with her? As a companion?"

"Oh, no, they are planning to marry me off still."

"Henrietta." His voice caught. He moved forward, forcing her to back into the corner of the balcony, into a shadowed triangle. "If I was a healthy man, if I could promise that you would not be stained in the future by my disease, thus harming both you and Louise, I would ask for your hand in marriage."

A shocking statement. Her head jerked up; she met his serious look with one of her own. "We could not."

"I know." He groaned, a deep, raw sound that tore at her conscience.

"It is not due to my reputation," she said, seeking to

alleviate the torture that wrote itself across his features. She had never seen him so distressed. Even though she had also thought of marriage, now that he said so, she realized how very terrifying it was. Chest constricting, she moved toward him, until only an inch or so of space separated them. "I just…and it is so very silly, but I cannot bring myself to cleave to anyone but myself."

"Is being alone what you want, then?"

"No." She shook her head, yet deep within, yes, that was it. Being alone was far safer. "Your words are most kind, my lord, but we both know that nothing could work out with us. I am far too practical. You are an emotional being, prone to quick smiles and flirtatious words. We are ill-suited."

And there was his disease to think of. He mentioned it as being a wall between them. He worried for how it would affect his family's reputation.

She did not care about reputation when it came to epilepsy. What kept her away was the knowledge that seizures could kill a man. And Henrietta could never again subject herself to the pain of losing her loved ones.

Just the thought of Dominic dying while in the thralls of a seizure rocketed her pulse. Could she subject herself to such pain? To add to that, he did not love her. Which was why what he had suggested would never happen.

"The only other option is if I stay on as governess, but I'm afraid I have no interest in that." She did her best not to flinch while speaking, to be careful and pragmatic.

Dominic stepped closer, and now they were chest-to-chest, heart-to-heart. Fanciful, and yet her pulse drummed beneath her skin in an unfamiliar beat. He bent his head close to her hear, his lips grazing the lobe.

"Are you afraid, Miss Gordon?"

"Never." The expected response, though indeed an ice-cold fear flowed like sludge through her veins. If anything ever happened to Dominic, she could not bear the thought. She loved him, she realized suddenly. She loved him so very much that the idea of losing him brought a real and physical pain to her insides.

No, it was better to be far away from him. To cut ties now.

"I am deeply terrified," he whispered in a husky voice that sent prickles down the nape of her neck. Before she knew what he was about, he wrapped his arms around her waist, drawing her flush against him. "But I am willing to take a chance, I think. If you are."

And then his lips were whispering across her cheek, to greet her lips with a tenderness that soon turned greedy, quick and moist, and she was returning the kiss. She could not stop herself, could not deny the love roaring through her in tumultuous waves that destroyed her inhibitions.

She curled the fingers of her left hand in his hair, trying to remember not to drop the punch, but his kiss was rendering her fuzzy, incompetent. No doubt he had kissed many women this way. The thought put steel in her spine. She jerked away, her lips swollen and tingling, her anger ignited.

"I shall not be swayed by your flirtations." Without thinking, without knowing why and acting in a way she had never tolerated before, she tossed the punch in his face, pushed past him into the ballroom and walked away.

Chapter Twenty-Four

Louise burst into Henrietta's room the next morning. The door slammed against the wall, startling Henrietta. She turned from her bed, where she'd piled various medical texts in an attempt to decide which ones to leave, and which ones to take.

"You're leaving?" Louise's pointer finger shook.

Sighing, Henrietta set down the book she'd been flipping through. "Next week."

"I can't believe it."

"But I told you I would be." Henrietta stood next to the bed, unsure. She'd spent a restless night, hardly able to sleep. Her stomach was sore, as if someone had punched her, and her chest hurt, though as far as she could ascertain, her heart rhythms were normal. She'd tried praying, but all she could utter were pleas for wisdom. Now she did not know whether to go to Louise and hug her, or perhaps just talk. Explain the situation in a rational way. Yes, certainly that would smooth things over. One could not argue with logic.

"It is the practical thing to do," she said in a calm, unaffected voice of which she was quite proud.

"No, it's not fair." Louise stomped her foot. "I told

them our plan wouldn't work and they didn't listen." She burst into tears.

"Them? Plan?"

"You two are supposed to fall passionately in love and marry posthaste."

Oh, this would not do at all. Henrietta rushed forward to hug the girl, but she turned and ran out of the rooms. She stared after her, that dreadful ache to her chest returning. Of course a twelve-year-old could not understand. It was unfair to expect her to.

It was, however, quite fair to expect her guardian and his lady friend to understand. Setting her jaw, she marched to the main hall. The entire way she fumed. A setup. Who did they think they were?

Had her love of medicine fooled her uncle into thinking she was no longer that strong-willed fifteen-year-old who had forged her own path? That girl was still inside, and she was seething.

She shoved the door to the study open, but there was no one inside but a startled maid, who let out a tinny screech.

"I beg your pardon," Henrietta said without thinking. And since she was already talking, she continued, "Do you perchance know where her ladyship is?"

"In—in the gardens, Miss Gordon."

"Thank you." She backed out and hurried to the gardens, fury strengthening her steps.

They were exactly where she expected, sitting in their chairs, chuckling and drinking tea. As though they had not created a disaster.

"You. Both of you."

Their laughs stopped. In unison, they turned to her. For the tiniest second, her anger paused at the sight of the silver-haired, meddling single people staring at her in wide-eyed wonderment. Perhaps even fear.

As they should, she assured herself, thus bolstering her resolve.

Lady Brandewyne was the first to recover. "Why, my dear, how lovely to see you. We were just discussing last night's soiree. Your uncle regrets missing it. He was sure something of note might happen."

They were not looking at her in fear after all. More like experimental analysis.

Huffing, she pulled a chair out from the table and sat. "There is a girl upstairs crying right now. And it's your fault."

"Mine?" Lady Brandewyne put her hand to her chest, looking positively affronted.

"And yours." Henrietta skewered her uncle with a glare. It wasn't hard to do, as she was impossibly upset with him already. "Do not act innocent with me. How long have you two been conniving?"

Lady Brandewyne gasped. "Conniving? Those are strong words."

"You're out of line, Henrietta," her uncle boomed in the deep voice he used when confronted with something he felt bound to fix, such as "hand me the saw" or "needle and thread."

In this case, "you're out of line."

Oh, the irony that she'd used the very same words on Dominic. In the broad light of day, she could almost believe she'd misjudged him. That she'd reacted hastily. She could almost forget what it felt like to be kissed by him.

But what she couldn't forget was the bone-deep dread of imagining a life in which he died.

Squaring her shoulders, she looked her uncle in the eyes. "You are quite wrong on that count. I am perfectly in line. What you two have done has not only made my life miserable, but you ballooned the hopes of a young lady who is now sobbing in anguish. How could you?"

Lady Brandewyne was sputtering, at a loss as to how to answer. Perhaps no one had spoken to her this way in years.

Uncle pushed to his feet, shoving his spectacles up the bridge of his nose in an impatient movement. "It is time for you to marry, to take on the role of a woman."

"The role of a woman?" Her temper rose, sending hot prickles across her skin.

"You know what I mean. Manage a household. Bear children. Don't you want that?"

"It is obvious to me that you have not listened to a word I've uttered or written. I do not want that." As she spoke, though, a nausea took hold of her. "At least not right now," she amended.

"The battlefield is no place for you." He turned to Lady Brandewyne. "She almost died. A week she doesn't remember because she was delirious, and now she pretends everything is fine. She does not see the danger for herself."

"Do not enlist her support in this." Henrietta put her hands on the hips. Perhaps she had lost a few days while ill. That had nothing to do with practicing medicine. "People catch sickness in England, too. I am no safer here than I was there."

"How can you not want a family?" Lady Brandewyne stood, a ridiculous gesture but nevertheless effective.

Henrietta rued her small stature. People always thought that standing over her would make their responses more believable. She lifted her chin. "I had a family."

"But my dear, I am your family," said Uncle William.

"Exactly. Which is why I don't need anyone else. Don't you see that you are controlling my life because of an unfounded fear of the unknown. You are making insensible decisions based on emotion. There is no way to control my safety. Surely you see that?"

Uncle removed his glasses, rubbing his eyes as though unbearably tired. A part of her regretted her outburst. She had no desire to hurt him, but this had to stop.

"Your machinations made Louise think that I would really marry Hodges. I will admit to a fondness for his eclectic style, but he is truly nothing but an acquaintance."

"Hodges?" Lady Brandewyne quickly covered her mouth, as though stopping the outflow of more information. "He is not the one we think is suited to you."

Uncle grunted.

More of her world crashed down, bits and pieces fluttering to the floor, as everything became clear to Henrietta. She sank onto her chair, her legs suddenly wobbly as she realized that it had not been Hodges after all.

"Who?" she asked.

"St. Raven."

"But why? When?"

"Because he needs a family as much as you do. I realized it when he came to London for the first time after the accident. I saw him at his sister's ball, and Louise and I have been planning ever since." The dowager countess dabbed at her eyes, a deliberate movement that did little to soften Henrietta's ire.

"I am speechless," said Henrietta.

Uncle William and Lady Brandewyne exchanged a glance, one fraught with meaning and guilt and possibly a bit of gloating.

"Perhaps we should sit," Lady Brandewyne suggested to her uncle.

They did, Uncle replacing his spectacles as though taking charge once again. A horrible emptiness opened in the pit of Henrietta's stomach.

"When you went to live with your uncle at the age of fifteen, it was determined that your nature was, how shall I put this...delicate."

Henrietta made a sound in her throat, a gurgle of frustration that she was desperately trying to tamp down.

"He came to me and asked for advice. As a successful mother of five rowdy boys who turned into responsible, good men, I felt both obliged and qualified to help your uncle." She paused for a moment, perhaps to admire her skills. "When you turned eighteen, he wrote that you had become besotted with someone in the Americas. At which point I suggested he send you home."

"That was during the war. He couldn't bring me home."

"Eighteen-twelve. Yes, I remember. A terrible time."

"So my illness was the excuse you needed to pressure me into marriage. And I would not say I was besotted with Daniel."

"You followed him everywhere," Uncle said pointedly.

"He was a good surgeon. He believed using boiling water on his blades would lower the mortality rates of wounded soldiers, and he was right."

"That has not been confirmed," Uncle insisted.

"Oh, pshaw," said Henrietta, feeling as though her world had turned upside down. "Every good midwife knows to use clean cloths and hot water. Surgeons should, too. That is not the point. Apparently you've been arranging to rip me from the life *you* gave me for years! How could you not say anything?"

"We are doing what is best for you." A rather weak rebuttal from Lady Brandewyne.

Exasperated, Henrietta pressed her palms against her forehead. "What you think is best. I find it hard to fathom that you've been planning such a life for me for years and never said a word. This is..." A betrayal. That was what it was. An ignominious travesty of everything he'd taught her to respect and value.

She covered her eyes. "You dragged Louise into this."

"We knew you are exactly who she needs." Lady Brandewyne's voice had grown subdued, perhaps understanding that her well-laid plans had just been annihilated.

"You have put me in an untenable position," Henrietta said quietly, looking up from the cave of her hands. "Now I must break a young girl's heart."

"Not necessarily."

Everyone in the room turned. Dominic waited in the doorway, having evidently pushed past the staff to arrive without announcement.

Her heart hitched. She pressed her hand against her chest as if that would stop the organ's erratic jumping. He looked so normal today. So unaffected by what had transpired last night. How very annoying. Even his hair was unruffled, combed neatly and amplifying his handsome features.

"Might I speak with Henrietta?" His voice was a low, husky blend of amusement and sobriety.

"Of course, of course." The dowager countess bustled up from her seat, patting Uncle William on the shoulder as if hurrying him along.

They left Dominic and Henrietta alone in the garden. There were windows all around and so they were not really alone. But the reason was clear. Her uncle and the dowager countess expected Dominic to propose.

Her throat closed.

"I have come to apologize for last night's uncouth behavior." He sat across from her, his eyes twinkling in the sunlight. "And also to beg you to reconsider."

"Governessing does not suit me."

"Perhaps wifery does?"

"If this is your attempt to propose, it is terrible." She stood, sweeping her skirts out of the way, and strode into the house. He was right behind her, worse than Smiles.

"Not an attempt. More of a feeling-out." He matched her progress on the stairwell. "Come now, are you truly angry over last night?"

She stopped on the landing, putting her hands on her hips, aware that downstairs in the hall, two traitorous sets of eyes watched them. "I am angry because those two—" she swept her hand downward "—have been matchmaking."

Dominic followed Henrietta's expressive hand to where it pointed to Mr. Gordon and Lady Brandewyne. They saw him and jumped out of sight. Presumably into the parlor, where they could continue their eavesdropping.

He didn't match Henrietta's outrage. Grinning, he shrugged. "What is wrong with that?"

Her eyebrows narrowed. "Because your niece believed their machinations and is now heartbroken. She actually thought that you and I, that you and I..." she sputtered.

"That is why I'm here, Miss Gordon. You were quite resistant to the mention of anything more between us last night, and I wondered if I might understand your reasoning."

"Reason. Yes, that's exactly what it is. I am leaving. Within the fortnight, actually. I received a letter in the post today that housing has been found for me."

"You're leaving?" Mr. Gordon popped back into view, his voice echoing up to them. "What are you talking about?"

"Uncle, I have accepted a position as an assistant to a Mr. Ledford of Italy. He is an old acquaintance of yours."

"Unacceptable," yelled Mr. Gordon.

"Unchangeable," she replied in a steady fashion.

Dominic looked at her gloved hands. They were shaking. "This is really it, then."

"You and Louise are welcome to visit, of course. I shall be taking a lady's maid with me. I've already hired the girl. It is all on the up-and-up."

"Henrietta…" His voice caught. He must be the brave one here, for he began to see that she lived in fear. "What if I told you that I think I might love you? Would that change anything?"

Her eyes widened. "You might?" Then she laughed, a broken sound that hurt to hear. "That is worse than no love at all. That is a 'you're almost good enough, but not quite.'"

"Not at all."

"It is my interpretation, but it doesn't matter, does it? Because I am leaving. I have dreams to pursue. A life to live as I see best. A talent from God to use and not let languish."

Dominic nodded, his features hardening. There was no use chasing a resistant woman. She didn't want them, didn't want him. Had made it perfectly, crystalline clear. "Very well, Miss Gordon. I wish for you the best."

He swept her a long, sardonic bow then brushed past her without a second look. She'd taken his words and stomped all over them. Never had he felt so maligned. Disrespected. He hurried down the stairs, only pausing when he heard Louise's shrill voice.

"I hate you!" And then a door, slamming, the sound echoing through Lady Brandewyne's cavernous townhouse. It was the sound of change, of promise, closing for good.

Mr. Gordon rushed to him as soon as he reached the

foot of the stairs. "Lad, don't give up. She's stubborn. She doesn't want to lose more people she loves."

"She's made her choice," Dominic said roughly, his voice scratching, his vocal chords chafing as he spoke. "Perhaps it would be best if the next time you two plan to match two people eminently unsuited...don't."

Chapter Twenty-Five

The earl of St. Raven was a big flirt desperate to keep his niece. He couldn't possibly mean what he said. He *might* love her. Pfft.

How Henrietta wanted to believe him, though. The temptation to follow her heart rather than reason was almost too much to bear. If he had told her he loved her, then perhaps she might have stayed. Because she was beginning to believe that she loved him dearly.

A one-sided love would never do.

Henrietta followed the footman who was hauling her luggage to the carriages. She was to be at the shipyard early tomorrow morning for departure to the Continent. The dreary day mimicked her mood.

Louise refused to speak to her, or to even emerge from her bedroom. If Dominic had returned to Lady Brandewyne's to collect his niece, she had not seen him. She inhaled a ragged breath of the damp air. Footmen loaded her bags.

"I forbid this." Uncle's voice came from the entryway of Lady Brandewyne's house. "Unload her things at once."

Behind him, Lady Brandewyne stood suspiciously quiet. A light mist began to fall, peppering Henrietta's face with cold tears. She walked to her uncle, close enough so that she did not need to yell, but far enough away to avoid looking straight into his eyes.

If she did, she might cry, and that was not befitting to the situation. Squaring her shoulders, she said, "If you do not let me use the carriage, I shall simply hire a hackney. I will not live beneath your thumb."

"Beneath my thumb? That is never how I treated you."

But a cold, hard block of something wedged in Henrietta's chest, and despite the feeling that she was making the worst mistake of her life, she couldn't bring herself to back down. "Nevertheless, you have made the serious error of attempting to control my future. That cannot be allowed."

"Henrietta…" Uncle stepped forward, holding out his hands. Utterly unexpected. "I love you."

She blinked. Hard. The prickling sensation beneath her eyelids did not cease. He had said such words perhaps four times since she had come to live with him. She had known he felt that way, but to hear him say it brought the pressure in her chest to a crushing pain. A tear, unbidden, slipped down her cheek.

He reached for her hands, took them in his own. "My dearest hope is for you to be happy. If that means staying with me and practicing medicine, then so be it."

"I have already given my word," she choked out.

He nodded, understanding. "Then go for a year. Learn. And come home to me. I will be waiting."

Tears blazed a burning trail down her cheeks. Her nose was becoming congested and her eyes puffy, stinging. She managed a nod, pulled her hands away and pivoted down the stairs to where her carriage awaited.

The ride to the room she'd rented for the night was fraught with tears. She managed to dry her eyes before arriving. The proprietor, a kindly lady with smile grooves beside her mouth, looked as though she guessed that Henrietta had been weeping. She showed her to her room.

It was clean and sparse, as Henrietta had been told from an acquaintance who recommended the place. She thanked the woman and then sat on her bed, suddenly aware that this would be her life now.

Alone.

She was not one to sit and ponder circumstances. She more often than not preferred to rise up in action and take charge of a situation.

Until tomorrow morning, though, she had nothing but a silent room in which to ruminate.

Uncle William loved her. He wanted her.

She laid down, staring up at the beamed ceiling. Until Dominic had mentioned her uncle's aloofness, she had not realized how it made her feel. Dominic had shown her many facets to herself that she had not realized existed.

Suddenly the thought of Italy was not so exciting. Perhaps pursuing medicine was her dream, but did it have any meaning without her family by her side? With a maid who existed only as a translator and preserver of reputation?

For the first time in months, she wondered if she ought to have prayed for direction. Since coming home, she had been so bent on getting her own way, on doing what she had planned, that she hadn't bothered to inquire of God what His plans were.

And now that she'd achieved almost exactly what she wanted, she still was not content.

"I appreciate you meeting me." Dominic studied Mr. Gordon, who had settled in a chair across from him.

"I'll confess, I've never been in White's before." Mr. Gordon studied the gentleman's club the way one might imagine a physician observes anatomy. As though taking in the bones and sinews of the place and determining health.

"Membership is select. An exception was made for you today."

"Why here?"

"It is conducive to a private conversation." Dominic tapped the side of his chair. He had often enjoyed White's in his less than circumspect past, but he had not been there in several months. "Here is the gist of the matter—you and Lady Brandewyne bungled. But it is not all your fault. I have something I must tell you. It is the reason why I can never marry your niece."

"Go on." The doctor folded his hands and leaned forward. Evidently used to secrets.

Dominic had been counting on that. One did not become renowned by exposing the secret illnesses of the *ton*. This man was trustworthy when it came to medical issues.

Dominic took a deep breath, feeling a rush of panic that lightened his head and shook his hands. He had never told anyone but Henrietta. Sharing the secret unnerved him. "I am not a healthy man."

At that, Mr. Gordon leaned back in surprise. "A remarkable thing to say, my lord. You appear quite fit."

"It is a falsity." Dominic leaned forward, glancing about to make sure no one heard. "I would prefer this to stay between us, as it could potentially affect my family."

Her uncle put his elbows on his knees. "But of course. Discretion is my duty as a physician."

"Even if you think I'm insane? If you believe me a menace to society, what then?"

"That is absurd. Lady Brandewyne has known you since a babe and vouches for your character. I have also observed and interacted with you several times. You're not insane."

"You may change your mind," Dominic said darkly.

"Doubtful. I am a man sure of my own opinion."

How he sounded like Henrietta. For some reason, that comforted him. The assertion rang with truth.

"I am an epileptic."

The doctor's face did not even twitch. "Why are you telling me this?"

"I want to be cured. I thought perhaps you might know of some procedure…and I am also telling you so that you can see why, though I care deeply for Henrietta, I can never offer her marriage." Dominic winced. "In a weak moment, I did offer it, but she wisely refused."

"Ah." Mr. Gordon leaned back, studying Dominic as though he was a new species. "When did your seizures first begin?"

"A year ago. I was in the accident that killed my brother and his wife. They broke their necks, but all I got was a bump on the head and a lifetime sentence of illness."

"Not unusual."

"Really?"

"I've a friend who has a theory that with epilepsy, some sort of electrical impulse is triggering in the brain. The fall could have caused a change in humors. Disrupting them perhaps. My friend has not published his thoughts on the subject, as he is still in the throes of research."

"Well, you understand why my secret must be contained."

"Yes, yes, of course, but epilepsy is no reason not to marry."

"I could die at any time."

"As could we all, lad. In fact, Henrietta just set me straight this morning. You see, I've been trying to keep her safe, but one should never sacrifice a calling for safety. Dreams for status quo."

"Status what?" Dominic was trying to follow the doctor's reasoning, but the events of the days had exhausted him. He shook his head when, for a second, there appeared to be two Mr. Gordons.

"What I am saying is that Henrietta is on her way to Italy. I couldn't stop her, though since she's left, I've had an idea."

Dominic straightened. "Today?"

"Her ship departs tomorrow morning," the doctor amended. "Since you asked me here, it has occurred to me that perhaps you are the man to keep her home. She wants a family, but she fears that she will lose them."

Dominic was aware of the blood rushing through his head. "Yesterday I bared my feelings, and she rejected me. Soundly and firmly." Though he remembered her hands, quivering and unsure, against her skirts. "I have taken her at her word."

"Does she know you love her?"

Did she? He had said *might*. Henrietta did not deal in halves. Suddenly he realized his mistake. "No, she does not know for certain. But I do. I love her in every way."

"Women are emotional creatures. She will stay if you confess your love."

"Henrietta?" Even as he scoffed at the notion of his practical, levelheaded governess succumbing to emotion, he recalled her heated tirade against the apothecary. And the way she'd giggled in a field of bubbles while Smiles and Louise rolled around, soaking wet.

"She hides them well," Mr. Gordon admitted. "If you are certain you cannot live without her, then I propose we stop her from leaving for Italy."

His legs itched to run out and stop her at this very moment. "Where is she?"

Mr. Gordon stood. "At a reputable boardinghouse near the wharf. Lady Brandewyne will meet us there, to preserve Henrietta's reputation. She will bring Louise."

Dominic's stomach sank. He had spent his entire life avoiding commitments, quitting whatever did not please him. "I've tried to reason with her. What if she says no again?"

"Then you can assure yourself you did all that you could, and you may move on with your life."

He thought of her impassioned words, the way she'd rejected his "I think I might love you." Perhaps she wanted… no, needed more from him. But was he strong enough?

All he knew was that he didn't want to lose her, and if that meant braving the murky waters of the unknown, then that was what he had to do. "Let us take our leave then."

"And no more nonsense talk of health. You have many years left in you." The doctor slapped him on the shoulder, an altogether unexpected gesture of affection.

Dominic called for his carriage, which was brought swiftly. He and the doctor climbed in.

Was he really doing this? She had rejected him many times. It was madness to try again, and yet her uncle believed she was saying no due to fear.

She *had* kissed him back.

He remembered clearly the feel of the woman he cared for in his arms, and the emotions he'd sensed in her when they kissed. If she left and he never saw her again… He set his jaw. He couldn't let that happen.

His vision wavered again and he blinked. He did not need a seizure right now.

Gordon gave directions to the driver and as the carriage

clomped over the roads, rocking with motion, Dominic finally felt a sense of purpose.

He closed his eyes and leaned back against the cushioned squabs. As he silently prayed, peace came over him. This was the right thing. At the very least, he would tell her his true feelings.

It wasn't just that he might love her.

He did love her.

To the dark, terrified depths of himself, he loved her. And if she wanted to give up, to cower in fear of living, then he would challenge her on that. She had made him feel as though he wanted to be a better person. That embracing his life did not mean embracing solitude.

And now it was time for her to see the same for herself.

Chapter Twenty-Six

Rapid, staccato knocking roused Henrietta from terrible dreams of smoke-clouded skies and unbearable loneliness. Sitting up, she rubbed at her eyes while her head pounded in frightening beats. The room carried a dusky stillness, interrupted only by the rapping on the door. Rapping that mimicked the clomping in her temples.

A frightful paralysis clutched at her throat. Who could be outside her door at this hour? She had no weapons. Perhaps the scalpel she kept in a side pocket of her reticule would serve to protect her.

"Henrietta, we know you are in there. Open the door." Lady Brandewyne, sounding as bossy as always.

"I'm here, too." Louise's voice.

She scooted off the bed, wondering if they had come to talk her out of her decision. Which could not happen, she assured herself as she opened the door.

Immediately Louise flew at her, grabbing her at the waist and squeezing so hard that a soft *oomph* fluttered from her.

"I don't hate you. I don't," she declared, her words thick with emotion.

Smiles pranced in behind them, jumping onto Henrietta's bed and making himself cozy. Henrietta patted Louise on the back.

"I know," she said, although secretly she had worried that the girl did. In fact, she had not been able to get out of her mind the notion that Louise would forever hate her, forever remember her not as a joyful time in her life, but a painful one.

She pulled Louise closer, savoring the contact, the proof of love.

And she did love the girl. It was a feeling that once known, could not become unknown.

"I love you," she said. Because a child should always know they were loved. In words and in deed.

"I love you, too," Louise muttered into the side of her dress.

"You look positively frightful," Lady Brandewyne announced, breaking the moment with a critical glare. "What have you been doing, sobbing since you left?" She swept a well-manicured hand upward. "Your eyelids are atrociously swollen. Your nose...why, no powder could disguise that color."

Henrietta tried to roll her eyes, but they were sandpaper-raw. "Why are you here?"

The dowager countess sniffed, managing to shut the door while keeping her nose in the air. "To aid you."

"If you have come to try to talk me out of leaving, then I fear you've wasted your time." To her relief, not even a wobble carried in her voice. "I have given my word."

"Ah, but what if another equally educated candidate could take your place? What then?"

Henrietta's mind blanked. "Pardon me?"

Lady Brandewyne smiled in a mischievous way. "If I found someone as educated as yourself, and sent him instead, would you stay?"

"I do not wish to be a governess." She lifted her chin. "And I've no desire to be on the marriage mart. I am too old, anyhow, for such nonsense."

"Yes, your age is showing now."

Henrietta scowled at the dowager. She may not care overly much for fashion, but that did not mean she wanted her looks publicly maligned.

"Let us fix you up." Lady Brandewyne bustled into the room, peering in corners and fiddling with her medicines on the small vanity. "Don't you have a brush? Where is that maid you claimed you hired?"

Louise played with the dog on the bed, giggling. Henrietta crossed the room. "She will join me on the ship. She is another reason I must go. I have promised her steady employment and knowledge. She has intimated an interest in learning."

"Bah. Let her work for me."

"Why are you so insistent? Did you really come all this way to stop me?"

"I came to tell you I don't hate you," Louise said.

"Thank you," she said drily. She eyed Lady Brandewyne, who was avoiding direct eye contact quite effectively. "However did you find me? I do hope you do not think showing up will change my mind about anything."

The dowager countess snapped around, finally bringing her gaze to focus directly on Henrietta's face. "You are the most stubborn woman I have ever had the misfortune to meet."

From the bed, Louise gasped.

"That is not my fault," said Henrietta. "I am simply living my life."

"Ruining it is more likely. Look at your face. Miserable. Do you think you will feel any better cavorting off to some strange place? Tell me, do you even speak Italian?"

"A bit of French."

"Which helps you not at all."

"Insulting me will not aid in changing my mind. And what do you expect me to do? Sit around London drinking tea and gossiping?"

"What a narrow way of looking at my world, Miss Gordon. For shame." Lady Brandewyne assumed a very square stance.

Henrietta had seen a pugilist stand that way once, right before he pummeled his opponent.

"I will have you know that I am a charter member of London's orphan society. We provide for more than fifty homeless children, offering them warm beds and plenty of food. Many women of my acquaintance pursue good deeds, using their money and their influence to better society."

A wave of regret engulfed Henrietta, not only because she had so soundly insulted Lady Brandewyne, but also because she did not want to spend her last day in England arguing with those she loved. Or at least had a modicum of affection for, she admitted, for the dowager's face was growing quite red as she continued listing her accomplishments and contributions to aiding those of less fortune than herself.

Henrietta held up a hand. The tirade stopped.

"What I said was a reflection of my own bias, and not knowledge." She drew a quivering lungful of oxygen. "I apologize, my lady, for my assumptions and rudeness. I do not wish to part on negative terms."

"In that case—" the lady shook her shoulders and assumed her usual haughty stance "—let us take you back to your uncle, where you belong."

If only she did belong. And it was not just her uncle she was thinking of.

Lady Brandewyne put a hand on her shoulder. "Dominic will be there."

"Will he?" She had rejected him. What man would accept her after such a blow to the ego, and Dominic's ego was exceptionally large.

"Miss Gordon, you are living your life afraid because of your past. You accused your uncle of not letting you live due to his fear, but here you are, committing the same mistake. You must move on." Lady Brandewyne's unusually gentle tone snuck past her defenses.

She was right. For all the practicality Henrietta prided herself on, she had not seen the truth in front of her face.

Perhaps Dominic thought he might love her, but she knew that she loved him. She had been making her decisions based on emotion and fear just as much as Uncle William. "You say my uncle has a man he can send in my place? One willing to apprentice on the Continent instead of beneath my uncle?"

She nodded. "He has already been asked and merely awaits word."

"I shall have to offer the lady's maid a better position."

"We will figure it out, dearest."

Smiles barked, his tail thumping hard against the bed, and Louise giggled. Henrietta did not feel she could laugh quite yet. She was giving up a position of surety for a risk.

Light-headed, she sank into the chair at the vanity.

A knock sounded. Urgent. Lady Brandewyne, who was nearest to the door, opened it. A footman stood there, twisting his cap in his hands.

"Bostick, whatever are you doing here?"

"There's been a terrible accident, my lady. Lord St. Raven's carriage overturned and he and Mr. Gordon have been gravely injured. Mr. Gordon requests your presence immediately."

"What of Lord St. Raven?"

Henrietta's head shot up. Together? She stood, observing Bostick's expression, the worry in his demeanor.

"They took him, my lady. He was severely injured, and then he…" The man swallowed, terror evident on his face. "He succumbed to a fit of sorts. Frothing at the mouth. The Viscount Winchester ordered that he be taken to Guy's Hospital."

"And my uncle?" Henrietta snatched her reticule.

"Mr. Gordon was taken to Lady Brandewyne's home, as it was closer. We sent for your personal physician."

"Well done," murmured the dowager.

Henrietta's head was clearing quickly and anger and purpose centered her. But where should she go? If Dominic was at Guy's… It was a reputable hospital for learning, but everyone knew that London hospitals were cesspools of disease. If he didn't die of infection, they might try to lock him up in Bedlam.

"Louise, pick up Smiles. Quickly." Lady Brandewyne turned to Henrietta. "You must go to the hospital, immediately."

She was already moving toward the door, panic and purpose warring within her, sending prickles across her body. "I'm leaving."

"I shall go with Bostick," the countess said to her. "Take my carriage."

She vaguely heard her as she pushed past Bostick and hurried down the hall. The French had been studying epilepsy for some time, but in England many still feared the disease, and Henrietta was not sure which type of doctor she might encounter at the hospital. Terror filled her.

The sooner she reached the hospital, the sooner she could rescue Dominic.

* * *

Dominic woke to pain. His body throbbed with it, hot flashes of shock that reverberated out from his rib cage to all his limbs. A metallic taste was in his mouth. Blood. He'd bit himself. Slowly he opened his eyes, several realizations hitting him at once.

His hands and legs were tethered to the bed. He could not move.

And his head ached. Bandages draped over his right eye, distorting his view. A smell pervaded this place. An unpleasant odor, coupled with sounds of despair, permeated his senses. Moans from the beds around him. The squeak of shoes on the floor as the place bustled with movement. A man walked past, holding a saw.

He closed his eyes.

Tired.

So tired.

Was this what God had planned all along? To let a silly accident due to a cat darting in front of the horses land him in the hospital? Or was it a seizure that had led him here? Had his secret been discovered?

He had not been sent to an asylum yet. Of that he was certain. This place reeked of sour and physical smells. Not to mention that surgeon with the saw. Terrible memories from the other accident saturated him.

Pain burned through his soul. When he next awoke, it was to a man calling his name.

He cracked open an eye. He tried to speak, but his mouth felt like it had been filled with cotton, dry and unable to formulate language.

"My lord, how are you feeling?" The man gazed down at him, his expression openly curious. "Perhaps some water." A cup was tilted to his lips. He drank, coughing and sputtering when too much entered at once.

"Terrible," he finally croaked. "What happened?"

"When your carriage tipped over, you were thrown. A concussion, contusions to the scalp and bruised ribs. A fractured arm."

"Why am I strapped down?"

The physician's eyelids flickered, but Dominic did not offer any information. He wanted to ascertain if they knew of his epilepsy. By the hesitation, and the tethering, he gathered they did.

"You had convulsions, my lord, perhaps due to the trauma? You frothed and a concerned viscount ordered that you be sent here for observation. For the safety of others," he added.

"Yes, of course," he murmured.

His worst fears at his door. No doubt his sister would take Louise and care for her while he was confined to an asylum for the remainder of his years. Henrietta was probably on her way to Italy by now. He wasn't sure what day it was, and he did not care to ask.

At the moment, he felt a failure in every way. It was though a dagger had gouged a hole in his chest, hollowing him out, making him emptier than the day he'd discovered he'd have to live with a dreadful disease alienating him from society, keeping him from a normal life.

He did not wish to succumb to pity, to solitude, but perhaps this was the culmination of all he'd avoided. Best to face it head-on. Alone. As he would always be.

"Unhand me, you fools." A strident, familiar voice echoed throughout the corridor. "I demand to see him at once." And then strong, sure footsteps.

Suddenly the hollow space inside filled. Longing, hope, amusement. Dare he smile at the annoying tone that he'd chastised her for using with his apothecary, and yet here she was, using it on physicians older and stronger than herself.

But not smarter.

"Do you know who I am?" she asked in an impatient tone that almost made him wince with its haughtiness. She was getting closer, her voice louder. Several lower tones responded with varying degrees of authority and confusion.

"Fiddle faddle, I'll not have it. I demand you send word to Mr. William Gordon. Surely you have heard of his work in Edinburgh? Imbeciles." The last was said scathingly.

And then she was at his side, the aroma of roses embracing him.

"My dear Dominic," she said in a tone he had never heard from her before. A choked, raw voice lilting with feminine pain that caused him to reach for her. He couldn't, though. The leather straps kept his arm from its intended journey.

He opened his eyes, and there she was, her dark chocolate eyes brimming with moisture, red-rimmed. Her lips the perfect color of a dusky, aged rose.

"They shall not keep you here," she said in a fierce whisper. Her breath brushed his cheek in a warm caress before she straightened.

"Your patient will be leaving with me," she announced.

He let his eyes close again, but this time when he fell back to sleep, he dreamed of lavender fields, of a picnic in the sun with Louise and Henrietta. Smiles snatched a biscuit, and Louise ran after him, her giggles a bright, sparkling trill in the afternoon.

The gentle gurgle of a baby's laughter lulled him into sweet darkness.

Chapter Twenty-Seven

One month later

Henrietta felt quite conventional as she stared at her reflection. The coral-colored silk dress pinkened her cheeks and somehow made her dark eyes look utterly exotic against the paleness of her skin.

She had never really felt pretty, and had never cared overly much to, but tonight she wished to look and be her best.

Tonight she would see Dominic for the first time since he'd been released from that terrible place called a hospital. Truly, London hospitals were a blight to England. She had seen many grievous places in her travels, but for a city of this size, with so much wealth available, there was no excuse.

She had already investigated several avenues of hospital reform and intended to be a part of changing the English methods of medicine. They were utterly archaic. It was as though no one had bothered to read the works of Hippocrates, or at least involve themselves with the Royal Society of Medicine, which published interesting although sometimes flawed articles.

In her opinion.

Which, she noted with an inner smile, was usually right.

She took one last look in the mirror, and then turned to go downstairs. Louise found her halfway there. She slipped her hand into Henrietta's.

"Do you think Dominic will be happy to see me?" she asked quietly as they moved down the stairs.

"Thrilled," Henrietta said.

"I have missed him so."

"As have I."

"Smiles missed him, too. He has already run ahead of me. I do not understand why we could not visit."

"Your uncle had multiple injuries. A quiet, uninterrupted regimen of good diet and exercise was necessary to help him recover." That, and other extenuating circumstances. In order to get him released into her care, Henrietta had to call in a favor from Mr. Moore.

Thankfully he had still been in London and negotiated Dominic's release. However, he'd asked to take Dominic to Edinburgh to recover. While there, they could study his epilepsy together, weighing their observations against recent articles published by French scientists involved in epileptology.

Henrietta would have accompanied them, but because Louise's governess unexpectedly quit due to a sudden marital engagement, she determined that it would be best to stay with Louise. To continue teaching her and to give her a home.

Seeing Dominic on that bed, strapped down and helpless…she could never forget the feeling. All due to an accident. One could not predict such a thing. And now he was back.

They reached the bottom of the stairs, greeted by quiet laughter coming from the parlor.

Louise raced ahead, but Henrietta found herself slowing as she neared the open door. What would she say? What if he had reconsidered all that he said he might feel? She wet her lips, stepping into the doorway.

Louise was laughing and hugging Dominic. No one noticed Henrietta at first.

When they did, both Uncle William and Dominic stood. In the candlelight, Dominic looked as startlingly attractive as he ever had. His eyes flashed a brilliant green, his eyebrows thick, black slashes over them. Perhaps he was a bit thinner, but that only chiseled his cheekbones into something more than handsome. When he smiled, his dimple curved like a second smile.

Meant just for her.

Her stomach fluttered, and she pressed her palm against the silk dress, embracing the feeling.

"Dominic," she said in a strange, breathy voice that might have once embarrassed her. "How well you look."

"And you," he said, his voice husky as he came forward, holding out his hands.

"Oh, I must check on something." Lady Brandewyne pushed to her feet.

"But we just got here," said Louise.

"Come, come," the dowager countess said, poking Uncle William in his shoulder. "You, too."

He started to protest, but one look at Henrietta and he left with the others. She knew, of course, why they were leaving her alone with Dominic, but she was far too nervous to summon amusement. Indeed, the way Dominic stared at her was strangely fascinating, as though he was a dehydrated man who'd found a fresh spring.

"You have grown more beautiful." He moved closer to her, his fingers reaching out to touch her bottom lip.

The words touched her deeply, for he had no reason to say such things other than that they were the truth.

"Before you say anything, I must tell you something," she said, dipping her head.

"A confession?"

"Of sorts. Louise and I were at your estate for several weeks. I confronted the apothecary, and he decided to retire."

"Miss Gordon, I'm appalled. Tell the truth. You scared him off."

"You should not laugh. I told him you would never pay him another farthing. That he could take his threats and stuff them. He decided to go live with his daughter." She shrugged.

"And you are telling me this because?"

"Well, I have been thinking a great deal."

"As you are often wont to do."

"You know me well." The taut worry that had been perching on her shoulders eased. It was true. Dominic knew her and understood her, even when he did not agree with her. How very comforting that suddenly felt. "I came to the conclusion that I never want to be apart from you and Louise. Since the apothecary's shop is sitting empty, perhaps you might be interested in hiring a female doctor?"

He broke into a wide grin, and she had a moment of fear that he was laughing at her.

"What a completely practical suggestion."

"I thought so," she said somewhat stiffly.

"What if I were to tell you," he said, eyes crinkling, "that I have also been thinking?"

He stepped toward her. She did not step back.

"I would say that I am quite relieved that your brain

has not atrophied after all. I would like to hear of your thoughts."

"Will you be making a list on how to improve them?"

"My lord, I would not do such a thing."

"Oh, but you would, my dear Henrietta." And now he was quite close, his arm encircling her waist, and she was not stopping him. "It is one of those impossibly annoying parts of your nature that I enjoy. In fact, one might say, I rather adore all the parts of your nature. The annoying bits, too."

This was not going where she'd expected, but rather where she'd hoped. "Might?" she ventured carefully.

"Ah, that pesky word. I do believe it's caused me more trouble than I anticipated." He was holding her now, his arms warm, no evidence of a break in the circumference. He still smelled the same.

She touched his left arm while trying to inhale is scent without him noticing. "There is no pain?"

"An occasional twinge."

"And your ribs?" She did not wish to return his embrace and cause pain.

"Still sore, but I do believe if you hug me back, it shall ease the ache in my heart."

"Hearts do not ache unless they're diseased," she said, but she returned his hug. Her head rested against his chest, where the sound of that particular organ thumped rapidly against her ear. "No disease that I can tell, though your heart rate is slightly elevated."

She leaned back to examine his face. "Skin tone appears normal. A slight flush to your cheeks."

"All that thinking has obviously ill-affected me." His dimple appeared, which made her smile in return. He had such a lovely mouth. It occurred to her how close they were, and that perhaps he might kiss her again.

And perhaps she might kiss him back.

"What were you thinking? I simply must know. You have teased me too much, my lord." She tugged at a strand of his hair, relishing the thick silkiness of it, the fact that he was here, he was alive.

He bent his head. "I was thinking," he murmured against her ear, "that it is madness to ask a woman for the fourth time to stay."

"That would be madness," she replied. "But as the woman has already made plans to stay, it is not necessary."

"I was thinking that our village could use an experienced doctor. One who often attends symposiums and panels paid for by Lord St. Raven."

"I quite agree."

"I was also thinking—" and now his lips were closer to her cheek, almost touching her "—that it would be most practical to marry the one you want to spend the rest of your life with."

"Most practical," she whispered, her cheeks burning, her pulse racing beneath her skin.

"I was also thinking that using the word *might* with love is most unwise. Either one loves, or one does not."

His cheek rasped against hers.

"Miss Gordon, I was thinking that I love you very much, and I dearly hope you love me in return."

Now his lips hovered near hers. Waiting, she supposed.

"Those are many thoughts to be thinking," she said softly. "But I must answer truthfully—I love you painfully so."

"Ahem."

The moment intruded upon, their heads snapped toward the doorway, where Louise stood with her arms folded and her foot tapping impatiently.

"I was thinking," she said, "that if you two do not get married, I may as well take up hoydenning for life."

"That is not a word," said Henrietta promptly.

"Keep it in mind." Louise winked at them, and then pranced off.

Laughing, Henrietta looked at Dominic.

"Yes," she said at the moment he did.

"I think our life will be slightly unconventional with that one around."

"Enough thinking." She pulled his head down until her lips touched his. "I am not interested in convention, my love."

* * * * *

If you enjoyed this book look for
THE MATCHMAKER'S MATCH and
A HASTY BETROTHAL by Jessica Nelson.

Dear Reader,

Henrietta, like many of my other characters, showed up fully formed. I knew she was stubborn, tenacious, and about to be confronted with a man who could calm her fears and give her a reason to love. Enter Dominic. *swoon* I really liked him myself, despite his flaws. He wants to be redeemed. He wants to change. And that is such an admirable quality in a human being. I felt he'd be perfect for Henrietta, a lady who has her entire life mapped out and who is resistant to change.

Enter a headstrong charge (Louise), and I knew I had a beautiful story worth telling. What I did not expect, however, was to be unexpectedly sharing the same circumstances as Dominic, caring for precious little family members who have lost both parents.

It makes this story especially poignant for me. I hope you enjoy it and, as always, I adore hearing from readers. Please forgive any mistakes I've made in facts and details. My imagination far outweighs my research skills.

You can find me by visiting my website, www.jessicanelson.net.

Happy reading and may God bless you in every way,
Jessica Nelson

We hope you enjoyed this story from
Love Inspired® Historical.

Love Inspired® Historical is coming to
an end but be sure to discover more
inspirational stories to warm your heart
from **Love Inspired®** and
Love Inspired® Suspense!

Love Inspired stories show that
faith, forgiveness and hope have the power
to lift spirits and change lives—always.

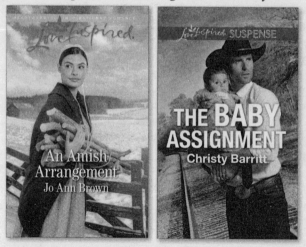

Look for six new romances every month
from **Love Inspired®** and
Love Inspired® Suspense!

Get 2 Free Books,
Plus 2 Free Gifts—
just for trying the
Reader Service!

SPECIAL EXCERPT FROM

Love Inspired HISTORICAL

*When widowed Anna Linford comes to Cowboy Creek
as a last-minute mail-order bride replacement, she
expects to be rejected. After all, her would-be groom,
Russ Halloway, is the same man who turned down her
sister! But when they learn she's pregnant, a marriage
of convenience could lead to new understanding, and
unexpected love.*

Read on for a sneak preview of
HIS SUBSTITUTE MAIL-ORDER BRIDE,
the heartwarming continuation of the series
RETURN TO COWBOY CREEK.

"I don't want another husband."

Russ grew sober. "You must have loved your husband
very much. I didn't mean to sully his memory by
suggesting you replace him."

"It's not that." Anna's head throbbed. Telling the
truth about her marriage was far too humiliating. "You
wouldn't understand."

"Try me sometime, Anna. You might be surprised."

One of them was going to be surprised, that was for
certain. Philadelphia was miles away, but not far enough.
The truth was bound to catch up with her.

"If you ever change your mind about remarrying,"
Russ said, "promise you'll tell me. I'll steer you away
from the scoundrels."

"I won't change my mind." Unaccountably weary, she perched on the edge of a chair. "I'll be able to repay you for the ticket soon."

"We've gone over this," he said. "You don't have to repay me."

Why did he have to be so kind and accommodating? She hadn't wanted to like him. When she'd taken the letter from Susannah, she'd expected to find the selfish man she'd invented in her head. The man who'd callously tossed her sister aside. His insistent kindness only exacerbated her guilt, and she no longer trusted her own instincts. She'd married the wrong man, and that mistake had cost her dearly. She couldn't afford any more mistakes.

"I don't want to be in your debt," she said.

"All right. Pay your fare. But there's no hurry. Neither of us is going anywhere anytime soon."

She tipped back her head and studied the wrought iron chandelier. She hated disappointing him, but staying in Cowboy Creek was out of the question. Russ wasn't the man she remembered, and she wasn't the naive girl she'd been all those years ago.

Don't miss
HIS SUBSTITUTE MAIL-ORDER BRIDE
by Sherri Shackelford, available May 2018 wherever
Love Inspired® Historical books and ebooks are sold.

www.LoveInspired.com